LINDISFARNE'S SECRET GOSPEL

Dedicated to **Christine Hutchings** and **John William Bremner** for the help they gave me to get this book published.

CHAPTER ONE

Holy Island. The jewel in Northumberland's historic and righteous crown. I'm sure it is, but a crown of gold ... or a crown of thorns?

It had a magic that tormented me, like no other place I had ever set foot on. Yet for the life of me, I couldn't explain why.

It was the place my husband and I wanted to settle to end our days, but that island became the dirt under my nails, and the haze of grey that had settled over my skin. I was hardly antiquated and grey-haired when I made that trip, still only 34, but I felt a hell of a lot older. And with the passing of time came the questions I hoped to find answers to. My husband had passed away two months earlier and we never managed to live out our fantasies, on Holy Island or anywhere else. Fate is indeed a cruel mistress.

There I was, back on that piece of land to banish ghosts or to walk in a dead man's shoes. I still couldn't decide which. Two months was not particularly a long time, but finally I had gained the strength to visit that place once again and I didn't even know why I was there.

I knew those crooked roads better than I knew my own home town. The beautiful thatched cottages greeted me on arrival, as they do all visitors, and I stood with my mind adrift until something burst into my memory. It didn't take much. Even the 'Welcome To The Holy Island Of Lindisfarne' road sign was enough to transport me back ten years to our very first visit when Craig felt we were being 'conned' by the mere description.

"It's not even a bloody island!" he snarled. "We drove here, so how can it be an island?"

He made a valid point. The place is a tidal island and access is by a paved causeway which is covered by the North Sea twice in every 24 hour period. Tide timetables need to be studied or you could get caught short and have to look for accommodation, and that happens often to tourists unfamiliar with the routine. Just because visitors crossed the causeway at 10am in June, there is no guarantee they can do the same in August. Cars sometimes get stranded out at sea as some gamblers take their lives in their own hands and chance their luck, with rescues as frequent as two every three weeks, on average, in the summer months. My husband was the sort of guy who never grew up. Some people never escape their childhood, and he simply never wanted to. It was like a part of him just didn't feel safe in the adult world. That was Craig. His clothes never seemed to fit, always too large for his body, and they only showed his shape on the parts that seemed to touch, and there weren't too many of them. A joker who constantly fished for laughs, which was what first attracted me to him, but he was more complex than I ever imagined. He could be a hurricane, but he was the eye of his own storm. Never violent or hurtful to others, but he would often go into battle with his own ego, and I often feared he had the ability to destroy himself. Sadly, in the end, he did just that. So, what made Holy Island so special to us? It has religious significance in abundance, but neither of us were spiritual folk, although we did respect its history. Who couldn't? On reflection it probably doesn't have much about it to be extra special to anyone. Situated on the far north-east corner of England near Berwick-upon-Tweed, it has a population of around 160 inhabitants and is famous for its Priory, which apparently is one of the most important centres of early Christianity in Anglo-Saxon England. There is also a tiny

16th century castle, which is about as big as a standard four-bedroomed detached home, stood on a massive rock, and I can only assume it was more a look-out post rather than a form of defence.

An old village of bricks and mortar locked in a constant battle against the forces of nature. No structure or building defends this place. It gets struck with everything the North Sea has to throw at it. And when Craig and I told locals we wanted to buy a property on the island the reply was pretty much unanimous ... "you must be mad!"

"We hear that all the time," said Murdoch Jobson, the owner of the Jobson Grocery Store. "But you see Holy Island in the summer, dressed up in all its finery. The flowers, the stooping swallows, the stunning view of Bamburgh Castle. Try staying here in the winter when that causeway is hit with sleet and snow, and visibility is down to the end of your nose. Sometimes we can't even see the Priory from my shop, and that is only yards away, never mind the Farne Islands or Bamburgh Castle."

I remembered that conversation well, word for word. Craig was not going to be put off by talk of bad weather.

"Bad weather isn't exclusive to Lindisfarne," he replied. "We only live 70 miles down the road at Seaham, and we live on the coast."

"There is no comparison," said Murdoch in a heavy Scottish accent. "We are exposed on every side because we are stuck out at sea. This place is only two miles across, from the Castle on the south beach to Snipe Point on the north sands. Nothing but a barren field lies between the two of them. Two miles of nothingness to stop whatever weather happens to come at us from Norway and the Baltic. Before you buy a property, if there are any on the market to

buy, try renting a bungalow and spending a winter here first."
His words were echoed by a local gentleman who overheard our conversation. He gave us his opinion without invitation.
"It's not easy living on Holy Island. Where would you work? Nothing is produced here. Yeah we know the Lindisfarne Mead is 'allegedly' distilled here, but I will let you into a little secret, it's imported from Scotland. As is just about everything else we have here. Even if you have a job on the mainland, your hours are dictated by the tide."
I'm not suggesting it put our ambitions on 'hold', because we didn't really have the money to uproot and move anyway. But we had thought about buying a holiday home and renting it out in the summer until we could clear the mortgage. But with so few houses on the island, Murdoch told us holiday homes were frowned upon by the locals: "It is a very tight and friendly community here. Very few houses are built and it takes a hell of a lot of 'pull' with the council to get planning permission. We don't encourage strangers unless they can contribute to what we have here."
I'm not sure what Craig (or myself) could contribute to island life, but he had a plan – and he was going to stick with it. All well and good if we were approaching retirement age, but we were only 34 and 36. Which probably spoke volumes about his approach to life. Everything was done by the 'seat of his pants'.
I walked down Sandham Lane through the beautiful village that was bathed in sunshine, but in this part of the country the weather changes on a whim. It is not unusual to have the weather of the four seasons wrapped up in thirty minutes, but I took a chance and dressed for the summer. It was August after all. Then I regretted it 15 minutes later

when black clouds appeared in the distance, although there was no guarantee they were heading in my direction.
It was at this point I understood my love for this place. That village comes with no logic for planning nor any great enthusiasm for architecture. Every building is different, erected in a bygone time when it was required. As though each and every person decided "We need a house, let's build one." And low and behold – they did - borrowing this and that from another era. It makes the place as glorious as a beloved grandmother's patch-work quilt, with every patch unique, and as eye catching as the one before. They may lack conformity, but that, to me, is the beauty. They built their houses the way they wanted a home to be, and the meaning of 'home' is evident in each and every one.
The cottage Craig had his eye on (not that we could possibly afford it) was on a pathway with the musical name of Crooked Loaning. How he wanted that address, as well as the building. As I walked towards it I realized I was now walking in 10-year old footsteps, imagining him by my side, holding my hand. But that was probably why I was there in the first place. Perhaps I wanted closure. A last walk down memory lane, to banish the past, no matter how beautiful the memories were. I must move on with my life, because for two months I had been on a guilt trip, blaming myself for everything that went wrong between us. I wanted to say "sorry" there and then, and there was probably no better spot to make my peace than at Craig's dream home.
The cottage looked as if it was straight out of a fairytale, but more to the point, a fairytale with a happy ending. That was my interpretation. Craig, however, saw it as a picture book for little kids. Hansel and Gretel's cottage built of gingerbread and cakes with window panes of clear sugar

and a candy-cane door handle. He was the child with his nose squashed against the window of the sweetshop - while my head was full of scented dreams and wild romance. We had never set foot inside that cottage but I imagined a large black stove; a comfy cream coloured sofa with cream carpets; perhaps two wooden chairs either side of the window; and a circular wooden table dominating the room. A two-metre high hedge surrounded the property. Vine grew up the archway and honeysuckle contrasted beautifully with two huge trees that showered the sky with red and orange leaves.

When we were back at home in Seaham, Craig and I would talk about the cottage often. It became an obsession with him, but to me it was all just wishful thinking. I had a 'bucket list' as long as my arm but half of the catalogue was dreams that would never come true. I'm no fool. Yes of course I wanted to climb Everest, see a tiger in the wild in Bhutan and learn to speak fluent Russian, and owning Crooked Loaning was another of those pipe dreams that would never happen.

I walked along the Maygate pilgrimage trail to the castle on the south bay, taking in the stunning view towards Bamburgh Castle. Thankfully the clouds headed in an easterly direction so a soaking became most unlikely. I sat on 'our' wooden seat at the base of the castle, looking out at the tiny fishing boats in what locals grandly call a harbour, when really it's only a bay with makeshift moorings. Then I'd swear I saw a seal bobbing its head out of the water for a couple of seconds before sinking without a trace. What a calm and therapeutic place. Even the chatter of the tourists could be relaxing, in it's own monophonic way.

Once again I drifted back to our many visits to this spot. This very seat. As though I was pressing the button on a CD player and our romantic past was being replayed. Only there, on that spot, could I give it all up, and banish the demons and get myself a new life. I couldn't imagine what the synopsis would be if a psychiatrist were to have shone a light in my eyes. Maybe it would be the push I needed, because what I was going through was purgatory. There was nothing there except me ... the victim; the torturer; the sinner ... the murderer.

Once I told Craig that I had no right to his heart, but I was blessed to love him with my own. He replied "I wish you could see yourself through my eyes, and you would see how special you are." That was his favourite quote and he told me that often.

I must have been in a spell for a couple of minutes, because when I turned to my right I was startled to see a rather well-to-do gentleman sat next to me.

"Sorry, did I frighten you? My apologies" he said, calmly touching my shoulder.

"No, no, I think I was dozing off," I laughed. "I'm pleased you woke me, it could have been embarrassing, particularly if I started snoring."

He was an attractive man in his own way, but he seemed confident enough to know it. Aged about 38 to 40 I would imagine. He had the kind of face that I can only describe as being like a seasoned warrior. I guess he must have been used to the sudden pause in a person's natural expression when they looked his way. That would no doubt be followed by overcompensating with a nonchalant gaze and a weak smile. His timid blush, that accompanied it, was a dead give-away. He played at being modest but he knew he was capable of turning heads. He had tousled dark brown hair, which was thick and lustrous. His eyes were a mesmerizing deep ocean blue, and his face was strong and defined.

But, despite it all, he was not my type. I so wanted to knock him off his perch, but he had done nothing to suggest he was on a perch in the first place. He was polite, and even seemed caring, so why did I take an instant dislike to him?

"Are you by yourself?" he quizzed nonchalantly.

"Yeah I suppose you could say that," I said, wondering if I should let him know that I was alone. Let's face it, you are either alone or you are not, so it was a pitiful answer.

"Yes, I am actually by myself," I said, trying to retract what I had originally said.

"Is it your first time on Holy Island?" he asked.

"No, I have been here often. What about yourself?"

"I was born here," he said, "I live here."

That immediately grabbed my attention, then he explained he was an author who wrote history books about the Northumberland and East Scotland coast.

"So tell me," I asked, genuinely showing interest, "is this Lindisfarne or Holy Island?"

He turned all official, as if he had prepared his answer previously: "Local people rarely refer to it as 'Lindisfarne'. That's its Anglo-Saxon name. The Vikings attacked the monastery in 793AD, when it was called Lindisfarne. But it was the Durham monks who first called it 'Holy Island'. Today it's official title is 'The Holy Island of Lindisfarne', so you would be correct using either name."

"Thank you Mr Author," I replied, and we both laughed. "So now I know. Another question, is it possible to live here in the harsh winter? Because, over the years, the locals have tried to discourage me from moving here."

He chuckled for some time before saying: "It's a code of conduct amongst the people of this island. They don't want strangers here, for sure. But to answer your question, the winters can be desolate. They really can. For example we had a group of ornithologists commissioned to stay for six weeks between December and January and they lasted three days. They still filled in a report, even though they were not actually on the island. They claimed we had 600 nesting pairs of Eider ducks here. We don't have one nesting pair, simply because we have foxes here. They are large ground-nesting birds and foxes would spot them a mile off. 600 pairs on an island this big? We would be tripping over them every ten yards, kicking them out of the way."

So he could crack a joke, too. He was charming, informative, but as my mother would say "a little bit too full-of-himself." Without being specific, there was something about him that made me feel a touch uncomfortable. There seemed more to him than than he was giving up, and I made my excuses and set off on the tourist trail.

I visited the tiny castle, which is probably the biggest rip-off on the island, because the only benefit from paying the money to enter it is the sea view from the top. But I could get the same view from the life-boat lookout tower, 500yds away, for free.

Sadly the clouds moved in once again, to switch the season from summer to winter and I was soon soaked in a cloud burst, stranded in the worst possible spot without cover. I made it to the village twenty minutes later and decided to take refuge in the Pilgrim Coffee Shop, have lunch, and hope the rain would stop.

There's nothing particularly fancy about this place, but it does have so much character. No elaborately decorated

French prints or fanciful etchings on the walls, just a room in a time warp. Like any other building on the island, you could pick up the whole establishment and send it back to the 1930s and it wouldn't look out of place. Lindisfarne doesn't 'do' modern.

At the glass-fronted counter there was an array of cream cakes and pastries, all with very English sounding names, but of course there were the obligatory Scottish scones. The local shopkeepers know the importance of catering for their near neighbours from over Hadrian's Wall.

They serve the tea in real white china pots and I ordered a cream tea with Earl Grey, as well as a cake from the enchanting selection on offer, then sat waiting for them to arrive. I was settled into a corner of the room, realizing I was lucky to get a seat because there was such a mad rush of customers. All around me other diners seemed to be competing with one another to be heard above their collective din. I probably wouldn't have noticed the chatter if I were in company, and it crossed my mind I never do pay attention to any commotion when I'm out with friends. From the corner of my eye I caught a young woman staring at me, her eyes piercing me through strands of lank, wet, mousey hair. I didn't want to stare back, so I gave her a passive glance and switched my attention to the window. The rush for the wooden chairs continued, and the one next to me on my two-seater table was about to be taken.

"You don't mind if I sit here, Linda?"

I jumped at the sound of my name.

'Mr Author' was next to me again, stood towering over my shoulder looking rather intimidating with his bedraggled wet hair coving half of his face. I felt as though I was being stalked, and what made it all the more frightening was the fact I could not remember at any point in our previous conversation giving him my name!

CHAPTER TWO

I wanted my own space, but how could I refuse? After all it wasn't my chair to keep hold of, so what would give me the right to tell him, "Sorry, it's taken," but that was what I wanted to say. So I tried diplomacy.

"I've ordered a meal. It's a bit awkward because the tables are so small, and I'd hate to crowd you out."

"I've only ordered coffee, I don't mind," he said, as though he was going to sit there regardless of whether I liked it or not.

"Can I ask you," I said, knowing full well that I was pulling a grimacing face, "how do you know my name, because I don't believe I told you? We weren't introduced."

"Oh sorry," he replied, "My name is Steve Campbell. Pardon my ignorance, but I thought I told you."

Then I started to doubt my own mind. Perhaps he had introduced himself when I was looking him up and down and I wasn't paying attention. Should I accept that answer? I didn't think I should.

"I'm not so sure you did, and I cannot remember telling you my name."

He sat down on the seat, crossed his arms in a defensive manner, and took his time to reply.

"I get the feeling I make you nervous, and I am sorry if I do. But I am just trying to be friendly. If you didn't tell me your name, I must have got your name from the keyring on your car keys."

He leant forward and picked my keys off the table and dangled them in front of his face. Sure enough, I have a keyring that my mother bought me years ago that says, 'Linda'.

My meal arrived at the table that precise moment. The room was packed to the rafters and our knees touched under the narrow table. Neither of us pulled away.

"So," I said, trying to kill a long difficult silence, "you were born here. Where does your family originate from?"

"My family has Lindisfarne roots that go back generations, as far back as records are kept. The Romans never ever set foot on the island, so records began with the monks at the time Saint Oswald arrived from Ireland."

He held my attention. Even though I wouldn't call myself a scholar on the subject, I did know the odd fact that I had picked up from Craig, who was an authority on the history of the island.

"Who arrived first - St Aiden or St Oswald?" I quizzed.

"Oswald came from Ireland to gain the throne of Northumberland at Bamburgh Castle. He placed a cross on the battlefield and fought under the banner of Christianity. He won the battle, took the crown, and Aiden was consecrated as a bishop and given 12 monks to spread the Christian faith. He could choose anywhere in the United Kingdom and he picked here. A good choice? That is still open to debate. Anyway, that's the short story."

Switching the subject, I asked, "You have lived here all of your life. Have you never married?"

"Yeah I married once, but ..." he said in a rather sombre tone, then stopped mid-sentence.

"But what?" I said, interrupting his silence.

"But ... she left me. Nothing more, nothing less."

I wouldn't let it drop. "Because she wanted to move to the mainland?"

"Probably. She gave a thousand reasons, but you probably hit the nail on the head. She was from the mainland, anyway" he said, "and it takes a very strange kind of person to live here. Very strange. Trust me."

He felt I was grilling him, and I could see the defence in his face. Particularly his eyes. He sat back preparing himself for the next question, and I wasn't going to disappoint. I wanted to break down his resistance. And why not, he had invaded my space, so why not invade his?

"So, Steve, I think you are a part of the Holy Island 'clan'." I smiled. "You are all trying to stop the flood of immigrants, like myself, because you all treasure your privacy. Discouraging people from moving here with your talk of 'strange locals'."

He took me by surprise by snapping back: "Oh there's a clan, alright. And as a local you get that shit rammed down your throat from childhood. They try and make you crawl, but why crawl? Let them carry you!"

I'm sure that was an intelligent answer. Sadly I wasn't that intelligent to work it out. He was a bright guy, of that there was no doubt, but he seemed a touch neurotic. I noticed that when he spoke he couldn't seem to figure out what to do with his hands. He clasped and unclasped them, as if in constant need to touch something. I knew a guy at university who had a slight stammer, and a lot of the girls took to him because he seemed so vulnerable. He made me feel that way too.

Seconds seemed to tick by like minutes, until he asked me: "Why were you looking in my home today?"

The question was well over my head: "Why was I looking in your home? What are you talking about? Why would I look in your home?"

The mood suddenly changed, and not for the better. I noticed he had a knack of doing that. Switching from being likeable and friendly to untrustworthy in the flick of a switch. I wanted him to go. I pulled out my phone and pretended I was checking it for messages, but I was reassuring myself that someone was at the other end of the line.

He looked at me fumbling, knowing I was using the phone as a security blanket, then repeated his questioning. "You stood looking in my home for about ten minutes today. The cottage at Crooked Loaning."

"That's YOUR cottage? Yeah I was there today. I didn't see you, though." I replied.

Once again the question was asked: "Why were you looking?"

"That was my husband's dream cottage. He wanted to buy it. Not that we could ever afford it. But it was our little dream."

"I understand that, but it has never been for sale," he said, and I was starting to feel this conversation had run it's course.

"Well, Mr Campbell," I said, before finishing off the last crumbs of my meal, "that was why I was looking at your cottage. I wasn't eyeing up the place to break in, I was simply admiring its beauty. So I will leave you to enjoy the rest of your coffee and I hope you have a lovely day – what's left of it."

I picked up my bag and glanced at myself through the mirror on the café wall.

"Dear me," I laughed, "what a mess I look. My hair is a disgrace."

"I wish you could see yourself through my eyes," came his reply.

I stopped dead in my tracks, "What did you say just then?" He didn't repeat it, he just stared back at me.
"My husband used to say that to me quite often," I replied. Why did I get the feeling this man knew that already?
"What time is the tide on the causeway tonight?" he asked.
"6.15, supposedly," I answered.
He looked at his watch, and I looked for tell tale signs about his person. He didn't wear a wedding ring but he had an ancient-looking gold-coloured ring decorated with an array of polished diamonds, with a brilliant red stone so vivid it couldn't possibly be the real thing. It had to be fake.
"Will you be returning to the mainland tonight," he asked, "or do you have plans to stay over?"
"No I will be going home, probably around three, and hope I miss the rush hour traffic," I said, checking my own watch and seeing it was 1.10pm.
"I couldn't tempt you to stay, could I?" he said, obviously knowing in advance I would say 'No'.
"I won't be staying. I don't even know you, and I don't have anything to stay for. Goodbye Mr Campbell," I said before heading towards the door, but the place was virtually standing-room-only and I struggled to get out.
He stood up, put his hand on my arm and said, "I have a proposition for you Mrs Wilson. At least hear me out."
He may have struck lucky seeing my keyring, but at no point in any conversation had I given him my surname. He knew more about me than I had given him credit for. I turned to face him and looked him full in the eye, "First and foremost … don't touch me again! OK? I don't like being touched or man-handled by someone I don't know. Secondly, I don't 'do' propositions. Thirdly, how do you know my name? Before you start, I don't have anything on

me that says Wilson, unless you have seen my credit card. And if you have seen that, I find that quite alarming."
"Can we go for a walk and talk?" he answered.
"No we bloody can't! But I want to know, how do you know my name?"
He leant forward to touch my arm again, but he had a rethink and pulled away: "I know your name because, just before he died, Craig approached me to buy the cottage."
I was dumbstruck.
Steve wanted us to move on: "Standing in the middle of a crowded café isn't the place to talk about this, don't you think? Can we go somewhere else?"
How did he know Craig?
We weren't together as man and wife when he died because we had been parted a few months. Well, I say 'died' but there was a lot more to it than that. He wasn't ill, he committed suicide.
"So," added Steve, "can we please get out of this place and go somewhere to talk?"
Let's get this right, he claimed he met Craig just before he died? So obviously Craig wasn't planning on buying the house to share it with me.
I suggested Steve and I walk to Coves Bay. I was going to do it anyway, so I may as well take the opportunity to find out how close my ex-husband, and his lover, were to owning the cottage of MY dreams.
After the sudden shower of the previous half an hour, we walked outside to be bathed in sunshine once again. We strolled through the village past Mapson's Corner Shop and off the tourist trail towards the north shore. It's not really a walkway at all, as we ploughed our way through thick springy grass, wet under foot after the rain. My new walking companion didn't help, as he had a way of walking

that made him seem perpetually in a hurry, obviously not comfortable about getting his pristine leather shoes wet. We hardly spoke a word until we arrived at Coves Bay, then I started the conversation.

"Did Craig actually visit your home or did he make the offer by phone?"

"He appeared at the door one day, said he would like a look around the place because he wanted to make an offer, but I said I had no intentions of selling my home. To be honest with you, it's not mine to sell. It's officially owned by the monks at the Priory. Craig seemed a nice guy so I invited him in. We had coffee and chatted for quite some time."

"Was he alone?" I asked, with a heavy heart, hoping he was not with his 'younger model' girlfriend.

"He was alone when he came to the house, but he could easily have had an accomplice waiting elsewhere," he answered. "We chatted for hours. He had a remarkable knowledge of the island, which surprised me, because he knew facts and specific details that are not available in guide books. We get people who come here from the Holy Order on religious occasions who know the history, but Craig had certainly done his homework. The Priory would never sell the cottage, no matter what he, or anyone else, offered. But I confided in him and showed him trinkets and jewellery collected over the years by the Elders of Lindisfarne. At one point I opened the safe, he was behind me, and I can only imagine he memorised the combination as I typed in the code. Later I noticed an extremely valuable item had been taken."

I may as well have been been shot with a stun gun.

"You are suggesting that Craig stole your possessions?" I mumbled.

"If you want a one word answer I'll have to say 'yes'."

I was shocked, and for want of a better word – I was horrified. I had known that man since my late teens but I was starting to doubt if I knew him at all. Yes he had been up to certain 'antics' as a teenager, and paid the price, but I didn't expect to go out for a day trip and find my ex-partner accused of theft. Craig was as open as a book. But, then again, he had travelled to Holy Island to buy a half-a-million-pound property, and I didn't think he had two coins to rub together. Where would he get the money to buy it? I tried a stab in the dark, "We are talking about the same man, aren't we? You haven't got him mixed up with someone else?"

"No," came the reply, "it's your husband. I can assure you."

"So what is the proposition you want to make?" I asked, fearing it was inevitable I was going to get tangled up in something I would later regret.

"We want the item back, and I believe you can help us."

"What did he take? Whatever it is won't be in my house because we didn't live together when he died. He left me."

He was quick to reply, "No it's not in your house, we know that."

"So what is it? How valuable is it?" I asked.

"It's a book and its value is difficult to calculate. That document is part of the history of this island and not something he could sell easily and get away with. He would have to know a private dealer. After Craig died someone asked for a ransom for it's safe return, so he was not acting alone. That makes it very messy. It's out there, we just don't know where it is."

"How much did that person ask for?" I enquired.

"A million," he replied.

Did I hear right?

"A million POUNDS?" I asked.

"Yes. It is a valuable piece of work, worth a lot more than that, but who will buy it? The Mona Lisa is worth £1.5billion if its sold by the museum. Pinch it and it's not worth 'Jack shit' unless it's offered back for ransom. But it's stolen property and anyone involved goes to prison."
It was not until seconds later that I realized what he had said.
"How do you know that the items are not in my house?" I wailed. "Have you been inside MY home? You have broken into my property, haven't you!"
"We know it's not there, Linda. Think about it, girl. We don't want to involve the police for a number of reasons, and I'm sure you understand we didn't want Craig hauled away for interrogation and the story appearing in the newspapers. All we wanted is our item returned and Craig to 'forget' about what he did and what he saw."
I was absolutely furious: "You broke into my bloody home. How dare you? The police could have hauled YOU away!"
But I got my reply: "He stole it Linda. It's not 'wealth-redistribution', it's taking someone's property. I will give him the benefit of the doubt, I don't think he knew for one second what he was getting himself involved with, and he couldn't handle the consequences. He couldn't sell it on or make a profit, and I don't think he had that intention anyway. He wanted a piece of Holy Island. He just happened to see an opportunity and he took it, but what he took - destroyed him. And what he took – we can't find."
The 'proposition' was put to me again.
"You and Craig used to stay in the Manor Hotel. I can organise for you stay there tonight, a place you are familiar with, and we can meet and talk later? I have things to show you, and perhaps you can help me find the item we want back."

"I feel I am being conned." I said, fighting my own corner.
"I am not used to anyone being so demanding. I do what I want – when I want."
The guy refused to take 'no' for an answer and I buckled under the pressure. He gave me enough rope to reel me in, and enough slack rope for me to finish off the job myself. His reply was just as relenting: "You just don't get it, do you? You still can't see the importance of what I am saying. Let me put it on a big blackboard with a 3ft piece of chalk and simplify it. Here is a question I will put to you. Do you believe Craig committed suicide – or could he have been 'helped' to carry it out? Because I know the answer."

CHAPTER THREE

That hotel room gave away more than it meant to. I always thought it was small when Craig and I stayed, stuffy even, but when I lay alone I could see how large it really was. The exact room where Craig and I lay on the bed and had a perfect view of Lindisfarne Castle. The view hadn't changed, I only wish I could say the same about myself. That was not the way I wanted to return to 'our' room. It was something that should have been left in the past. My bundle of happy memories had been packed up in a brown paper parcel and thrown in a wheely-bin. Although, realistically, that was probably the whole plan of being there.
What the hell was I doing?
Having convinced me I needed to talk this out, Mr Campbell barged through every barrier I put in front of him. I made it known I didn't have a change of clothes. No dress shoes, make-up, etc, and he took me to the one and only fashion shop in the village and told me to take

whatever I wanted. The finance wasn't covered by his credit card, every obstacle was hurdled over with the aid of one little business card placed by the till. It was the same in the Manor Hotel. I picked my room but no money transaction was made. The business card was placed on the receptionist's table with the kind words "give the beautiful lady whatever she wants."

We arranged to meet at 8pm, and no matter if I viewed this bizarre scenario with a change of heart, I couldn't get off the island. The causeway was flooded and I was stuck there until the tide turned.

For one whole year, loneliness had been my one dependable friend – it was there morning, noon and night. But at that precise moment, I had never felt so isolated in my entire life.

The time arrived. I give myself a quick glance in the mirror, and muttered to myself "Well Mr Campbell, you take me as I am, because this is the best you are going to get with the tools available."

The colour scheme was conservative, white blouse and black skirt, but we weren't going on a date. What was this? Business or personal? I couldn't decide. It was a guy wanting his stolen property back and myself wanting answers to how (and why) my husband died. It was personal alright.

I could see Mr Campbell waiting in the hotel reception, dressed very smart in suit and tie, and I tried to walk down the stairs with an air of sophistication. However, I had been pacing up and down in my new shoes five minutes earlier as if determined to wear out a thin trail in the carpet, trying to get used to those high heels. He greeted me with a formal handshake, said I looked "fetching", and then I tried to negotiate the walk to the door. What with my stomach shifting uneasily, and my legs shaking fearing I was going to trip, it was a relief to get as far as the door! Then I had to face the cobbled pavement to wherever we were going to go. Nightlife is rather limited on Lindisfarne. Take away the 'Crown & Anchor' pub, which just happened to be over the road, and there wan't much else in the way of recreation. I suggested we "pop in for a quick one" simply to give myself a target to aim for and head to in a straight line.

The 'Crown' is a place that can get very busy, but we were in luck. It was rather quiet. Just four old guys sat in a corner; a family of four having a meal; and no background music to battle with.

My gentleman friend bought the drinks and we moved to a table well out of ear-shot from the other customers and settled down to talk about recovering stolen property and who had been rummaging around my house. He said he preferred being called Steve, so we were now on first name terms, and I was rather comfortable with that. At no point did I feel he was trying to flirt with me, which was how I wanted the atmosphere to be, and he genuinely tried to make me feel relaxed in his company. I was nervous, and having learnt from experience, I'm not the best at humour. It's never a great plan when my conversation-to-be sounds hilarious in my head, because it is usually followed by a big fall. So I saved us both from embarrassment.

Two young women walked into the room and went to the bar looking so casual, not even a touch of make-up. Maybe I should have done that. I felt on show, even though I had dressed down.

"So Linda," he said, switching the dialogue from idle chatter to more pressing matters, "I take it Craig didn't mention to you about his offer to buy the cottage?"

"Not at all, you could have knocked me over with a feather," I replied, before getting to the point of me being there in the first place by asking, "What do you know about Craig's death?"

He sat back in his chair, giving himself a moment's grace, recalculating his next pre-prepared sentence. It had better be good, and he knew it.

"I met him for only a short time, perhaps three hours tops," he said, picking his words very carefully. "I am generally a good judge of character and he seemed a very likeable guy. But I got the impression he was running away from something. He wanted to move here to Holy Island, but he was desperate to get a deal done as soon as possible. I told him to check the property market, but he had done that already. You don't get properties for sale on this island, and even if one was to become available it would go to a friend-of-a-friend."

"He took his own life," I said, waiting for Campbell to correct me, but he didn't. "He was in a poor state of mind." Steve went down my path rather than over-ruling me and leading me down his: "What changes had you seen in him leading up to that day?"

"I have thought about that often," I replied. "And I've gone over it a million times in my mind. I blame myself because I wasn't there for him."

I asked myself if I should I tell him the whole story, or save the tragic details for another day? To hell with it, I kick-started the engine, ready to see where my motor-mouth would take me.

"About two weeks before he left me he started to act strange. I thought it could be the pressure of work, and I noticed he was taking medication for stress and anxiety. That was a first. I cannot ever remember him having problems in the past or certainly not during the time I knew him. He told me he was taking Celexa and Prozac tablets, and I noticed big changes in his personality. Everything became 'level', that's the only way I can describe it. Level in that he didn't become anxious because he had no feelings at all! He was miles away. He couldn't get excited about anything, or happy, he just behaved strange. He looked like a marathon runner who had 'hit the wall'. The legs had gone and the brain wasn't far behind. The doctor says that it was related to an OCD depression and could possibly be Post Traumatic Stress Disorder. All of this confused me because that man had never suffered depression in his entire life."

I looked at Steve and he hung on every single word.

"What about his work?" he asked.

"He never brought his troubles home with him," I replied, feeling guilty that I never really showed an interest. "He had the mentality that the trouble with the rat race is that even if you win, you're still a rat."

"So where does the guilt trip come into it?" He said, as though he knew more about our relationship than he was making out. He looked deeply into my eyes as though he understood the pain I had suffered. I decided to tell him the truth.

"The things I loved most about Craig had been trashed every single day because I couldn't accept what he did. With suicide comes the guilt for those left behind. I didn't help him. I found a text on his phone from another girl. Perhaps I read it wrong. I thought he was having an affair, and like the stupid cow I am, I slapped him and threatened to divorce him. I crushed his spirit. I cut up his expensive clothes and smashed up everything that was of value to him. He just sat and watched, not even showing an emotion. He sat through it all as though he deserved it. He didn't deserve that! It was just a stupid text that I took out of context."

I continued, "There, I have finally poured out my grief, but to a stranger. I have never spoken those words before, not to family or friends. You measure each day by the imaginary cuts you inflict on yourself. Every time I remember his suicide, there's another cut engraved on my person. None are enough to kill me, but over time their accumulation will probably do it."

Steve asked the question: "How did you find out about his death?"

"I was working at home, I'm self employed, and a policeman came to the house and broke the news that Craig had been found in a friend's flat where he had been staying for a couple of days."

I had to ask the question, "What makes you feel it wasn't a suicide?"

He was prompt with his reply: "You have put yourself through so much cruelty and I don't think it's justified. Perhaps you should look at the bigger picture, Linda. You need to look at his troubles and answer two questions. Question one – was he having an affair? And you are kidding yourself because you know the answer. Question two – was it suicide? If it was, it will go down as the first horizontal hanging in history!"

We gazed at each other, both looking for a response. How did this man know so much?

I found myself in a quandary. Did I have anything to hide? Perhaps I really was fooling myself all along and maybe I should have named-and-shamed guilty parties, as my friends suggested. But I am far bigger than that. I had suffered with shame and remorse ever since Craig's death. Feeling prying eyes piercing me every time I walked down my own street, questioning why I drove a man to suicide. What was to be gained opening a can of worms when my husband was dead? The very word 'affair' suggests I was a failure as a wife. I didn't want to add another burden on my own shoulders.

"What do you know about the affair?" I asked.

"Enough. Probably just as much as you pretend not to know. June Banks, wife of a drug-dealing smack-head; mother to a small population explosion; six kids – three different fathers. Trouble with a capital 'T'. Bonny little thing, apparently, if your taste is in red-heads."

I was astonished: "Where did you get this information from? Earlier today I couldn't figure out how you knew my first name. Now I'm starting to wonder if there is anything you don't know about me."

I couldn't deny any of it. Those were not allegations, they were the facts. I certainly couldn't fault his research. I had suspected Craig had been seeing her – or someone – for months. The usual signs were there – emotionally detached; critical of everything I did; unreachable by phone; he started to pay attention to his appearance. A woman just knows.

"What I don't understand," Steve said, pointing an accusing finger at me, "why did you keep quiet about her? The police must have asked you questions when they arrived asking for a statement."

"I suppose I didn't want to believe it." I replied. "What would I have gained? I couldn't bring him back. I must have been doing something wrong for him to wander off in the first place. I wouldn't have an affair with anyone because I loved him. I thought he had the decency to do the same. Naming that 'slapper' wasn't going to make any difference. Anyway, how do you know all of this?"

"Your darling husband put his hands in my safe and took something that is very important to a lot of people. So we researched."

"That's a mighty impressive CSI team you've got there, mister," I said, shaking my head in disbelief.

"Somebody staged Craig's death," he said showing genuine concern. "Why, and for what reason, we still haven't established."

"Why are you so sure Craig was murdered," I asked. "The autopsy plainly says it was suicide. There was no reason to suspect anything."

"Trevor Banks, June's husband, found out about the affair. We know that, and we suspect that was why Craig wanted to sell up and clear out of Seaham."

I didn't believe that for a second. "He didn't have the money to move anywhere. It slipped through his fingers as soon as he got it. He often told people 'if anyone tried to rob me they will just be practicing'. Where would he get the money from? How would he live?"

"He had money, alright," said Steve. "In a Luxembourg bank. It's still there. Computer fraud ran by a syndicate of three - Craig and two French guys. It's a complicated ring of bank accounts set up across Europe but based in Paris. They get the money in – get it out – close down each individual account and move it from bank to bank until it is untraceable. It's untraceable to those being ripped-off, but we hacked into Craig's bank account and he grossed £1.6 million in the last year alone."

"Impossible," I argued. "Are you serious? I never saw any of it."

"It's true. Threats were made from his lover's husband, and Craig wanted out. Trevor Banks had it in for him, alright, and blew out the windscreen to Craig's car with a shotgun. He meant it, Craig was in the car at the time! Could a drugged-up 'waster' have the intelligence to stage-manage a murder; carry it out; and get away with it? I don't think he could. That's three things – I don't think Banks can count to three! Yeah he can fire a shot gun or use a knife, but I'm not convinced he could murder your husband and get away with it."

"Well I'm not convinced Craig had – or has - £1.6 million in a foreign bank account, either!" I replied. "The guy you talk about is NOT my husband. You have the wrong man, and I'm convinced of that."

Craig was the life of any room he was in. I heard him tell the same stories over and over, but in each rendition they became just a little bit more entertaining. Tales of ordinary people and everyday humour but the truth became a sideshow. I'm not suggesting he would lie, but he could 'tell a good tale'. He could turn normal common people into comic book heroes and mundane modest holidays into momentous never-to-be-forgotten adventures.

Was Steve suggesting that under that extroverted exterior, beneath the mask of a clown, he didn't know where he belonged or who he was. His mother told me at his funeral: "At his core he was probably the most complicated human being I have ever known."

Why did I not see it? He was my world – my everything. Every love story is beautiful – but ours is my favourite.

What happened to him devastated me. To be told he was murdered brought out a true bitterness in me I didn't even know existed.

No-one at any time questioned the suicide. Neither the police nor the doctors, so why would a total stranger know more than the authorities? Who the hell was this man?

He explained his theory in great detail: "Your doctor stated that in his opinion death resulted from asphyxia, caused by compression of the neck due to suspension. In other words ... a typical hanging. But, in forensic medicine, the course which the ligature mark makes on the neck indicates the difference between hanging and throttling. Are you with me?"

I was, to a degree, "Yes, I follow you."

He continued, "Doctor Sinclair came to the conclusion that the cause of death was asphyxiation but he neglects to consider an examination of the course of the ligature mark. The bottom line is - the precise course of the mark is not given in Sinclair's autopsy report. Neither the position of the strangulation mark on the neck, nor its position to the larynx, has been described or assessed. He bodged it! As simple as that. He saw Craig hanging and accepted what he saw. That was not a hanging – or if it was - he was hung while lying flat out on the bed! He recorded the burst blood vessels in the face, but that was caused by strangulation. I suspect he was placed on the floor when he was dead, while the murderer set up a suicide scene. Only then was he placed in the noose. The question is, could one man plan it and carry it out? There was an accomplice, perhaps more than one. There were no bruises on his body so there wasn't a struggle, and no trace of drugs. It was a professional job."

CHAPTER FOUR

The 'Crown & Anchor' was filling up with tourists, and a party of boisterous Americans were determined to take over the pub and let everyone in on their conversation ... whether the clientele wanted to hear it or not. Patty from Alabama and Chuck from Delaware were on a mission to spread the American word, and we could not hear ourselves think. Suddenly this was not the place for a quiet conversation so Steve suggested we go to his cottage. We had plenty to talk over and I wasn't in the mood to visit a restaurant or have another alcoholic drink, so I politely accepted the invitation.

There were many thoughts flashing through my mind as we approached the beautiful old wooden door. How often I pictured Craig carrying me over that threshold, like two teenagers in a 1930's black and white motion picture. I always fancied myself as Jean Harlow and Craig as Clark Gable. But this visit to Crooked Loaning was no movie. Steve placed the key in the lock and when the door swung open the strong odour of garden flowers gave way to a stronger smell of, what seemed like, a lemon fragrance. A lot of old cottages have that humid, muggy smell of dampness, but this was most pleasant and took me back to my time at university when my house mate, Emily, would try and stifle the smell of our home cooking with scented candles.

There was a natural softness and warmth about the place, which is most unusual for a man living alone. Everything in its place, putting my own home to shame. He stooped down to remove his shoes, so not to be rude I did the same, and then wondered how I was going to get them back on later as my feet would swell to twice the size by the time I left.

Perhaps he had a pair of wellingtons I could borrow, and I smiled at my own thoughts.

The floors were polished concrete and the room was furbished with beautiful antiques and statues, nothing like how I imagined it to look. A pair of Scottish broad-swords crossed elegantly on the main wall, giving the room a touch of regal elegance.

"Would you like tea or coffee?" asked my affable host.

"Tea please, milk, no sugar," I replied, and soon it was presented on a tray with biscuits and cake.

I couldn't help but ask the question that had bothered me from the moment I arrived: "Where is your safe?"

Pointing to an elegant oil painting of Lindisfarne Castle on the far wall, Steve replied: "Behind the painting over there."

"Is it secure?" I asked, and rather regretted it as soon as the words came out of my mouth.

"It's about as secure as you can get, I suppose, as long as someone else doesn't know the combination and how to turn off the alarms" he replied. Did I detect a hint of sarcasm? "It's hidden from view and has two infra-red sensors on the safe and another on the main door. Nine-inch steel housing that would take probably three or four hours to get through with welding equipment. Unless someone bulldozed the entire house, I would confidently say it was unbreachable. It has a security camera inside and outside the safe, and a link to the police station in the village. There is also another security link to the police station on the mainland. All-in-all a mini version of Fort Knox. The Bank of England isn't as secure … or so it said on the packaging." He said with a quaint giggle.

"How did Craig walk out with your possessions? How did he get - whatever it was - off the island?" I asked.

"I must have been lost in conversation and let my guard down," replied Steve. "Because I knocked all the security off for half an hour. Craig mentioned a ring that had been found in a grave on an archaeological dig in the mid 1980s, and I happened to have it. It's not mine personally, it's part of the Lindisfarne history. I opened the safe and Craig must have memorized the combination. He must have taken the book sometime when I was making coffee. It was very clever the way he got away with it because the book isn't small. He is caught in CCTV. He took the book, quietly opened the door, and placed it outside in the garden and returned for it after I waved him goodbye. It took me two weeks to realise it had gone, and we have been chasing our tails ever since trying to locate it."

"So Craig just 'seized the moment'?" I said, expecting to be abruptly put in my place. But Steve seemed a nice guy and kept a level head.

"I don't believe you could plan anything like that," Steve replied. "Yes I believe it was an opportunity he couldn't resist."

"I'm not defending him," I replied, being careful how I phrased what I had to say next. "But a moment of selfish desire ruined his life. What was the book he took?"

"I'm sure you know about the Lindisfarne Gospels, their history and their importance," said Steve.

"Yeah," I replied, as I had travelled with Craig to see them in the London Museum many years previous. "The Gospels of Matthew, Mark, Luke and John."

Steve filled me in on the story: "The Gospels are the most exotic and explicit religious books ever made. The Lindisfarne monks took 24 years to produce them 'for God and the people of this island'. 518 pages made from calfskin. But there were more gospels produced here, and

sadly – as history has it - they didn't survive. They were lost off the coast of Ireland when a boat taking them to the Emerald Isle capsized in a storm. However, one does still exist. Its called 'Codex Usserianus Primus' and it was the first book to name the two thieves who were crucified with Christ as Ioathas and Capnatas. It was produced here in Lindisfarne and it holds within its pages many secrets about this island. Trinity College in Dublin claim to have a second version of the book, but it is badly damaged and what pages that are left are fragmented and impossible to read. Our book was created at the same time as the Lindisfarne Gospels in 722. However the pages in Dublin were carbon-dated in recent years and found to have been produced in the 12th century. It's not even a copy of the true book, it's some Italian text of something else entirely." Steve's voice changed tone slightly as he pointed to the wall and told me, "The original book - Codex Usserianus Primus - was in that safe the day your husband arrived here."
"Oh my God!" I thought out loud.
Craig never did anything by halves. While petty thieves may pinch the odd wallet or handbag; my husband went to Lindisfarne and took home part of the great Gospels!
"You say it explains secrets of this island," I inquired.
"What secrets?"
He didn't answer me at first, but instead walked to the window and looked out towards the illuminated Bamburgh Castle in the distance. I got the feeling he didn't want to tell me anything I didn't know already.
"I've spend my whole life on this island trying to use the past to escape the present," he said. "Nothing on this patch of land is as it seems. It hides the past and it holds no grudges."

He still wasn't giving me straight answers. So I probed more. "What secret is here?"

"Imagine you are wrapped up in a kind of nostalgia. Imagine the day Jesus of Nazareth was crucified. The King of the Jews impaled on a wooden cross."

I nodded my head. "OK, I can imagine the Crucifixion."

"Jesus died at a place called Golgotha, or Calvary if you want it's Latin name. Described as a hill, but there is no Biblical record suggesting it was. There is only one article from that scene that is still on this Earth today. And it lies here."

"And the Gospel you are looking for would tell me what it is?" I questioned.

"Yes, it's in there."

This had to have been the weirdest day of my life. It was just ridiculous.

"So there is only one article from the crucifixion that is still on this Earth today, and you happened to have it?" I said in disbelief. "It's not in Rome or the Vatican, it's here on a tiny island in the north-east of England? And you expect me to believe that?"

He stood his ground, "Linda I could not give a shit if you believe me or not. You asked a question and I gave you an answer."

Steve offered to walk me back to my hotel, and the more I thought about our conversations the more I needed a reality check, because this was not right. I wanted to be honest with the man because I didn't believe he was being honest with me.

So I charged in with all guns blazing: "It hurts me to say this but I think you are leading me down the garden path. I don't know why, but you have gone to a lot of trouble to string me along. Craig's death was suicide, the doctors said

so. You say he stole – but where is the evidence? Why didn't you get the police, because you have the CCTV recording? Where do you hope to find this 1,300 year old book? How could I help you, when I didn't even know of its existence until a few hours ago. It's utter bullshit!"
Either he realized his cover was blown or he was genuinely shocked that I doubted him.
"Why don't you believe me?" he said. "We still have to talk Linda. You are the only person who can help us. Can I see you in the morning before you head home?"
I really was at my whit's end, "Who the hell is 'WE'? You constantly say that. And 'OUR' property. Who are you - the voice of God? Because that is what you are trying to make me believe - secrets that you can't explain."
He didn't seem to have an answer, or he was giving me a 'time out' to calm my emotions.
"Listen Steve," I said. "I don't think it's a good idea we meet again. I took notice of the causeway crossing times listed on the wall in reception in the hotel before I met you. The causeway is open from 10.45 this evening until 6.45 in the morning. In effect I don't have to stay tonight, and I think I should head home. I've had one alcoholic drink and I am well below the limit, and it's time for me to take my leave. Let's just say the whole day has been an 'experience' and leave it like that. I'm sorry but I can't help you."
He wasn't going to drop this without a battle.
"You don't know how easy it is to manipulate the truth, Linda, or make bad decisions made on partial evidence. You believe it was suicide, and I cannot sway you from that thought. I cannot make you believe something you don't want to believe. It was a life vs money issue, but there is a hell of a lot more going on other than that. Someone is

currently trying to make money out of what was stolen, and he will get hurt very soon unless things are resolved."
I stepped back and retaliated, "Are you threatening me?"
"I'm trying my hardest to help you," he instantly responded.
"Help me ... how?" I tried to recapitulate the essential points of our talk and how we first met. "Did you meet me by chance? If you did, that was an extraordinary coincidence. Twice in half an hour, so in essence, that was two strokes of good fortune you stumbled upon. How did you plan it? How did you know I would be on the island today? How did you recognize me?"
"I think it's time to cut to the chase, Linda. I knew you would be here. I know everything about you, from the colour of your car to the colour of the carpet in your front room and I even know what you said to your mother this morning. What time you get up on a morning to what time you go to bed, and everything in between."
I was starting to feel terrified.
"Shall I continue?" he said smuggly. "I know you texted your mam at 11.34 this morning and you phoned your friend Corrie from your hotel room around 7pm. On your way here this morning you pulled in for petrol at a service station on the A1 near Bedlington, and called off at Alnwick for a coffee."
"How the hell do you know all this! You had me followed!" I bawled.
"Not at all, it would be a total waste of manpower," he replied. "Your phone is tapped and your little Kia car has a tiny location device fitted somewhere you will never find."
"That's against the law!" I shouted.
"Phone the police, then." He snapped back. "You know the number – 999."

"What the hell do you want from me?" I said, virtually with tears in my eyes.

"You are in danger, girl, and I mean real danger." He said, and I was in no fit state to doubt him. He continued: "It doesn't matter what you believe about the Gospel and what I told you, there are people out there who believe you have it – or at least speculate you know where it is. They are religious fanatics – and they are after you. You haven't accepted a single word I have said all day, but I would suggest you start believing me, because I am probably the only man who can get you out of this mess."

"I'm leaving now Steve," I said, knowing that the half mile walk to my car was going to feel like a marathon, regardless of what shoes I was wearing. I grabbed my bag and headed for the door, giving no wave and no goodbye. But he caught me at the door and pushed a business card in my hand asking me to phone him when I arrived home. I assumed he wasn't going to stop me leaving but perhaps he would follow me.

This was an escape rather than a parting, and there was no looking back. Outside the road was illuminated by two street lamps, probably picturesque and atmospheric at any other time, but all I wanted was to find the road leading to the car park. After about ten yards of seemingly walking on broken glass, fighting the pain as I tried to look dignified in a duck-like fashion, I took off those absurd stilettos and made a run for it. I didn't pass anyone at any point along that road, and even if I had, I'm sure the dim light would have hid my discomfort because I ran in the shadows. My ears were closed and my mind put up barriers to anything that threatened to distract me, until I reached the grass underfoot that was the car park. Only then did I glance behind me, only to see a shape of a man peering over the stone wall close behind. It could have been him, but I don't think it was. I wanted to scream out for help but nothing came out of my mouth. But what was I actually running from? Was I in any real danger? I wasn't going to be a hero this particular evening, I just wanted get on that road home. My car was there, one of only about eight spread out over a stretch of land about the size of a football field, so it was not difficult to spot even though the street lighting was poor. I grappled with the keys. Why the hell did I have so much junk hanging off that bloody keyring? Finally I found the key fob and opened the door, thrusting the key into the ignition, and give praise to the heavens when the engine sparked up on the first turn.

I was at the exit of the carpark long before I started to struggle with my seat-belt, and I noticed the figure who had been looking over the stone wall had evaporated into thin air. I was at the junction of the road, left would have taken me back towards the village or right onto the causeway. For a split second I was actually tempted to go back along the road to see if that figure was Steve. I was in the safety of my little car and it's amazing how much bravery and courage can flood over a person in a tiny tin box. But common sense won the argument. It may have been Steve following me, but then again it could have been no more than a dog walker bemused by the sight of a very strange woman 'legging it' bare-foot down Lindisfarne main street swinging a pair of stilettos in the air.

CHAPTER FIVE

The drive home was quick and trouble free, but I had a nagging thought at the back of my mind that the stranger at the wall could easily have slipped into a car parked by the entrance as I left the exit of the car park. Heading South down the A1 I spent a good percentage of the journey looking into my rear view mirror. The traffic was minimal for such a normally busy road, and the cars I viewed in my mirror came and went without any one vehicle standing out from the rest.

But if my car was tracked (as he claimed) there was hardly any urgency to follow me, he would already know exactly where I was.

I noticed a person on the street corner as I drove up to my house. The brightness from the street light stuck to him, as though he was standing in his own personal glow. I stared at him and he stared back. He wasn't hiding, more observing or waiting for someone. Perhaps he was nothing more than a father waiting for his daughter to get off the last bus, but no buses (or transport of any type) go down my street. The area is a cul-de-sac so no-one walks down there unless they have a purpose. Ordinarily I would have drove right past, but my senses were on red alert and this guy didn't seem to be wanting to go anywhere in any great hurry. His piercing eyes peeped out from above a baggy dark brown winter coat and below a black woollen hat. This was England in August for God's sake, not Christmas in Moscow. His coat was shabby and that made him look almost destitute, or was I just being a drama queen conjuring up a crisis?

When I pulled up at my house he was about twenty yards away, still rooted to the spot. I pretended to check the boot of the car before putting the key in the lock of the front door and I turned quickly to try and catch a fleeting look at his face. But there was nothing to see. He was well covered up, and whether intentional or not, he gave nothing away.

I crossed over the threshold of my home and slumped myself into the large cushions on the couch. It was just before midnight so I'd made decent time getting back to the sanctity of my very own abode. It was so homely it was almost as though my mother was in the room. I felt safe and secure, as though those four walls were impregnable ... until I glanced at the floor. Didn't Steve say: "I know the colour of the carpet in your front room" when he spoke of my house? He had been in my home, and that immediately took away my feeling of being safe. Was there someone there now? Perhaps that guy outside was a look-out and his friend was in my house.

I had to take a look, for my own sanity. The stairs are extremely close to the front door so I convinced myself perhaps I should open the door just in case I needed a swift exit? But what about that spooky man outside? I would just be playing into his hands.

After freezing to listen for a few moments, I began to ascend the stairs against the advice of my anxiety. There was no way I was going to get up to the landing quietly, as each step creaked and groaned, seemingly ten times louder than normal. Who was I kidding, if there was someone hiding in a wardrobe or under the bed they were well aware I was there. The stairs were lit up, then I flicked the light switch as soon as I got to the top to illuminate the landing, and I did the same in each bedroom as I peered through each door. I braved my fears and checked wardrobes and cupboards, but there was no sight of anyone, or anything. I was alone, but the fear still remained.

I lay on the bed looking around the room, and it was then I noticed the picture frame on my dresser had been moved. I always had the photograph of Craig tilted to one side so he was facing my bed, but at that moment it was in line with everything else beside it. Each photograph and ornament had been placed in regimental order. It was as though someone had been in my house that very day and tidied up the room. That smiling face of my husband was always the first thing I saw when I woke up, and I remember it was looking at me that very morning. It wasn't facing the bed anymore.

I immediately checked to see that everything of value was still there, although probably the only items worth stealing with a decent re-sale value were my laptop computer and a tablet. But I noticed they were all in their usual places as soon as I returned home. I always keep a reasonable amount of ready cash in a CD box tucked away with the rest of my music collection, but that was a secret I shared with nobody, and the only way that would disappear was if the thief cleaned out the whole stockpile of CD's. I picked out the specific box but I scattered twenty pound notes all over the carpet as I carelessly forced it open and dropped it to the floor.

I shuffled the bank notes together and counted them. No money had been taken, it was there in full, and I placed the box back on the shelf. The more I thought about my house being 'visited', by Steve or whoever, the more I became unnerved. Well, scared stiff, to coin another phrase.

I thought of phoning the police, but what would I tell them? I could hardly say "My house has been broken into and all they did was tidy up the place!"

Steve had no fear of the police, because when I threatened to phone them earlier that night he was decidedly comfortable with the suggestion, and at one point even seemed to encourage it.

My phone must have been tapped, as he said, otherwise how else would he know my conversations? He proved that conclusively by naming times of calls and the conversations I made. I'm no computer wizard but I know it is easy enough to track someone by their phone. The app is standard, so he wouldn't have to be part of MI5 to watch my movements, just log onto Google maps.

Someone had broken into my house that particular day, but it couldn't have been Steve because he was with me. I had no intention of staying in that hotel on Holy Island, I just played along with his little game to see what he had to say. I knew the tide times before I left home that morning, and I confirmed them in the hotel later to be double sure. I knew I could leave any time after 10pm, but I didn't want him to know that. Once he offered to buy me clothes, and the causeway was closed, I was in unknown territory and wary of everything that could happen to me. But I knew that was just for a few hours, and I spent half that time in the hotel alone.

Before I left, Steve gave me one of his business cards and he asked me to phone him as soon as I got home to confirm that I made it safely. Who was he kidding? I never wanted to see him again. But I knew I hadn't come to the end of this little tale.

I decided to make contingency plans as I made a coffee, but the kettle hadn't even started to boil when my phone started to ring. It was an unknown number, obviously him, because who else would phone me at the witching hour? I decided to ignore it.

I glanced outside through the front window as I closed the blinds and the stranger was still propped up against a neighbour's wall, casually smoking a cigarette. He wasn't looking in my direction, which was comforting in some small way.

Then my land-line phone started to ring. That too was an unknown number. Could he possibly have that number too? It's ex-directory. This was starting to terrify me. All I had to do was lift up the receiver but I couldn't summon up the courage. I let it ring out, and then the silence became deafening. I wanted company ... I wanted someone there ... immediately!

The stillness was suspended with the muzzled ping-pong tone of my mobile phone, a text notification.

"Don't ignore me, I will call you on your house phone – please answer! It is very important!"

It was Steve, and I had no sooner read the words when the land-line rang once again. This time I did answer his call.

"Linda, I don't want you to say anything over this phone. Don't say a word, just LISTEN! In the morning I want you to buy a 'pay-as-you-go' mobile and phone the number on my business card, or use a friend's phone. Someone you can trust. If anyone comes to your house and you don't know who they are, or you feel threatened, be prepared to phone the police. Don't hesitate. OK? Please, phone me in the morning."

I simply said, "OK", and put down the receiver.

This was a double-edged sword if ever there was one. It was nice of him to show some concern, but that just confirmed I was under threat from someone. Originally I perceived Steve as the threat, but he was clearly on the right side of the law if he was encouraging me to get help from the police. But that call was the last thing I needed. Photos of Craig adorned every room in my home and I could see his face wherever I turned. I talked to them as though he was still a part of my life.

All my friends had tried to console me by urging me to change my reasoning: "Get rid of the memories and move on." But everything takes time and I was work in progress. My close friends consisted of Corrie, Grace, Emily and Joe, each with an opinion on how I should run my life, and presumably each well within their rights because they know me better than I know myself.

Corrie is the more vocal of them all, always demanding of me and always wanting to control what she can of my life. But I love that girl so much and I knew her major concern was to help me get through the mourning period and onto a better life.

"Living in the past is not healthy," she insisted. "Get rid of everything that hurts you. And that is everything that reminds you of Craig. He cheated on you Linda. Never forget that!"

I would LOVE to forget that, trust me, but does anyone know how difficult it is to believe you can blank out everything negative in your life and then actually achieve it? I had to learn to promote what I loved, rather than bash what I hated. I thought I could make that pivotal step when I went to Holy Island. Instead I came back with more baggage than what collects on the luggage carousel in Heathrow airport!

I grew up with Grace and Joe from our school days, and Emily was my closest friend at University. But for different genuine reasons, none of them were at hand to help me over this. Corrie lived close by, but she had a family and I couldn't take it upon myself to knock on her door in the early hours of the morning and ask for a bed for the night. Yet, I'd have given anything I owned to have any one of the other three there to help me through that evening.

I turned to switch off the standing lamp before heading up the 'wooden hill' to bed, but I was stopped dead in my tracks by a heavy-handed rap on the front door. Two knocks that just about took the door off its hinges.
I glared at the clock, it was 1.03am. I took a couple of paces backwards and instinctively picked up the phone. I waited about a minute for a third knock but it didn't come, so I replaced the phone and built up my courage. I peered through the blinds to see if anyone was standing outside. It was dark as there are no security lights anywhere in the area, only a street lamp up the road, but there was enough light to assure myself there was no-one there. I ran upstairs and looked down from each of the bedrooms and there was no movement at all in the street. One of the neighbours must have been disturbed because her bedroom light was switched on and I saw her peering through the window. Whoever knocked didn't seem to expect me to answer the door, they simply knocked and did a runner in an attempt to terrifying me. It worked.
This was the straw that broke the camel's back. I didn't need the police, I think I'd have been better off phoning the ambulance because I felt I was close to having a nervous breakdown. Was it fear or adrenaline making my heart beat faster? Either way, I'd had enough of this. Now I had to spend a night in a bedroom where someone had visited earlier that day. If he (or they) had wandered around once, what was stopping them doing it again?
I had a lock and chain on both the back and the front doors, so it was more secure when I was actually in the house, but I was going to call a locksmith first thing in the morning. Whoever got in obviously had a key, and that was another issue to address. How the hell DID he get it?

Even on good nights I can only sleep when I'm exhausted. This particular evening I was exhausted from the travelling and the ordeal of a frenetic day, and I could only manage to doze off for sporadic periods. I was starting to understand how sufferers of insomnia must drift through monotonous hours of misery every time their head hits the pillow. Who was it who said "I sleep like a baby – I wake up every ten minutes crying."
Time takes on a different form when you are afraid at night. It is more plentiful but there are more wakeful hours to worry and fret. And if you cannot sleep you are compelled to be afraid.
When I finally dropped off to sleep I woke as if a whole night had passed, but it hadn't. It was 3.16am, and I turned my head towards the door because I was sure I was roused by a muffled noise coming from the spare bedroom.
There was someone there, without doubt. There were footsteps, three or four, coming from the room next to me. But I had checked the rooms when I first returned and there was nobody there, and how could anyone possibly get up the creeky stairs without me hearing them?
I was too fearful to even move a muscle, and if I was going to move my body in any form it was going to be down the road in a gallop! All I needed was another bang on the door and I would have passed out. I couldn't take any more.
Could I conjure up the enthusiasm to go and find out what it was? I could either settle in for the long haul hiding under the bedclothes and wait until they showed a face, or I could phone the police. There was no choice in the matter, I leant forward to pick up the bedside phoned to dial 999 ... then the bedroom door opened.
In that moment the quiet had become like ice dripping onto my already cold skin and there I was face to face with that

stranger who had stood by the lamp-post outside. I stared back at him, my eyes trying to take in every detail in the shadows, but just seeing, sensing and feeling unmitigated fear.

"Where is the Gospel, Linda?" he questioned in a weird accent I couldn't fathom out. "You know where it is."

He certainly wasn't English, probably eastern European. I started hypo-ventilating, and as much as I wanted to reply I wasn't making a sound. Each second seemed to play on forever. I lay listening to the footsteps of my likely murderer as he paced the room getting more and more agitated. I couldn't see a weapon but that was not to say he didn't have one.

"Where are you hiding the Gospel?" he asked, as he finally stood still by the door, almost hidden in the darkness.

"Honestly, I don't know where it is," I cried out, "I didn't even know of its existence until today. I promise you."

I could feel every beat of my heart pounding, the sound of my own pulse throbbing in my ears. Suddenly, the serenity of silence surrendered to the deathly scream of his voice and he lunged forward pointing a finger right in my face.

"WHERE IS IT?"

This was the moment I thought I was going to die. I tried to protect my face, as I cowered back and pulled the blanket up to protect myself, as though a bed sheet would keep me safe.

"I honestly don't know!" I cried, but he grabbed the blanket and pulled it back. I lay there in my bedclothes as vulnerable as a day old child. I held my breath, daring not to make a sound. Each second seemed to last an eternity as he stood over me coiled like a cobra ready to strike. What other answer could I give? I was telling the truth.

He grabbed my face, squeezing my cheeks, forcing my jaw open. I grabbed his boney wrist and for a split second he seemed stunned that I was willing to put up a fight. It was then that I realised he wasn't the strong man I thought he was. He pulled away, twisting his arm so I lost my grip, but this time he forced himself onto the bed and grabbed me by the throat. I couldn't fight back. He was on top of me, pinning my arm to the pillow and squeezing my throat. I could smell his pungent, stinking, cigarette-fuelled breath as his face moved nearer to my mouth.
"Listen you bitch ..."
At that very second, cutting him off in mid-sentence, a narrow stream of light meandered through the room as my next-door neighbour turned on her bedroom light once again. It wasn't enough for me to make out his face but it perplexed him and made him rethink what to do next.
He looked towards the window but continued to pin me down. This time he lowered his voice to a whisper and put his rancid mouth to my ear: "Raise your voice and I kill you!"
He slowly eased the pressure off my throat, ready to grasp again should I scream. Then he whispered: "Make one move out of place and I will tear out your windpipe, do you understand?"
I understood fully, but I couldn't stay silent because I was choking.
I composed myself after coughing and spluttering for a second or two, then I told him all I knew: "I know my husband took the book but I honestly don't know where it is. I can't help you. Please believe me."
Was he prepared to kill me? I don't know. Would he have tried to rape me? I cannot answer that either. But neither happened, because, for some miracle, my neighbour opened

her front door. He got off the bed and looked for a quick getaway, threatening me with all manner of atrocities should I scream for help or get the police.

His words didn't mean much, they just came at me with such venom I was too frightened to make them out.

The neighbour knocked on my door, and the stranger retreated to the bedroom door, leaving with a volley of words: "If you get the police, you will be hanging from the nearest tree before the day is out!"

Then ... he was gone ... as fleeting an exit as the Scarlet Pimpernel in Emma Orczy's novel. I lay on the bed and woefully cried my eyes out. My neighbour returned to her own house and closed her front door, and I was so glad I didn't have to explain my tears.

What is fear? I remembered the saying - "When fear comes, walk with confidence right past, because like the ghosts of children's nightmares, fear is an illusion."

Fear is not an illusion. It is as true and as real as anything we can touch. The precursor to bravery. To cry or to fight? I didn't fight against him, but fought against the urge to scream, cry and have a melt down – and it probably saved my life. I'd recommend it to anyone.

He left by the back door but I was convinced he didn't enter by it. The chain had been put in place the previous morning immediately before I left for Holy Island, and I did the same with the front door when I returned. Replacing the locks on doors was hardly going to make the place impregnable, because I believed that whoever was treating the place like Paddington Station was not using the doors at all. I had no idea how they were getting in.

I learnt many things from that experience that night - that Steve seemed to be on the right side of the law; he wasn't the only party searching for the Gospel; and I was now totally convinced that Craig was murdered.

CHAPTER SIX

Should I phone the police? Would the intruder carry out his threat if I did?

I struggled to find an answer to either question, but I understood that the latter was a possibility.

My past brushes with the boys in blue proved a total waste of time, and those memories swayed me towards "don't bother." And that was despite the fact that my dearly departed father used to be a copper! He been part of the Old Bill all of his working life, so what does that say about the public's lack of trust in the law enforcement agency?

My Dad tried to tell people that everything was "done by the book" but I don't believe there even is a "book." The police hold all the cards and I've seen first hand how they work. Many of them up to their eyeballs in corruption.

I shared a flat with Emily during our days at university in Leeds. Harehills was not the safest area in the city, I must admit, but the rent was affordable. My God, those memories. The locals had 'looking poor' down to a fine art, even the ones with money. The newcomers, the students, knew it was advisable to keep a low profile. If you wanted to stay 'healthy' you did just that. However, if you broke the golden rule and reported an incident to the police, it was a waste of time anyway, because the they would never respond. Nothing was ever done.

I saw a young kid (about 13 years old) firing pellets from an air-rifle into my car, for no other reason than to use the vehicle for target practice. Not only did it cost £585 to repair, but there was the danger that someone could have

been blinded by the jerk. I took a photo of him in the act, and showed it to the police to identify him, but later I was informed that his parents wanted to take ME to court for taking photos of a minor without their permission!
The police advised me to "drop the case" because I was "treading a fine line". That day I lost all faith in the legal system. I became aware that plain and simple 'honesty' is only the truth when the police say so.
Back to the intruder in my bedroom. If I reported the incident how could I characterize him? A nondescript face; average height; medium weight and build. In fact if it wasn't for that distinctive trench-coat he could have walked past me in the street and I wouldn't have noticed him.
My words would feel small and inadequate, and the officer would expect more. I know how it works. It was excruciating torment but what could I do?
Some say there are good cops and bad. But I say that's an oversimplification. They can be honest; courageous; corrupt; devious; malicious; cunning; or just plain stupid. And that was just my dad! He was all of those things. Not all at once of course, but the right blend of circumstances could bring out any one of those emotions in him.

I visited my neighbour to ask what she had seen the previous evening, in the hope that perhaps she had seen more of him. She had heard noises as though someone was trying to get into the house through the upstairs toilet window. She too saw the stranger outside in the street that evening, but her description of him was just as poor as my own. However, I had a lot to thank her for.
Being self employed, I can work when it suits, but I was starting a two week holiday, so I had all day to catch up on my much needed sleep. But I had a list of things to do and

top of that inventory was to call in to see Corrie, knowing she would be up with her one year old son, Jack. She only lives up the road and the sun was now beating down on the pavement, encouraging me to walk rather than take the car.
I needed someone close who I could trust, to let out some of the emotion that hadn't already been spilt all over my pillow.
Sadly, Corrie has two sides to her. She has a forthright opinion on everyone else's lives, but she gives away very little about her own.
Her main weakness is her own relationship with her husband, Derek. It's hardly harmonious but she keeps her feelings under lock and key. She has a dark side that she never reveals, and it upsets me that she never shares anything with anybody that could taint the fantasy of their 'perfect' marriage.
My mind flickered back to her wedding, when she exhibited an acting masterclass. I assumed she didn't want to marry Derek that day because her make-over covered up bruises from yet another heated debate. They happened often. Derek didn't seem over enthusiast about the wedding, either. After the ceremony he spent the entire evening in deep conversation with his ex-girlfriend!
I didn't know how much I should tell Corrie, or even where to start?
I didn't think I could make Steve's character believable. Should I have portrayed him as the villain or the hero? I couldn't decide which because I didn't think he was either. I was still up in the air about that myself. Although he didn't seem frightened by any police involvement, he still hadn't won me over. The stolen Gospel was probably believable to her from the stand-point that she had a big distrust of Craig after his infidelity, and she would make

any negative thought a tool to hammer his memory. Probably because she sensed Derek was doing the same behind her back.

I started by telling her the tale about the night visitor, and that had her eyes almost popping out on stalks. However, suggesting Craig's death was murder had her shaking her head in disbelief. Nope, she wasn't falling for that one.

"He wasn't murdered, Linda," she said most profoundly. "That's a ridiculous thought."

It was the burglar that concerned her most.

She made no effort to hide her disgust. "You are joking me? Why the hell didn't you phone the police? Oh my God!"

"That was an experience I never want to relive," I said, and it upset me even talking about it.

Corrie poured boiling water from the kettle into two brightly coloured mugs, and I could see her mind ticking over.

"It's a lot to take in, Linda. My God, I would have died if a stranger grabbed me by the throat. You must have been petrified!"

I didn't answer.

Corrie continued: "As for Craig being a thief … has he ever stolen from anyone? Is he that type?"

There were patches in his life that he refused to talk about to anyone. He spent time inside Low Newton young offenders prison in Durham when he was a teenager. He would never admit to me the charge, but his mother said it was for burglary. She would occasionally drop it into a conversation when he was being obnoxious to her, much to his disgust. But although he always played it down when talking about it to me, he never denied it in front of her. I didn't think it appropriate to mention it in that discussion with Corrie, so I skipped the question.

"I'm supposed to phone Steve this morning using a different phone," I said. "Could I use yours?"
Corrie immediately went on the defensive.
"Errrrm, if he can tap your phone, I'd rather he didn't have my number. I'm not being nasty, Linda, just cautious. I'd rather not get involved in this if you don't mind."
She turned away and tidied up the breakfast table, doing anything to avoid looking me in the eye.
"Yeah, I understand," I replied.
But for someone who didn't want to get involved she asked a lot of questions.
"Are you going to inform the police?" She asked, but wasn't that the '$64,000 Dollar Question.' Should I or shouldn't I?
"I've thought about that all evening," I answered. "I don't know what to do."
Then just when I was about to give a couple of reasons why I should … and why I shouldn't … my mobile phone rang.
"It's him! It's Steve!" I shouted, "He's phoning me!"
We both stared at each other, she took the phone from my hand and looked at the number, "Here, you have to answer it!" and handed it back to me.
"Hello," I said timidly, although I was pleased there was someone there to witness this man really did exist.
"I asked you to call me this morning," he said in a demanding voice.
"Yeah, well I've had a lot to think about since I got up and I'm thinking about phoning the police," I replied, half expecting him to try and discourage me, and he did, but in a roundabout manner.
"If that's what you want to do … go ahead. But can I come with you? Because I would like to report a theft from my home by your ex-partner." he replied. "Linda, I think we

should talk. You only know half of the story and it's probably time I put my cards on the table. Can we meet now?"

Corrie heard it all and started to shake her head, mouthing in silence "No, don't do it!"

"A man broke into my house last night and threatened to kill me," I said over the phone. "At one point I thought he was going to rape me!"

"He wanted information, Linda, he didn't want to rape you. Rape is a big word."

I wasn't having any of that, "How the hell do you know? Were you there? 'Murder' is an even bigger word, and I believe he was capable of that too! Do not patronize me Steve!"

Brick by brick, my walls came tumbling down. I started crying and a sharp pain ripped through my chest. Corrie pressed her forehead against my face and my spirit crumbled. I dropped the phone to the floor. I wasn't interested in what that man had to say.

As much as I tried to hold it in, the pain finally came out. I picked up the phone and shouted, "I wish I had never set eyes on you! In less than 24 hours you have tried to ruin my life!"

Then I switched off the phone and hugged my friend.

At that moment my world became a blur of colour that melted to black.

Ten minutes later my phone rang again. No guessing who it was.

"I'm at a friend's house at the moment," I said, before Corrie finally broke her silence: "Don't tell him you are here!"

"Can you PLEASE return to your home so we can talk?" he said.

"Are you at my house?" I questioned, "Right now? How long have you been there?"

I was starting to panic, but not as much as Corrie, who was on the verge of having a heart attack.

"Oh my God, I've got Jack here Linda, you have to keep him away from this house!" she screamed. "I'm going to phone Derek ... and the police!"

"Listen," I said, trying to calm down a woman who was totally off the rails. "I will leave, don't worry, I will sort this out. Steve and I will go to the police together. OK, Corrie? Don't worry, I will not bring trouble to your house, I promise. So DON'T phone the police because that really WILL involve you!"

I picked up my bag and briskly headed out of the door. She literally threw me out onto the street and tried to close the door before my feet were even over the threshold. So much for everlasting friendship. However, she did say "Take care" ... through the letterbox!

I knew there was no way I was going to end this fiasco anytime soon. No matter how ridiculous the situation, it would not be solved until they (whoever they are) got what they were looking for, but what could I possibly do to help them?

"Enough is enough," I mumbled to myself as the distance shortened to my house. Every emotion shot through my head and I wondered what to do next. What I wanted to do was pack my bags and head off for a holiday. The destination didn't matter, just give me the first flight available.

Steve was stood by a silver grey Mercedes.

"Where did that pop up from?" I thought to myself. It was not parked at his cottage the previous day, and it was a car I would certainly have noticed.

He gazed at me but seemed unmoved as I trudged forward, and that annoyed me somewhat. I stopped, just short of colliding with him, but I steadied myself before speaking.
"Someone is trying to ruin my life, Steve," I said calmly. "He was here last night and you are involved with him. What are you playing at?"
"Can we go inside, please? Let's take this … misunderstanding … off the street," he replied, then tried to lead me by the hand. That made me even more annoyed. The fact that he was inviting, and leading me, into my own house!
I wasn't too happy about letting him into my home but there wasn't really much of an option. Before we stepped inside I sarcastically remarked, "Shall we use your key or mine? You obviously have one."
He took what I had to give and wisely kept his mouth shut. I hung up my coat and we both sat facing each other across the small living room waiting for the other to start the conversation. I finally broke the silence.
"So, Mr Campbell, what brings you to sunny Seaham?" If you cannot say anything constructive, hit them with a bit of sarcasm. Something I learnt from my father.
"Linda this isn't quite going to plan," he said looking for every reaction in my face, as though he expected me to jump into a fit of rage at the drop of a hat. And, to be honest, he wasn't wrong. But I was fighting it.
"What is the plan, Steve? Pray tell me."
"I told you what I am looking for but I didn't get to finish the story," he continued, and dare I say, he looked most sincere. "You dashed off before I could get into detail. I hoped you would stay on the island. I wanted to gain your trust, because you don't believe a word I say. But everything I tell you is the truth."

He was going to extremes to get over his point. Once again, like at Holy Island, he leant forward to touch my arm and again we clashed: "Don't Steve! I mean that. Do NOT touch me!"

"What can I possibly know that Craig didn't?" I said, meaning every single word. "I haven't seen your book; the only thing I know about it is what you told me; and you know for a fact it isn't here. What else is there to add?" Although Craig was my soul mate for many years, I have to admit there was a large percentage of his life that I knew nothing about. Corrie called him 'devious', and perhaps she could see through the charm and I couldn't. I'd prefer to think that Craig just wanted to keep our relationship as simple as he could. Telling me his problems meant involving me in them, and all the obstacles in his life were kept in some fictitious tin box hidden under the bed. He didn't want to burden me with them.

That was how I perceived it at the time, but obviously he was pulling the wool over my eyes. There was a lot going on in the shadows that I knew nothing about, and I don't just mean hopping into bed with Little Miss Slapper from up the road.

His friends were never part of our social gathering. He mixed with my pals, but I was never allowed to mix with his. "Allowed" is probably too strong an expression. He called his mates boring and uneducated. My father's description was more graphic - "scum of the Earth" – followed by "uncultured halfwits".

Most of them were involved in petty crime, and my father had crossed paths with them many times. He had 'nicked' all of them (quite often) over a period of years, and I sometimes wondered how Craig always managed to keep his nose clean.

My husband and my Dad never built a friendship beyond idle talk at birthday parties and Christmas gatherings. Neither wanted to meet the other half-way, and I understood their reasons. So I left them to it. But during the last days of my Dad's life he told me he had regretted he had not made the effort to form a bond with Craig. He knew he only had days left of his life and perhaps it was his way of making me happy and clearing his own conscience. I don't know, and I will never know, how serious he was with those words. My Dad didn't know about the 'affair', having passed away three years before that came to light, but I think he would have been very shocked if he found out about the suicide. Everybody associated with Craig, friends and family, were unanimous in the shock of it all. So many loose ends.

However, perhaps my father was right all along. I dread to think how he would have reacted to the news that Craig had stooped so low as to pinch from the church. My father was not a regular paid up member of the 'Bible Basher Club', but he was religious. And you don't have to be religious to curl your toes up at the very thought of what Craig did.

At the end of the day, although Steve had a peculiar and somewhat 'mystifying' way of going about things, he was only wanting back what my husband had taken. And as things stood, he was trying to keep Craig's dignity intact by not involving the police. But did Craig deserve that privilege?

"I have tried every possible way of doing things without involving you, Linda," said Steve, and he was coming close to winning me over.

"I don't want any harm to come to you," he continued, "and no harm WILL come to you. But PLEASE help me. I am responsible for what has happened. I was stupid enough to give your husband the opportunity to do what he did. I hold my hands up. It was moronic, and I am suffering the consequences. Because of my actions, everyone is a loser. Although I cannot alter what has happened or change the past, I have a duty to find what was taken and return it to Holy Island. Can you understand that?"

"Who was the man in my house last night?" I asked. "You say no harm will come to me. I was pinned to my own bed!"

"What did he look like?"

"His face was hidden and it was dark," I replied as I tried to relive that terrifying moment. "He wore a baggy dark brown winter coat; dark trousers; big heavy boots; and a black woollen hat. His breath stunk of cigarette smoke and his clothes did too. I would be grasping at straws suggesting his age, but he wasn't young. Around 50-ish probably."

"Did he speak with a foreign accent?" he asked.

"Yeah, he did. Nothing particularly strong. He must have lived in this country for a long time because I could make out very word, but there was an accent. Polish perhaps?"

"How about German? And was the coat like a regimental type of garment?" asked Steve.

"Possibly, yeah," I responded, trying to rewind to his threatening words. "Yes, I could live with that. German more than Polish. An army coat? Yes, certainly. Who is it?"

"I have a decent idea who it could be," he replied, but he knew who it was alright. I could tell immediately but he wouldn't say. Anyway, a name wouldn't have made me any wiser. I didn't know the man … but I wanted to know about him.

"Well, then, who is it?" I demanded to know.

Steve got up and started to pace the floor. Whenever I confronted him he would reply in a tone as though whatever he said was pre-packaged. Like an educated statement.

"I think it's a guy called Buchtmann," he replied. "I'm not sure, but the description fits. We have a past history, and if anyone has an interest in what we are looking for … it's him. He won't touch you again. I will make sure of that."

I suppose you could call it a 'Eureka' moment. Not a memory per-se, but after a ten minutes in-depth conversation he had me believing I was safe. In this environment – on my home turf – I was willing to listen. When I was on Holy Island it was a whole different ball game. I put up barriers because he was in my face, probing and pushing, and he gave the perception that he was a little too enthusiastic to get what he wanted.

Now I was willing to be attentive and listen to what the 'teacher' had to say.

"The Gospel Craig took is more than a book of pretty text and paintings," he explained in layman's terms. "It's not like conventional books of today, it has very little punctuation and the text is set in 'sense units', which is a little like poetry. The Lindisfarne Gospels were taken from the island, along with the body of St Cuthbert, after an invasion of the Vikings. After seven years of journeying they settled in Chester-le-Street before eventually ending their travels at Durham."

Steve continued with his tale: "As for the other book, the one we are concerned about, it remained on the island and for most of its early years it was hidden in the walls of the Priory. However, Holy Island monks took it to Rome to the Apostolic Palace, which is now Vatican City, and it caused so much outrage it was denounced by the Pope as evil propaganda. It was castigated as being the work of evil and the Catholic clergy ordered it to be destroyed. The Bishop of Catholicism in the Vatican pronounced it a fake and many witnessed claimed they saw it being incinerated. But it survived. We have no idea how it ended up back on Holy Island. That is as much an enigma as the book itself. Some suggested the Pope handed it back to the monks in a pact of secrecy, insisting it should 'never see the light of day again.'"

It was a lot to take in but I accepted the importance of what he was saying.

"That book makes a declaration that we, on Holy Island, own the most important relic in Christianity. The only remnant that survives from the time of Christ and the only fragment of anything that displays his name."

"So why," I asked, "would that be a problem to the Pope?"

"Because every relic in the Vatican, and all of Italy and Spain, are fakes. Whatever they profess to own from the life of Jesus is a forgery. Every last item!" he said with robust conviction.

He continued, "While experts debate whether Christ was crucified with three or with four nails, at least thirty 'Holy Nails' continue to be venerated as relics in Italy in various churches. The St. John Lateran in Rome claims to have the 'umbilical cord' believed to remain from the birth of Christ. Utter rubbish, but millions of people flock to see it. The Veil of Veronica, which according to legend, was used to wipe the sweat from Jesus' brow as he carried the cross, is kept in Saint Peter's Basilica in Rome. It was carbon-dated and comes from the 12th century. The Holy Shroud of Turin is the most studied artefact in human history. Radiocarbon dating proved that the shroud was made during the Middle Ages. Another is the Holy Chalice, the vessel which Jesus used at the Last Supper to serve the wine. It gave rise to the legend of Holy Grail. It is not even part of Catholic tradition, it's just mythology, but at least eight such vessels are found in numerous churches throughout Europe. The most significant religious artefact in history is hidden on Holy Island. The Vatican claim to have it but what they have on show is a forgery, just like everything else they have."

Curiosity got the better of me: "Well then, what is it? And does the Vatican have a right to it?"

He was quick off the marks with his reply: "Not at all! The monks of Holy Island held it for 500 years before the Vatican even came into existence."

"OK," I replied, "what is the artefact?"

Finally I got an answer: "The wood placard that was placed above Christ's head on the cross. John describes it as reading: JESUS OF NAZARETH, THE KING OF THE JEWS.' It was written in Hebrew, Greek and Latin. Hebrew was the national language; Greek was the language most widely understood; and Latin was the language of Rome. Although John's gospel refers to the writing as a 'title,' Mark and Matthew both refer to it as an 'accusation.' It was customary to name the crime for which they suffered, and the name of the criminal. Jesus had been condemned by Pilate for claiming to be the King of the Jews."

"What about the cross itself?" I asked, "Did that survive?"

"Once again many Italian churches claim to have fragments, but carbon-dating proves them all wrong. It was most probable that the cross Jesus was crucified on had been used for previous crucifixions, and it was subsequently used for many more after his death. But the 'Titulus Crucis', the piece of wood baring his name, was unique to Christ and it survives. It was taken to Holy Island by Emperor Hadrian, along with many other treasures." It was as though he was reading from the pages of a guide book and I still wasn't sure that everything that came from his mouth was legitimate.

Steve changed the subject of our discussion and asked about Craig's last Will and Testament.

"He rewrote it just days before his death," I replied, "and the financial side of it was fairly straight forward. There is no mention of any millions of pounds in an off-shore account. If that money did exist, don't you think he would have accounted for it in the Will?"

"No I don't," he replied rather assertive. "That money is not legal! And it remains illicit whether he is alive or dead. It can't just suddenly appear in a Will and immediately go back into circulation. It was a felonious act. But I'm sure he will have made contingency plans for it. It will probably land through your letterbox in various brown paper parcels, periodically. That's how scammers work. They will take the money from a blind beggar's tin pot, but they are loyal to each other."

"Ah well," I replied, "I will look forward to the first installment."

Steve continued to check out the living room as he spoke, looking at clocks, ornaments and my music rack. His mind only half on what he said.

"What are you looking for?" I asked as my eyes followed his vision around the walls.

"Back to the Will," he said, looking up at the ceiling as though he was waiting for religious intervention. "I know I'm grasping at straws, but did Craig leave any unusual items for people you wouldn't have expected to benefit from his Will?"

"You've seen too many movies, Steve," I laughed. "How do you think it was conducted - 'The grieving family gathered in the Solicitor's office as the last Will and Testament of the deceased was read out. Great Aunt Ethel expected the off-shore millions, but all she got was the toaster, prompting uproar amongst the relatives'."

I knew there was a cryptic clue in the Will. It dawned on me as soon as he mentioned it, but I wanted to know how Steve knew. No-one – other than our solicitor and myself – was there when it was actually read out.

The Will was as good as making a personal statement that something was going to happen to Craig. That was why the suicide was never disputed, because his Will was virtually a suicide note. It was indeed a last testament, with some rather crazy personal instructions. I was the named Executor so I carried out his wishes. His solicitor confirmed it was legally valid, made by the deceased, and it was established that it had not been superseded by a later Will. He left just about everything to me, apart from some army memorabilia he promised to his mates. Some of it was borrowed from friends, and some he bought himself. It included funeral wishes, and odds and sods for his friends, but some of the beneficiaries named lived abroad. They could have been work mates, but they could also have been the hackers and scammers Steve talked about. There were keys for safe deposit boxes in London and abroad, all dealt with (under instruction) by one of Craig's best friends.

But there was a cryptic clue at the end that had me confused. As though he had a secret he only wanted to share after his death, but for who? Our solicitor couldn't work it out. It mentioned an address but I checked it out and it didn't exist.

CHAPTER SEVEN

The more I looked at Steve I could see a man who almost 'belonged', but not quite. He had the right persona, someone you would be proud to take home to meet the family, but I constantly wondered what was ticking inside that head? Something was not wired up quite right.
He was like no-one I have ever met before. No man who seeks to be mysterious can truly be, because there's something about wanting the attention that gives them away.
So what was Steve hiding?
"There is a cryptic clue in the will," I said. Well I had to come clean sooner or later.
I had his full attention.
"But you knew there was, didn't you?" I added. "How did you know? And don't fill me with bullshit!"
He looked studious, and I thought immediately he was cooking up a cock-and-bull story to see what he could get away with. But when he spoke he always sounded so convincing.
"I get everything second or third hand," he replied. "Craig had told someone the key was in the Will he had written."
"What I don't understand," I said, trying to piece together this gigantic jigsaw, "why would someone kill Craig if he was the only source of information? They were never going to find the Gospel if he was dead, were they? That doesn't make sense."
Steve agreed: "Exactly! Which is why we are chasing our own dead-ends. But every now and again we get the flash of a rabbit's tail. I believe whoever killed your husband knows where the Gospel is, and he was making sure nobody else got to know."

Now that made a lot of sense.
"What was the cryptic clue?" he asked.
I took my time to reply as I didn't want to make a mistake. I don't have a photographical memory but I took a stab at it: "'Whatever he is hiding can be found at Thomas Street in a place called Meadas.' He also names two individuals called Trevor and Ronald, who I don't know personally."
"Where the hell is Meadas?" he asked rather abruptly. "That sounds Arabic, but Thomas Street? That's an odd combination."
"I checked," I replied, "and the only place with the name Meadas that I can find on the internet is near Faro in Portugal. But Craig never visited Portugal. I would normally say that I know that for a fact. But it seems as though he has travelled far and wide without me knowing. So perhaps he has."
"Who is Rob Mitchell?" quizzed Steve.
"Why do you ask? He is a close friend of Craig's."
"You sent a number of texts to him recently," said Steve, and once again it was disturbing to realize he was checking my phone. "You mentioned a letter included in the Will with directions to some place you hadn't heard of. So I take it he knows about the address and the people you have been talking about."
"How can you be allowed to tap my phone," I replied. "That is an invasion of privacy. I can get you jailed for that!"
He instantly ignored the question, as though I hadn't even spoken.
"Why did you send the text to this guy called Mitch? What does he know about the Gospel?"
That immediately got me wound up: "I only found out about Craig stealing the Gospel – from you – yesterday! So

obviously there had been no mention of it verbally, in texts or on the phone. I didn't know the Gospel existed until yesterday!"

But it got me thinking. "Hold on ... I did think at the time that Mitch seemed unusually intrigued by the contents of the Will, especially as he wasn't involved in any part of it. I thought perhaps he was expecting a windfall and he was disappointed that he missed out."

"Did you tell him the address?" Steve asked, as though he was onto something.

"No, I didn't tell him, but he did ask for it. I thought that was strange and I didn't want him getting his hands on something I knew nothing about."

"Yeah," said Steve, "I noticed. But was the only communication by texts?"

"Yes," I said, making sure I was correct before I spoke. "Everything was said in texts, there was no other correspondence because I don't like the guy. I didn't tell him anything more than that. Why? Do you think he is involved?"

"I KNOW he is involved," he replied, making his point profoundly, "but does he knows where the book is? How would you describe him as a person, his personality? Wise-guy, shifty, on the wrong side of the tracks?"

"Yeah, probably all of those, but 'shifty' more than anything else. He's got a name in Seaham, and not for anything good. He did time as a teenager for petty crimes – burglary; GBH; car theft; and he beat up a copper once. I think Craig met him for the first time in Borstal. They have been pals ever since their teens. I didn't trust him and Craig knew my feelings so he made sure our paths rarely crossed."

"He knows something about the Gospel," said Steve in a strange satisfying manner. "And it's what he knows that concerns me. I get the feeling he was the brains behind the deal offered to the Priory when they wanted a million pounds for a safe return of the book. A deal that obviously went wrong for Craig."

I wasn't convinced: "If this book is as precious as you say, I don't think Mitch has the contacts, or the know-how, to get to the money men. He's 'small time', in his own little small time world. He can get you a knocked off HD TV or top of the range phone, but that's about his limits."

"Perhaps he saw the opportunity of a lifetime," replied Steve, although I felt he was probably giving Mitch more respect than he rightly deserved.

"It depends on what Craig told him," he added. "Rob gets himself a goldmine plonked right on his lap. How could any petty thief resist that?"

Steve asked for my copy of the Will and I went straight to the bedroom drawer where I kept all of my personal documents. But as I flicked through bills, long forgotten love letters and birthday cards, I realised it had disappeared. I was convinced I had put it in the drawer, so delving any deeper down the pile of discoloured envelopes and shards of paper was futile. Somebody had taken it. Anger boiled deep in my stomach. The pressure of this rigmarole returned. My space had been violated. My house, my home, had been treated like a walkway from one street to another. My personal property had been taken … not taken but stolen!

I walked into the living room smouldering underneath a blue flame.

"It's not there," I said. "But you knew that already, didn't you?"

"First and foremost can I tell you I have not been in this house before!" he insisted.

"So," I retorted, "if you didn't take it, somebody else did! I may as well throw open the doors and let you all get on with it. I'm so sorry for getting in your way." I wasn't just angry, I was about to get nasty. "Nothing is sacred to you, is it? You are trying to destroy my life. Treading on my feelings and destroying every emotion I have had for a person I adored."

"Quite the contrary, Linda, everything is sacred to me!" he answered, "And you have no idea how much I want to help you and put things right. I have been honest with you, every word, but I need your help just as much as you need mine. We BOTH want answers."

"Who were the witnesses to the Will?" asked Steve.

"Two workmates," I answered.

"Who would benefit from his death?" he responded, "He could have been killed by his new girlfriend's lover, and no matter how unlikely it seems, that is a possibility. He was deeply troubled. He must have had threats from quite a few people. I believe he tried to sell the Gospel to a private collector, probably with Rob Mitchell involved, and they got themselves in deep shit. I can picture it all now. Mitchell knows he's next for the rope unless he produces the goods. The problem is, Craig hid it away and Mitchell can't do a deal because he doesn't know where it is!"

"Do you think Mitch has the letter?" I asked.

"I don't think he has," he replied, thumbing through the contact numbers in his phone. "I think he has been here, but I don't think he found it. But it's missing, so somebody has it! But Mitchell is in big trouble."

"Did you see Craig's flat after his death?" asked Steve.

71

"No, his brother saw to all his possessions. I never set foot in the place but his brother said it was distressing."

"Before Craig died he had painted across his apartment wall 'I REPENT - Jesus of Nazareth – King of the Jews' in big letters. It was in three different languages – Hebrew, Greek and Latin. He was a petrified human being."

That struck a chord with me: "When I viewed his body at the Chapel of Rest to identify him I noticed a tattoo on his back. Words in different languages. That probably explains it."

There is a well known saying: "There is a book in everyone". But if my life was made into a book, the reader would be bored on page one, and after page two throw it in a bin with the trash. The most excitement I had ever experienced in my life was probably a package holiday in Spain, drinking wine and eating paella before dipping my toes into the Mediterranean Sea. In university Emily and myself, like every other Fresher on campus, had big big dreams. I wanted to backpack across New Zealand, sail up the Amazon in a little wooden boat, and swim with dolphins. She wanted to explore rural China, see the Northern Lights, and trek across America on a Harley-Davidson. She achieved them all while the closest I got to the Amazon was downloading a book.

In a nutshell – nothing of note ever happened to me. But if I was going to write a book, at least I now had at least ONE exciting chapter.

"If the Gospel is such a secret," I asked Steve, "why did you show it to Craig?"

Steve explained he didn't show him what was in the safe: "I didn't actually show him anything apart from a ring that was excavated from an archaeological dig that Craig happened to mention. I explained the rest to you yesterday. He got inside my safe and obviously found what was there."

Steve then produced a couple of photos, "This is the Gospel. It's made from calfskin and weighs in at around one and a half kilos. It is unmistakable. The book's secrets are its true value. I don't know if your ex-husband could read Latin, but I think he found out more than he was expecting."

The book cover was decorated with a monogram formed with a large jewelled red cross and a mesmerizing haloed bust-figure of Christ.

"That is breathtaking," I whispered, and that was no understatement.

When I said I was going back to Lindisfarne, my friend Emily warned me to leave things be and not to go walking into the past.

Holy Island may be beautiful, bewitching even, and Craig described it as "The Elysian fields of a Promised Land." Don't worry about going to Hell, the bible tells us, just be good. But Craig couldn't even do that!

Then, suddenly, those very thoughts jogged my memory. It was at that precise moment that I remembered where I had left the letter!

CHAPTER EIGHT

'Last Car To Elysian Fields' by James Lee Burke was the novel Craig bought me for my birthday just days before he died. We lived apart but that 'connection' remained. I wasn't ready to forgive, and I wanted him to accept the consequences. So we lived in a time warp of nothingness. What we both wanted, neither of us got. But I blame myself for that. I was magistrate and jury all rolled into one, and wouldn't give him a pardon. He apologized, what more could he possibly do?

You know when you feel as though you are lost in a maze and you are not sure which path to take, then in a split second there is a spark of light and you walk right through the walls as though they weren't there? I saw that light. "Follow me," I said pointing to the dining room door. "I know where the Will is!"

'Elysian Fields' was my favourite novel but I lost my copy on holiday when I left it in a Spanish restaurant. Craig replaced it and I remember putting the letter between its pages and positioning it on the bookshelf.

I remember the book had gold lettering on a black binding, so it wasn't that difficult to find. It was there, thankfully, untouched since the day I placed it on that shelf. I flicked through the pages and the envelope fell to the floor. I picked it up and handed it to Steve.

"I'm so sorry. It slipped my mind," I said, showing more gratitude than regret. "But the fact it was lost may have been for the better because no-one else got their hands on it."

The clue was meant for a specific person, but what was the point if there was no name attached?

"It's not in Seaham, the only hope is in Meadas.
Don't waste your time in Moats Street, go to Thomas Street.
3-3 is the score.
Look for Ronald, but leave Loran alone.
Trevor has it, but it's not in his Rover.
Father of the bride confesses to being on the Beech."

One moment I thought I had something, but the next minute I was back to square one, and I couldn't say which one I preferred. Believing I was getting somewhere when I was nowhere near; or accepting it was beyond me. I didn't know a Ronald or a Loran, and the Trevor I did know didn't have a car because he couldn't drive. Obviously none of the names were going to make any sense to Steve, so he didn't stand a chance of cracking it.

"Can I take this?" he asked, holding the piece of paper up against the light for whatever reason.

"Yeah, no problem," I replied. Then asked: "What are you looking for?"

"It's an old piece of paper," he said. "Do you know which notebook it came from? There could be clues in the notebook if we can find it."

"He had lots of notebooks for varied reasons – his tax; his spending; his artwork. They are all in the spare bedroom. I will get them," I said, then hastily ran upstairs and collected together about eight or nine books.

I spread them on the table and immediately Steve picked up an old battered ring-binding book that looked well thumbed.

"This is the book he used for the letter," he muttered, flicking through the pages. "He's had this book most of his life judging by the brown edges. It smells like a dusty old attic."

"No," I replied, "I believe that was his dad's book. He died about a year ago. Craig kept all of his old books."

Bound in red, cracked and dry with age, the pages of the thin volume were brittle and what remained of the book's original stitching barely held it together. A faint scrawl on the inside of the cover declared that the journal once belonged to John Wilson of 15 Moss Gardens, Peterlee.

The first page began in the middle of a sentence, suggesting that pages were missing. Steve seemed enthralled with it and asked if he could borrow it. He stayed for another ten minutes then, after he made a couple of phone calls, he headed off on "business". He didn't say if he would be returning, he simply said he would phone.

"Can I get back to my normal life?" I asked, "Or will I be required again?"

He thanked me for all of my help but pleaded with me to keep quiet on everything we had discussed.

Before he disappeared out of the door I asked him, "Have you been truthful with me about everything you have told me?"

He turned around and thought very deeply before replying: "What part of this do you doubt?"

"That's not an answer," I retorted. "Have you told me any lies?"

"Everything I have told you about Craig is true! And I say that hand on heart."

There were still more questions than answers. And Steve knew the damage he had done to me.

"It must be excruciating for you," he said in sympathy. "I don't want to crush the love you have for your husband, Linda. You knew the man, I didn't. But I HAVE told you the truth, no matter how much it hurts. You know in your subconscious what you feel about him. I don't want to destroy anything you had together."

"What about you?" I asked. "How would you describe yourself?"

"How would I describe myself? You know, I have never been asked that question before. I'm not perfect. I have my negative side. I admit. But I am a decent man, and everything I have told you is as accurate as I can possibly be. I am not a con man."

"So what happens now?" I asked, "Will you find your Gospel?"
"Oh I will find it," he said in a confident manner. More confident than I expected.
"Because of your help, and I thank you for that," he added. Then he left. I looked around the house and reflected on what had just happened, then that lonely feeling returned. What was that all about? It's not so much the fact that nobody is with you, its the fact that nobody cares.
Would I see Steve again? Did I want to see him again? He had caused me nothing but stress and anxiety during every second I was with him, but all that time he showed he cared.

I had the locks changed on the doors of the house and latches added to each upstairs window. It was all well and good keeping intruders out, but what if I had a fire?
I decided against buying a new phone, because I couldn't see the point. If they (whoever 'they' were) could tap the phone I already had, what was stopping them doing it to any new phone I purchased? I would revalue that at a later date. If listening to my every day mundane conversations gave someone a kick, all well and good. Each to their own. On the subject of phones, Corrie rang me that afternoon.
"It's just me, Linda," she said in that friendly but 'what's the latest gossip' type of voice of hers. "Has that gentleman gone? Shall I pop in for a few minutes?"
I don't think Corrie ever meant to be selfish, I really don't. But, for her, the world that mattered stopped at the tip of her nose. Which was probably why she had such a stormy marriage, because Derek was just as egotistical. She interacted of course, she laughed and joked, but ask her a personal question and she would recoil faster than a

snapped high-tension spring. After that you'd be in her no-friend zone for a while, isolated until you learnt your lesson.

On this occasion I was just as bad. We had coffee and I spent the entire time trying to avoid every question she threw at me ... and she knew it! How can you hold a conversation and tell a friend your own husband has been murdered, then retract it? So I said I had mis-heard Steve and I put it all down to tiredness and hormones, the escape clause in many an emotional moment. But she didn't fall for it ... and it would insult her intelligence to believe she would.

"There's a sudden change in your attitude towards that man," she said. "You were petrified of him earlier today. What's changed? I'm worried about you."

"Perhaps he is just trying to look after me, Corrie."

She had an answer for that, "Personally I think the opposite! The man is a stalker. He meets you for the first time, knowing more about you than some of your best friends, then next morning he drives from his home – almost two hours away – and he turns up at your door! Is that a normal thing to do? Do you get that often?"

She was right, of course. It was refreshing to have someone give me an 'outside looking in' perspective, because that man had sucked me into a world where nothing made sense.

Corrie continued with the interrogation: "Is your phone tapped, or is it not? Did Craig take his own life, or was he murdered? Just random topics that we talk about every day over a cuppa. Yes I'm being sarcastic, but you need a reality check, girl! At this moment, Linda, your head is full of his bullshit."

I sensed earlier I would regret confiding in her, but credit where it is due, every question she asked, and every point she made, was valid and deserved to be answered. But I didn't have the answers.

"Linda, listen to me. I don't know what this guy wants from you but, whatever it is, it isn't good. This is a man who thinks he is bloody James Bond, for God's sake. That's how f***ed up HE is!"

Three days passed (this was now the Wednesday) and when I returned home from a day shopping there was a parcel waiting for me. A brand new Apple iPhone, with a letter from Steve saying he wanted me to have this 'gift' but I only had to use it in conversation with him. All the bills would be paid and everything was in his name so I wouldn't get any statements or charges.

He phoned me later that night around 11pm, and after pleasantries he told me Mitch had tried to find a buyer for the Gospel in France and Italy, but did it when Craig was alive.

"I admire his nerve," said Steve with a cutting tone to his voice, "a two-bit arsehole trying to mix it with the elite of the art under-world in Paris and Rome. And can I tell you one thing, he selected the wrong city when he cherry-picked Rome."

"Has he got the Gospel?" I inquired.

"Nope, apparently Craig had it all along. Mitch didn't even get to see it. He says he was the 'brains behind the operation', working on behalf of his 'client'. It get's more like Butch Cassidy and the Sundance Kid the more it goes on."

"Did you see Mitch yourself?" I asked.

"No, that is not my department," said Steve. "I just supply the blow-torch and the thumb-screws."
He laughed, so I laughed with him, although I don't quite know why.
The conversation was rather short and I was soon in bed, but at 2.04am precisely my new phone rang.
"I've got it!" shouted Steve down the phone.
"Why are you phoning me at this time of the morning? Are you mad?"
"I know where the Gospel is and I have a good idea who has it." he said, demanding I listen. "What's in Meadas that isn't in Seaham? The answer – the letter D. What's in Thomas Street and not in Moats Street? The answer – the letter H. The 3-3 score had me baffled but don't you see? It a post-code! The post-code is DH3 3DT and guess where that is?"
"Come one then, surprise me Sherlock Holmes," I said.
"The answer, dear lady, is St Mary & St Cuthbert Church! It all ties together now."
Steve really had done his homework.
"Where is St Mary & St Cuthbert Church? I don't know it?" I asked.
He then laid out every minute detail:- "That old red book that belonged to Craig's father. I've found the page where Craig wrote the letter and tore it out," he said in a victorious voice, "The pieces fit perfectly. And I notice he scribbled random notes on the previous page. There is a mention of that particular church. Did you ever go there? A wedding perhaps? Were you married there?"
It meant nothing to me. "Where is it? Craig was a fanatic on history and church buildings but he was never religious. I couldn't even get him to marry in church!"

"It's in Chester-le-Street. Does that mean anything to you? Did you ever go tghere together?" he asked.
"Never! I know the town but I don't know the church."
"The original Lindisfarne Gospels were taken there," said Steve. "They arrived, along with the monks, when they fled Holy Island with the body of Cuthbert. It was Cuthbert's resting place for seven years. Pilgrims would flock to the Church and hand over money, gold or their jewellery, to see the body and expect miracles in return. And quite often, by hook or by crook, miracles did happen. Cuthbert's body was a money-maker, whether the miracles were for real or devised, we will never know. But those funds helped build the most iconic building in the North of England - Durham Cathedral. The bulk of the fortune was generated from that church in Chester-le-Street."
I pictured Steve sat in his 'Crooked Loaning' cottage, his brain ticking over like some old grand father clock. He may have been slow out of the blocks but when his plan came together he could explode his thoughts to the world.
"Sadly, I don't think you knew Craig as well as you thought you did, Linda," he said assertively, then probably winced waiting for my reply. I was starting to think he enjoyed winding me up.
"Obviously." I couldn't disagree, could I? "But he always had his own friends, and I never interfered. Perhaps that was my downfall, I should have interfered more often."
"Let's take the last sentence of Craig's letter. The one line that ISN'T part of the post-code. 'Father of the bride confessing to being on the Beech'. Beech is spelt wrong in terms of sea and sand, but it is a surname. I checked out St Mary & St Cuthbert Church on the internet and there is a Reverend Beech. Not a 'Father' because it is not a Catholic church, but I can only imagine Craig thought it was

Catholic. With the name St Mary's, it's an obvious mistake to make. Now then, why would Craig take the Gospel to that particular church? For the reasons I explained before. The monks of Lindisfarne took the original Gospels to that very church, and I feel your husband was wanting some form of sanctuary. The theft put his life in danger, even more so being caught trying to sell it. Put something as unique as a book of the Gospels on the market and the word soon spreads. The longer he held onto it the more danger he was in. He was extremely frightened, but I'm sure he wasn't sure what he was frightened of. The word 'confessing' could solve the riddle. I believe that he went to, what he thought was, confession and intended to give 'Father' Beech the book."

"That doesn't explain anything," I said, knocking him off his stride. "What difference does it make if he was a priest or a reverend?"

"Because of 'absolution' dear lady," he said proudly, confident he had solved the mystery.

I was showing my ignorance but I did not have a clue what that meant, "Can you explain please?"

"Basically it is confession, when people go to confess their sins in church," he replied. "The person doing the sinning is called the penitent. He or she makes a sacramental confession of the sins to a priest and prays for forgiveness. The priest then assigns a penance and imparts absolution in the name of the Trinity, on behalf of Christ himself. Absolution forgives the guilt associated with the sins, and removes the eternal punishment of going to Hell. I've put it in layman's terms, but that is how it works. I believe he took it there believing the gentleman doing the confession could not, under any interrogation, say a word to anyone."

"He wanted forgiveness?" I asked.

"It seems that way. He went to the RIGHT church to return the Gospel, because I'm sure Craig knew it was there at some point in the past, but he went to the WRONG church to make a confession. Anglican churches don't do confession. A priest cannot disclose to anyone what is said between the two parties. That is the strict rule. What Craig intended to say that day would remain in the confessional box, or that was his intention. But what actually happened, only one person will know. It's probably a stab in the dark, but it's the best lead we've had to date."

None of this was fact until it was actually proven, but every piece of the jigsaw was on the table just waiting to be slotted into place.

Steve asked me: "Would you come with me tomorrow morning? They have Holy Communion at 10.45pm. Let's go to church and meet the Reverend Beech."

"Why do you want me there?"

"I thought you would like to see this through to its conclusion," he answered, "And a couple draw less attention than a man by himself. I will pick you up at 10am."

"You are very presumptuous for a man that hardly knows me," I replied. "Do people always jump to your beckoning call?"

"I asked you, Linda. I didn't presume anything. OK, I will ask again, will you please come with me to the church tomorrow?"

If nothing else, this history lesson was improving my IQ. I now know what 'absolution' means.

Steve picked me up at 10am - 'bang on the nail' - not a second late. I do like punctuality. Another one of my father's saying: "Punctuality is a show of respect."

We drove to the church with time to spare, and we filled in a few minutes by wandering around the grounds of that stunning building. Why do churches make you want to whisper when you talk? And we weren't even inside the place!

If parts of this church were 1,100 years old, as Steve proclaimed, the guy that designed it certainly made a statement. What a timeless, beautiful, masterpiece.

"What is it about buildings like this that make your heart skip a beat, and I'm not even religious?" I asked.

Steve looked up at the spire then said: "It doesn't make my heart do anything. It's a cage for God. And God isn't contained within those walls. Religion is pomp and pageantry, and in all its many forms. The old stone walls and stained glass windows hide the hypocrisy. Religious folk keep up the pretence that all is well in their own particular divinity, but the world would be a better place without the lot of it."

I was startled to hear that. "That's a bitter statement to make. At least admire the beauty."

Then he held council, as though his rant was cleansing him. It was like a mini form of exorcism.

"Why did Cuthbert believe that being a hermit would make him closer to God?" he asked, as though little me, little Linda from Seaham, would know the answer.

I took a stab in the dark, "Errrm, more time to think?"

"This place was built for Cuthbert, and the unique feature of this Church is the little two-storey Anchorage beside the west door at the base of the tower. In the 14th century it was built as the home for an Anchorite, or hermit as we would call him these days. Having been approved by the Bishop, he took monastic vows and was sealed in for the rest of his natural life. Two small holes allowed limited access. One

with the passing of food, and the other to dispose of waste. There's an angled slit in the interior wall which forms a 'squint' through which he could observe the Mass in the side chapel of the church. When he died he was replaced, and that went on for more than 160 years. What a waste of life! They were given a religious book that was a type of bible, and a book of psalms. That was the entertainment for the day ... every day ... for the rest of their lives."
"You certainly know your stuff," I said.
"I've written more books about St Cuthbert than J.K. Rowling has written about Harry Potter!" he said, rubbing his hands in a circular fashion on the wall of the Anchorage. "But I'm sure writing about Harry Potter was more fun ... and profitable," he added.
We could hear the organ music so we headed to the door, wanting to be last in so we could hide ourselves at the back. The aroma of the fresh flowers overpowered the occasional whiff of dust that always settles in high places in churches. "How often do they get a feather duster up in the alcoves?" I asked myself under my own breath.
The more he spoke about religion, the more I was astonished at Steve's attitude towards anything holy. For a man who was so knowledgeable about the doctrine, he certainly didn't do it any favours.
"These places let the devil in their doors long ago – because of the worship of money, gold, and power," he said in a dour tone. It was certainly uncomfortable listening. I sat and listened to the service, hoping it would be more optimistic, because he was starting to get on my nerves. When the congregation left we made a point of being last out of the door, with Steve asking me to "pass the time" while he had a conversation with Father Beech. "Pass the

time" doing what, exactly? I felt very conspicuous so I stepped outside and a lady came over to chat.

"Is this your first time here?" she asked.

"Yes, it is. Isn't this a beautiful church?" I replied. "My friend came to see Father Beech, and I'm at a lost end."

"Would you like to look around the place? I work here part time as a guide and organise tours for the local schoolchildren, teaching them about the history. Not that they listen," she laughed. "Children these days have very short attention spans," she added. "All they seem concerned about is their mobile phones."

"I would love to look around," I replied. "My name is Linda, Linda Wilson."

The lovely Jenny got herself in tour guide mode and away we went.

"We are a welcoming church family," she said, punctuating every syllable, obviously well rehearsed. "We gather each week for worship, fellowship, learning of God and prayer. There has been a Christian worshipping parish here since 883AD, when monks from Lindisfarne, brought the incorrupt body of Saint Cuthbert."

I felt I was now that brain-washed on the subject of Cuthbert that I could teach her a thing or two.

At no point did I lose interest. Jenny did her job remarkably well. The Anchorage, the place that housed the hermit, was the place I most wanted to visit and it didn't disappoint. How could anyone possibly live their life in a place no bigger than an average-sized bathroom? But the story of the spire and bells impressed me too.

Jenny had me hooked: "In 1409 the spire was constructed and three bells were installed that same year, one of which is still here. Two became cracked, and in 1883, their metal was melted down to make new bells. The 1409 original bell

is still rung for the last few minutes before each service, and is dedicated to Saint Cuthbert."
Still, to this day, they ring a bell for a man who died 1,300 years ago. How incredible is that?
The tour concluded with a cup of coffee and a biscuit as we waited for the two gentlemen to return.
It was while we were in mid-conversation that my phone started to vibrate, and (probably to Jenny's disgust) I had to give way to modern technology and answer it.
The name 'Dawn' flashed up on the screen, one of my Mother's friends from home.
"Can you please excuse me Jenny, it's a very good friend of mine," I said, pointing to the phone, before stepping outside.
"Hello, how are you?" I said, noticing that Steve was in the church garden still deep in conversation with the Reverend who was acting in a rather agitated manner. Probably more animated than troubled, but whatever the conversation was, all did not seem well.
"Linda, it's Dawn here. Sorry to bother you. Can you talk?"
"Yeah, no problem."
"Have you heard about Rob Mitchell?" she said.
"No, what's up?"
I sensed the worst.
"He was found dead yesterday. I've just been told. The police haven't made a statement yet, but his brother told me he was found hanging from a tree in Dawdon Park just a matter of yards from my house."
"Oh my God!" I shouted, "You are joking me! Suicide? There seems to be a bloody epidemic going on at the moment! Oh my God, Dawn. What else do you know?"
I looked across the garden at Steve and my blood ran cold. He must have had something to do with this. Had he been

to see Mitch himself or did he send one of his heavies? His conversation with the Father had ended and they both headed towards me as I stood in the doorway.
"That's all I know," she replied. "I will keep you updated."
"OK Dawn, thank you so much for phoning" I stammered, watching Steve walking closer and closer, and I was growing more and more anxious.
I flicked off the phone and looked directly into Steve's eyes. He introduced me to Reverend Beech, who seemed as nervous as myself, and that was confirmed when I shook his shaky hand. We both were as uncomfortable as each other being around this man.
Steve sensed from my expression something was wrong. I'm not saying he knew me well enough for us to be joined at the hip, but he knew enough to spot a signal. I don't know what gesture I was sending out but he looked at me as though he wanted an answer and he hadn't even asked the question.
The reverend's eyes stayed glued to the ground. Head bowed like a scolded kid stuck in the 'naughty corner'.
"Business is done, Linda," said Steve. "The book isn't here but I get it back at 3pm. Craig did come here to talk to the Reverend."
I didn't know what to say, I just gazed at them both, leaving the conversation open. What I wanted to ask was: "Are you a murderer?" But it would probably have given the poor Reverend a cardiac arrest, and I wouldn't have got an answer anyway.
"We should be happy!" he proclaimed in a joyful manner, as though he was about to burst into song. I wanted to end that friendship there and then, but I wanted answers about Craig first.

I turned to the Reverend, "Can I ask you sir, what state of mind was my husband in when he came here?"
The gentleman turned and looked at Steve as though he was asking his approval to reply to me, and that immediately made my blood boil. He leant forward to hold my hand in such a pitiful fashion before finally saying, "I don't think he was well, my friend. He looked a sad figure."
Suddenly, I felt a mourning inside of me that sapped away my defences. I had a lot to say and I summoned up the strength to say it. "That conversation he had with you was probably the very last that he had with anyone. The official conclusion is that he went home and hung himself. So, if all confessions are kept within the walls of the church, let's take a walk inside your church and hold another one. Because I want to know what he said to you."
The Reverend was well outside his comfort zone and I was on a roll. Wild horses wouldn't stop me getting to the bottom of this.
Steve was not happy, "Linda, come on, let's ..."
I raised my voice and stopped him in mid sentence: "LET'S DO WHAT? If you want to go – GO! I'm not moving until I hear what my husband said to this gentleman. And if I'm treading on your toes ... the gate is over there!"
The Reverend stepped between the pair of us in a sort of benevolent manner, taking the heat out of the fire by calmly answering what I asked.
"He was extremely distressed and I cannot make it any easier for you by saying any other. He gave me instructions of what I should do with the possession he had with him, and then he prayed – in English and in Latin. All he wanted to do was to make his peace with God."
"That was a man who didn't believe in God," I replied. "He never prayed to anyone."

But the man of the cloth stood his ground: "I can promise you … he believed in God when he walked into this church … and he believed when he walked out!"
Steve was growing increasingly agitated and tried to take my arm and hurry me away. "Come on Linda, let's go."
"You are doing it again! How many times have I got to tell you? Don't touch me! Don't lay one finger on me, not now, not EVER! I was living a life in blissful ignorance until I met you. You've got your book back so this is where it all ends. I won't require a lift home, thank you. Goodbye to you, and thank you for your time Reverend Beech."
I turned and walked down the stone pathway, but before I got to the gate I asked the question that was dearest to my heart: "What were the last words Craig spoke before he left the church?"
The Reverent answered: "The same words he spoke continuously at the alter - 'I repent, Jesus of Nazareth, King of the Jews.' Then her ran out. No goodbye or thank you."
I headed right at the exit and proceeded downwards towards the park. I wanted to get a half-decent head start on Steve. Distance was all that mattered – the distance between us! After 50 yards or so I looked back but thankfully he wasn't following me.

CHAPTER NINE

I believed I got to Chester-le-Street park without being followed, and I was relieved in one sense, and somewhat surprised in another. Steve didn't seem the type of guy to let me get away without him having the last word.
The park is my kind of place. Particularly on school days, when the swings are stationary and the place wallows in its own absolute stillness. That was how it looked this

particular day. But I was still anxious, if not a little bit frightened. I thought about my actions and the words I spoke to Steve back at the church. But on reflection, I didn't regret any of them. I didn't particularly want to humiliate Steve, but he got what he deserved.

Then I thought about Mitch. I don't know why but there was guilt festering inside me, as though telling Steve about him wasn't the best plan I had ever conjured up. But did it matter? I wasn't the one who put a rope around his neck. Then I thought of poor Craig begging for forgiveness in the church. What the hell was going on? He would turn on the TV, watch the news, and repeat himself almost daily, "All these wars are caused by religion."

The Bible, in his opinion, was the most dangerous book ever published. Yet he ended up in a coffin because he stole a Gospel.

How on Earth did he suddenly find religion? He was intelligent, without doubt, but I must admit he was a man who could switch his loyalties simply by losing an argument. He was a maverick. I knew he wouldn't see old age, and I told him often enough. And me? To him, I was the nagging bitch who knew everything. I was never going to change him. You can never tame a free spirit, so why didn't I remind myself, you should never try?

I sat gazing over the slow moving river Wear. Nothing much had changed since my childhood when I used to come visit the place with my family. Those hot summer days that we all seem to remember. I'm sure it rained sometimes but why spoil the 'good bits'? I've never had good powers of retention anyway, so whatever I recall I probably embellished anyway.

But just as I was starting to take delight in the moment, the silence was shattered.

"I don't quite know what happened back there Linda, but if I've done something wrong I'd like to know what it is," said the man I had hurried away from.

I looked up and there was Steve, looking all shy and retiring. Yes, he was a charmer alright.

"How did you find me this time?" I said in jest, "Don't tell me, let me guess. I have some form of tracker inserted up my backside."

"What upset you?" he asked.

"OK, why should I beat around the bush, I may as well go straight for your jugular," I growled. "Do you know Mitch is dead?"

He either put on a remarkably impressive act, which he was perfectly capable of doing, or he was genuinely shocked.

"What happened to him?"

"I got a call while you were outside talking to Reverend Beech. Suicide apparently. But we don't know what suicide is these days, do we? Perhaps he slipped and accidentally strung himself up."

He didn't reply.

"I don't suppose you had anything to do with it?" I added.

He sat next to me on the rusting metal bench, but I moved uncomfortably to the edge keeping a distance between us.

"Don't worry," he said raising his hands up in surrender, "I won't touch you."

"I didn't go to see Mitch," he said. "But I ..."

"Yeah," I snapped, "you know because you sent them!"

"Linda we are going to have to calm down here. I am trying to have a rational conversation and I'm not getting one. Let me talk."

I did what he asked, took a deep breath, and let him continue.

"We knew about Mitch some time ago, but when my partner give him a visit he only got out of him what we expected to hear, but that was as far as it went. I know Mitch ruffled a few feathers in Rome but he did not know where the Gospel was. His failing was that he pretended he did know! You do not hold people to ransom, as he did, and expect to walk away."

Everything was coming together and I was starting to realise what this whole charade was about.

"And you thought I had the book," I said.

"Not really," he replied, "but there was that possibility. You seemed our only hope of finding it."

I had to ask the question: "How many times was my house broken into?"

"I don't know, I wasn't involved in that." he replied. "A couple of times I think. I'm sorry."

"What happens now that you've found the Gospel?" I asked.

"It's in a secure place at the moment, in pristine condition apparently, and I will get it at 3pm and take it back to where it belongs."

"So this is the end as far as I'm concerned?" I asked.

Steve looked around, as though he had a sense that we were being watched, then finally answered the question, "Yes, this is the end for you. I wish it was for me too, but the show goes on."

"Well that is what I am concerned about," I replied, "Because the people who know about this 'Secret' of Holy Island tend to end up in body bags. I know a couple of dead people. Do I know too much? Craig and Mitch knew too much."

Credit to him, he tried to take any blame away from me. "Craig and Mitch were a pair of thieves trying to line their own pockets, and you were not involved in that."

But he didn't convince me.

"Who are you looking out for?" I said, scanning the horizon myself. "Is someone looking for you ... or perhaps me?"

He wasn't in control, and he didn't like it. At times I half expected the wind to ask him permission before it was allowed to blow. But he was edgy, he couldn't hide it.

"Did you see two men sat in a black Audi outside the church?" he asked, back-tracking the scene.

I had seen a black car with two men inside, but I wouldn't have been able to pick them out from an identity parade. "I saw the car, yeah."

He thought for a moment.

"You're scared," I said, interrupting his train of thought. "You are genuinely scared. Someone is after you, aren't they? Why would they do that? Do you know them?"

He chose not to answer. He was like a meerkat popping his head up every few seconds, looking in the direction of Lumley Castle. There was activity behind the bushes, but it was a golf course so nothing that was out of the ordinary. Perhaps a golfer looking for a lost ball.

He was still very much on 'red alert', and that created a tension. Then I suddenly became aware that Steve wasn't the only one seeking the treasure. He had competition. Possession is 90% ownership, and the Gospel was not in his hands.

"You know what I think Mr Campbell," I said before starting my spiel. "I think there is a 'rabbit off'. That's an old Geordie term for suggesting there are people not happy at the way you messed up. You lost the Gospel on 'your watch.' All you had to do was keep it safe for a smidgeon of time and you blew it! Picture the scene. Some guy walks into your cottage, you open the safe and you give him the opportunity of a lifetime. You turn your back ... and hey Presto ... it's on the open market in Paris and Rome. What a Wally! You either get it back or you have to pay the piper. Am I right?"

I felt his ego deflating, because he didn't reply ... but he knew I was right.

"I'm not finished," I said, taking centre-stage once again. "As the saying goes - 'a speech is like a love-affair, any fool can start it, but to end it requires considerable skill'. And I will end it by saying I think someone has taken you for a ride. They now know where the book is and you are surplus to requirements. You have been the brains and they have been the brawn, but they have been mopping up behind you. Disposing of the evidence, and all that goes with it. Are you one of 'them'? I don't think you are ... not any more. They didn't tell you what they did with Craig, you found that out yourself. You didn't even KNOW what happened to Mitch, not until I told you half an hour ago. The Women's Institute is getting to know details quicker than you, Steve."

There had been times when I didn't like this man. He was controlling; intrusive; but for the first time he was vulnerable.

"I've been shadowing you these last few days to keep you fit and healthy," he said. "You don't deserve what you have been through. You have lost your husband and the last thing you need is me ruining your life."

"To keep me 'fit and healthy'?" I replied. "So you admit there was a potential threat to my life?"

He didn't reply.

"I think I should know what I am dealing with here," I said. "Exactly what AM I dealing with?"

He tapped his fingernail on his teeth, making a drumming sound, seemingly conjuring up some cock-and-bull story. But, no, he wanted me to know the truth.

"I will tell you exactly what WE are dealing with. Not just you ... both of us. Every religion has its fanatics, its extremists. They believe they are right – the rest of the world is wrong. There are many religions in this world, each and every one of them believes they are the ultimate faith. Christians believe that faith in Jesus brings eternal life, but others don't. It is more than a simple obedience to a set of rules. To extremists there is no debate, nothing is up for question, they do what they do. In this case, when something goes missing, it is found. No matter what it takes – they get it back – with the minimum of fuss. I am a cog, I do what I'm told, then get the hell out of Dodge City. Others do stuff behind the scenes that I know nothing about, and I don't WANT to know. You were in a room today where years ago they housed the Anker, the hermit who gave up his life for Christianity. Locked away for good, because that was what HE wanted from his life. Extremists do ridiculous things, like blowing themselves up with suicide vests. Religion does that to people ... well, certain people."

My mind wasn't taking it all in. I didn't quite know which sentence to concentrate on first.

"So," I asked, "we are dealing with suicide bombers?"

"We are dealing with the four horsemen of the Apocalypse as far as I can make out," he replied, "Not quite, but that's about as good a description as I can come up with at the moment."

Steve wanted to get away from the park but he didn't want me to be alone, so he asked me if I would like to go for lunch somewhere to kill time before his reunion with his piece of history. I could have walked away, and looking back, I wished I had walked away. But if Steve was concerned about my safety, perhaps I should be concerned too.

I know the area well so I suggested we go to a bar at the top of the Front Street.

We walked in, picked our table, and ordered our meals at the bar. The place doubles as a nightclub on weekends, and transforms from a teenager's pick-up joint into a rather respectable restaurant on week days. OK, it's not an establishment I would hold a wedding reception but there are worse places in town.

As we waited for our meals to arrive, a trio of giggly over-weight drunken 'ladies' invaded the table opposite and tried to include us in their conversation. Having been asked if we were a couple, I replied rather too convincingly that we "hardly know each other" and it became 'open season' for bagging some game. Two of them took a shine to Steve. One twiddled her blonde hair in a sexy fashion as she sipped a Barcardi Breezer. Giving her the benefit of the doubt, she was probably unaware she was flashing her pink knickers that were in full view to everyone else in the pub, but then again I could be wrong. The girl in the middle had faked tanned skin that seemed to have been applied by the gallon, showing streaks on her arms and legs. When she blinked her heavily made up false lashes in Steve's direction I knew the movie was ready to begin. These two wanna-be film stars were casting for the part. The girl on the right was otherwise occupied, texting on her phone to, I assume, her boyfriend. Her mind was in another place.

'Tan girl' fixed Steve in a sort of Marilyn Monroe stare that must have been cultivated in the bedroom (or on the toilet). Meanwhile 'knicker girl' folded one leg over the other, dangling her high heels, showing more leg than should be allowed in a public place.

Steve stayed aloof, looking everywhere but at them, which must have been very exasperating to the girls. But I became aware of a slight pang of jealousy that was most unusual for me. Mainly because of all of the years I had known Craig I cannot ever remember him attracting female attention. Although, to be fair to him, it was only when he was in another relationship that I realized I should have been taking notice. What was obvious to many was invisible to me. In art, creating the 'obvious' is a sin. In my marriage the 'obvious' simply didn't even exist.

The girls didn't stay long, they drank their drinks and headed off to the next watering hole. Steve pretended he didn't notice they had gone, but the sudden silence was a dead giveaway.

Once again the black Audi car was dropped into the conversation, showing Steve was very concerned. But I suggested the driver could have been waiting for anyone, most probably some old granny from Father Beech's congregation.

"They have I got you thinking," I smiled. "Come on, you must have a clue who they are."

"I think the guy in the driver's seat was Waldermar Buchtmann."

"The burglar in my house?" Now that was the last thing I wanted to hear. "Oh my God!"

"He's not after you, Linda. He wants the Gospel. I'm not 100% sure it's him."

There were questions to be answered and I led the way: "Tell me about Buchtmann. What does he have to do with Holy Island?"

"When I was telling you about the 'extremists', Buchtmann is one of them. His only link to Holy Island is what we have there. Pilgrims have flocked to our island for hundreds of years, to be blessed, healed, and saved from hell and damnation, by the three Saints ... Cuthbert, Bede and Aidan. It is an island that held so much, in religious terms, but in the early years it was robbed of everything it had. These days we have the 'Lindisfarne Holy Trinity' and these 'believers' are genuine fanatics who will go to any length to defend what we have."

"Lindisfarne Holy Trinity?" I asked. "What else is there?"

"You will find out in the course of time."

Getting information out of that guy was like drawing teeth!

"What religion are we talking about?" I had to ask. "How fanatical can they be? We have established they are not suicide bombers. Is that right?"

"They are a cult called the Rosicrucians, and they have very strong links to the Freemasons," he replied. "Some historians claim the Masons were formed because of them. They originated from Germany in the early fifteenth century and their extremist religious views took over the country. Their founder, Rosenkreuz, emerged from a background of alchemy, and they spread across most countries in Europe. They were backed by the Freemasons and other fraternal orders in later years. Their beliefs are a brotherhood of learned men, preparing for a revolution that will transform all of Europe. They really DID start a revolution, too. They had an influence on the formation of what is now Russia! Afterwards they went underground, became very secretive, but they never entirely went away."

"It still survives here in Britain?" but I stated the obvious.
"Yes, its still ongoing," said Steve. "They are still rumoured to be using occult practices. Some religious sects call them the 'College of Invisibles' or the 'Invisible College'.
"Why is Buchtmann following you?" I asked.
"He obviously knows why we are here. Someone is giving him information … the information that I'm passing onto the island. That's the concern. I knew your phone was tapped, and I'm starting to think mine is too. I have to make a phone call. Give me five minutes."
At that point he disappeared outside to make that call. Several minutes past before he returned and I could tell by the look on his face something was not right. He glanced at me, gave a forced smile, but I know anxiety when I see it.
"Well then, what's the latest news?" I asked.
"They claim they don't know Buchtmann is here. Reading between the lines we are either in a bit of trouble here, or else I'm being fed a load of bullshit!"
The "we" metaphor had me worried.
"I'm starting to look at this rationally," he said, looking me straight in the eye, "I'm starting to think that every word you said to me in the park is true. I'm a stool-pigeon. I'm being set up. What an IDIOT I am!"
"Haven't you done your bit?" I said, thinking he had recovered the book so what more was there to do?
"I've told my colleague that once I return the book my job is done and my conscience is clear," Steve replied. "The problem at the moment is getting it from point A to point B. I told them that I'm getting the book tomorrow morning, because whatever I seem to say over the phone gets passed on. That could give me breathing space. I get the book at

3pm and I head straight up to Holy Island and the job is done."

He offered to take me home but I wanted to see the book which had ultimately been the cause of Craig's death. However, while I dwelt on the finer details of his mess, the bigger picture was escaping me.

"I'd rather take you home, Linda, this is not the place for you. I don't want you involved any more. You can walk away from this. I'm the one with the responsibility now."

His words made perfect sense but I didn't believe this was over. I knew too much. We must have been seen together and even a 'blind man on a galloping horse' could see we were working as a team. If I hadn't gone to the church I may have got away with it. But now I was right in the firing line. I was involved, whether I liked it or not.

"I'm going with you," I said in a commanding voice. Much to my surprise, he didn't oppose it.

He gave a gentle smile and softly said, "Ah well, let's do this."

CHAPTER TEN

I wanted to be in this escapade right up to the point when the Gospel was handed over. For my own sanity, but mainly as a duty to my ex-husband. I'm not suggesting it would 'right every wrong' but it would banish the monkey off my back.

I wasn't even asked, I just took it upon myself to invite 'me'.

"My major concern is Buchtmann," he said. "Where is he right now?"

"You aren't even sure you saw him!" I added.

"The mind plays tricks. But I know he's here. I can smell the Kraut bastard."

I didn't need a second opinion to work out the pair of them were not bosom buddies.

"We are to meet the Reverend at his home at the rear of the church this afternoon," said Steve, running through the plan of action. "If Buchtmann is tapped into my phone conversations he will be expecting the drop off at the church in the morning. That is what I told them. I told the Reverend our meeting was confidential and it must be kept a secret, so let's hope he keeps his word. We get the book then we head up to Holy Island by train. If Buchtmann is here, as I suspect he is, he has a tracker on my car or phone. I will dump them both."

We took the five minute walk back to the church, looking out for a black Audi car on our way.

There was no way to get to the Vicarage at the rear, so we couldn't sneak in through the trade-man's entrance. It was by the front door, at the end of the church yard.

Steve knocked on the big brash wooden door and the Reverend was home. But he didn't seem 'at home' in his mind, if you understand my meaning. As the saying goes: "The lights were on but ..."

That worried me.

Steve couldn't hide his enthusiasm. "Have you got it?" he asked before we had even set foot in the door.

"Yes, it's here," came the reply, although the Reverend didn't say it with much conviction. Was I going to see money changing hands? Was it acceptable to put a brown paper envelope on the table? I didn't know the procedure with stolen religious artifacts.

The holy gentleman didn't like Steve, for whatever reason, and he wasn't shy in showing it. But I noticed that earlier at

the church, too. There was friction there, and I don't think either of them wanted to conceal it. Steve could be intimidating. He seemed a true gentleman, I'm sure of that, but there were moments when I knew when to keep quiet. We were invited in and entering such a charming place was like reliving my experiences when I visited my grandmother in my youth. Her home was a living museum. I don't think she had ever bought anything 'modern' in her life. I often thought she even frowned upon electricity, as she always boasted that her cast iron wood burning stove was far better than the "new-fangled electric rubbish" that was available in the shops. Here, right in front of me, was the very same make of stove.
"I love the effect the wood has when it's all stacked in the corner like that," I said. "Doesn't it make it so homely?"
Steve laughed, "It's not an 'effect', it's used on the fire."
I suppose he had a point.
In the lobby sat a big black old fashioned telephone; the type with the large dialing disk and curled cable dangling from the receiver. It had to be a modern imitation, surely it couldn't possibly be a 1950's original and still work.
"Take a seat young lady," said the charming Reverend (well he was most engaging to me, it was Steve he had the problem with). "Would you like a tea or coffee?"
We declined, Steve was still aggitated and made it plain he was eager to get away. I was enjoying the moment and I felt a little bit embarrassed, as though the kind gentleman was trying his hardest to make us feel at home and we were desperate to leave.
Steve sat down for a couple of seconds, but I noticed him glance back at the front door and immediately his expression changed, as though the blood had run from his

face. He grew increasingly edgy, looking towards the old wooden door leading into, what I believed to be, the study.

"Go on sir, yes we will have coffee if you don't mind," Steve said, surprising the Reverend, and me even more.

"Two cups, white, no sugar."

"No problem," said the old gentleman and he scuttled away into the scullery.

Steve got up and whispered in my ear: "Where is the nearest taxi rank?" putting his finger to his lip as though instructing me to keep my voice down.

"Opposite the market square down the road. A minute away. Why?"

"Go now, run down the road and get a taxi and get the driver to wait in the market square. I will be as quick as I possibly can. Don't go back to my car under any circumstances. OK? Get a taxi."

"Why?" I asked, totally confused.

"Buchtmann's old army trench coat is hanging by the door. I'd know that coat anywhere. Go now!"

That explained a lot. Reverend Beech looked petrified because he had unwelcome company.

Steve paved the way for my exit, leading me to the door, telling the Reverend, "Linda is just popping outside for a cigarette, Reverend Beech. A terrible habit, I know, but old habits die hard."

A forced laugh from Steve, a smile from me, then I opened the door and made my exit. I didn't want to draw attention to myself by running, so let's say I 'shuffled along with haste'. I was desperate to get to the curve in the road to get out of view of the church, very aware that any man would be able to outrun me down that road. I decided to move off the path and head for the busy traffic on the front street, but I had to climb over a small wall about 2ft high then cut

through a dark tunnel next to a pub. That slowed me down no end, and I had to feel my way down the wall of the pub in total darkness for about 20 yards. I got to the end, ploughing over old discarded cardboard boxes, empty beer tins and God knows what else, then took a turning. Abruptly and unexpectedly I felt a hand touch me on the shoulder. I staggered back in total shock, pushing away the grimy hand as I cowered against the wall.
"Where the hell have you come from?" shouted a man in his late 60's, clasping a cigarette in his other hand. "You nearly frightened the shit out of me!"
I didn't speak, I didn't acknowledge him in any way, I brushed past and suddenly I was out onto the street amongst shoppers and I felt safe again. From that corner I could see the taxi rank at the bottom of the street and I knew I was out of harms way. Nobody was going to abduct me on a busy street in broad daylight.
Gasping for breath but feeling a lot more secure, I jumped in the first taxi at the head of the four car queue. I told the driver to pull up across the road in the market square.
After about two minutes, the stroppy young Asian taxi driver told me the obvious: "You do realize the meter is running, don't you? We can stay here all afternoon if you want, but you will be charged the rate."
"Yes, I do understand," I replied, "We won't be waiting long."
The last thing I needed at this point was somebody with an attitude problem. Some trumped up individual who felt his troubles were of a greater importance than mine. I wasn't sure whether he felt that giving out deep sighs periodically was going to encourage me to start my journey, but it only added to an already stale atmosphere.

There is a kind of waiting that feels like time has stopped and you want to kick-start it again. I stared so hard down that road my mind was willing Steve to appear and each person that did was an instant disappointment. Meanwhile the driver looked around, killing time, with the face of a man who seemed convinced the world was as tragic as the newsreaders have us believe.

"This gentleman we are waiting for, did he give a time?" he uttered in an aggressive manner, when I had already explained the situation.

Waiting needn't be a pain. But I felt like leaning over the front seat and banging his head against the windscreen.

Then, the waiting was over. Steve appeared at the corner of the main street and headed our way, carrying (what I took to be) the Gospel wrapped in his coat. I opened the car door to attract his attention, waving frantically, and he upped his pace to a gallop. I shuffled along the back seat and he clumped himself next to me before the driver could barely formulate a thought. The door clashed shut and Steve instantly wanted to get that car on the road.

"Birtley High Street, as soon as possible please," he instructed, and Mr Happy obliged.

Steve had a big cut to his forehead and blood ran down the side of his cheek, missing his eye by a fraction. He didn't utter a word and gave me a hand gesture telling me to keep quiet, as our taxi driver tilted his mirror to look at us both in the back seat. I couldn't resist the temptation to look behind to see if we were being followed, but Steve sat unmoved, staring straight ahead. Not a word was spoken on that journey, and as the driver kept glancing at his mirror, Steve glared back at him. The driver's attitude changed dramatically from being rudely offensive to "I'd better not say a word or I might get a punch in the mouth."

We took no longer than seven minutes to get to the destination and, after paying the fare, we made a quick detour away from the High Street up Station Lane.

"You've got the Gospel I see?" I said, trying to keep up with his sprightly pace.

"Yeah, eventually," he replied, still not giving much away. Steve dismantled his mobile phone, removed the sim card, which he bent and disfigured, then dropped it down a water drain. He ushered me up the road, physically dragging my arm. I still didn't know what was going on and he was in no frame of mind to tell me.

"What happened to your face?" I asked knowing full well he had been in a fight.

"Buchtmann and his friend wanted the Gospel ... and me in a body bag."

"So he got neither." I replied.

"Well the book is here," he said in a semi-humourous manner, "and I can still feel my heart beating."

"What about Buchtmann?" I asked, "Is his heart still beating?"

"Does it matter?" he sternly replied.

"Does it matter?" I roared, "I think it does!"

He didn't answer the question, but prompted me to get into the back seat of a waiting taxi.

"Why did we dump one taxi to get into another?" I asked as we approached the car.

"The last guy knew we were on the run from something," said Steve, "now we can act as a married couple and not draw attention to ourselves. Or alternatively, you catch the bus home if you want to bail out. I would understand. We can drop you off at Newcastle."

I was starting to favour the latter option. I was out of my depth. There is excitement, which is one thing, and there is pure undiluted stupidity.
He had made up his mind where he was going, and I was free to make my choice.
"Am I a convenience or the opposite? If you are on the run, I want no part of it, do you hear? I'm not going to be part of a Bonny and Clyde double act. I don't want the fame if it comes with a prison sentence!"
He was obviously used to this kind of adrenaline rush, because he never gave anything away. I never, at any time, knew what was going on in his mind. He was like an ocean liner in the middle of nowhere. Calm on the surface but with so many deep under currents, all of them heading in a different direction. Me, I'm a 'people watcher', proud of the fact I can suss out a personality in a minute. The perfect hobby for a daydreamer like me. But he had me beaten all ends up. I could not read that man.
"I can't make you do anything, but, for a couple of reasons I would like you to go with me to the Island. Reason number one … I want you safe. Reason two … I want to put a proposal to you. The chance to make you rich beyond your wildest dreams."
This whirlwind encounter with the stranger from Hell was starting to take yet another twist. I didn't doubt he wanted me safe, he seemed to make that a priority throughout our time together, but to make me rich? What was that all about?
"I am starting to wonder to myself," I said, "Am I safer with you or without you? At this moment my gut feeling is telling me to go home."
"Tell me the alternative then," he responded quickly, "To go back to your house where you feel safe? Do you feel

safe there? Buchtmann and his College of Invisibles have known you were the key to finding the Gospel ever since Craig died. Even more so now. They found it, they lost it, and only two people know where it is at this precise moment in time – you and me. I've become a lot wiser today and I don't phone people anymore to keep them updated, because our location suddenly becomes common knowledge. We are on our own Linda, just you and me. And until I get this Gospel to the island and back in safe hands, WE are wanted. Not just me. You wanted adventure. Welcome to my world."

I should have been scared. All that stopped me from being pulverized on impact was the logic behind it. I had to go with him. Craig and Mitch had given these people answers but that didn't get either of them off the hook.

There was no point worrying about the past, that was done and dusted, but I had anxiety about what was about to happen next. I would rather the immediate future be in the hands of someone who showed me genuine concern, as Steve did, rather than return home and rely on neighbours who went into hysteria the week after Christmas when the bin men didn't arrive!

I made the decision – I was going back to Holy Island.

"OK Steve, you have won me over. What happens now?"

"We could take a taxi straight to Holy Island but we will be 'hit and miss' for the tide. It's 3.53 now, and the causeway closes around 4.30pm. They won't have any idea where we are right now, They will have realized we aren't going back to my car, and if I was in their shoes I'd be watching Newcastle train station. It's approaching rush hour so they will have their work cut out watching every single train that heads North. We bypass Newcastle and head to Blyth and a friend of mine will hopefully take us to the island by boat.

The more confusion we leave behind us the harder we are to track."

"Please tell me Steve, is Buchtmann alive?" I had to know. He responded half-heartedly, "Buchtmann won't be troubling you ever again."

Now things were on a very different level.

We got in the taxi and headed towards Blyth. The journey gave me time to let my mind escape the past few hours, and not even bother to think beyond the next few. While Steve attempted to fill in every minute of the trip holding pointless dialogue with the driver, I sat and let my mind empty.

The transfer was completed at Blyth and we were dropped off at the harbour. I didn't realize how big the port was. Blyth hardly shows up on the map, but there were ships flying flags from exotic countries like the Bahamas, Sierra Leone and Panama. Who would have guessed it, little Blyth a big player in a big world.

At the south of the port were the small fishing boats and private vessels moored along the embankment, and Steve, still hanging onto his prize possession hidden under his coat, made conversation with a couple of the fishermen. He called me over and put me in the picture. An oldish fisherman rubbed his hands on his thick wool jumper before shaking my hand.

"The guy I'm after is still out at sea," Steve said, "and nobody knows what time he is due back. But this kind gentleman will take us to the island."

The man was probably younger than he appeared, as his thick, bushy white beard made me think of TV adverts for Captain Birdseye. His skin was tanned and I wondered if all fishermen were like this, or did we just happen to stumble upon the picture book stereotype?

I wasn't expecting an ocean liner, but when I was invited into his tiny boat I questioned if it was seaworthy! We were about to set sail into the North Sea, for God's sake.
"Will we be OK?" I asked with genuine concern.
"It's a mild afternoon, we will be fine," said Steve, knowing I felt my life was at risk. "This man goes out in all weathers, he knows what he is doing."
I wasn't dressed for this occasion and several fishermen who were watching from the harbour wall were most amused as I dithered my way down into the vessel. Thankfully, I couldn't hear what they were saying and it saved everyone the embarrassment of me giving them a reply. At the end of the ladder there was still a long drop onto the deck. I say "deck" but there wasn't much of it I could see, only piled up fishing nets. So in one adrenaline fueled warrior-like yell I leapt into the nets knowing the worst damage I could do was to my clothes. I landed nose-down, which was probably the worst part of my body to place into a net that stunk of fish, and I immediately felt physically sick. This was, of course, top rate entertainment for everyone watching, and I earned myself a round of applause from the men on the wall ... and Steve.
Within seconds we were at sea, leaving drag marks behind us, half erased by the waves. The engine roared us on and we chugged our way out of Blyth northward. Steve hung onto his book as though his life depended on it (which was probably more truth than I considered at that time) and the Captain had an expression that looked like a gargoyle from a Gothic church.
We reached the island, passing the skeletons of a couple of old fishing boats that were visible beneath the water, making it a bit of a minefield for the skippers of small fishing vessels who didn't know the waters. We scrambled

to the top of the jetty and I had never been more delighted to get my feet on dry land in my life.

Steve paid the Captain for his trouble and we were back to where it all started.

"What happens to your book now?" I asked.

"We go to my cottage, you do whatever you need to do to brush up, while I take this to the Priory."

"Will there be a welcome party at your cottage when we get there?" I asked.

"I was thinking exactly the same thing," he replied as he scanned over the harbour, taking very careful notice of who watched us arrive. The tourists were small in number, but we did draw a certain amount of attention. Every beady eye made me feel even more conspicuous, and I wasn't helping my own cause by staring back. Steve was doing it too. He focused on a fisherman sat on a boat smoking a pipe. Steve's gaze was unwavering and unabashed, clearly wondering why the guy was sat in a boat that was moored and heading nowhere. Was there a reason? Did there need to be a reason … it was his boat after all. Steve said he knew all the local fishermen because they were so small in numbers on this stretch of the sea, but he didn't know this particular guy. We had to walk directly past him. I said "hello" in a friendly matter, but he looked at me sourly, giving no gesture of recognition. Steve stared elsewhere as he quickened his pace and marched straight ahead almost in regimental fashion. I followed like a scatter-brained poodle.

"What if they are waiting for us?" I asked.

"I'm trying to keep one step ahead of everyone," he answered, "but from this moment onwards I think it's a level playing field. Your guess is as good as mine."

We reached the cottage and no-one was waiting for us, but '007' went through all the procedures of making double sure ... just in case. He checked the doors; windows; behind every piece of furniture; every room; and even the garden. Meantime, while he was doing his tour of duty, I abruptly paused to close my eyes and steel myself into thinking things could only get better from this moment on. We were now in command of our own minds, body and soul. The Gospel was home, so what could possibly go wrong?

CHAPTER ELEVEN

We both had risked life and limb to recover the book and the very least I wanted was to see what all the fuss was about. I expected the Gospel to be cracked and dry with age, but that was not the case at all. Yes it was aged, a thousand years worth of antiquated goat skin can hardly look as though it had just been taken out of its plastic wrapper, but it was in remarkable condition considering it was centuries older than the Magna Carta. There was a strange smell about it that was nauseating but certainly not over powering. I half-expected it to be a bit rancid considering what it was made from, but that was not the case. It was absolutely spell-binding in every way. The cover was more a treasure chest than a book binding, covered in exotic jewels with an exquisite painting of Christ. I opened it and as I ran my fingers over the gold lettering I noticed the text was written in Latin but with a faint scrawl in pencil above each word translating it into English.
Words appeared and disappeared as my eyes flitted across the pages, quickly trying to pick out anything familiar from the jumble of sentences. The colours; the text; the artwork; everything about this volume of words was spellbinding.

"Are you happy now?" asked Steve.
"I don't think 'happy' is the appropriate word, but I'm pleased I've seen it, if only to ease my curiosity" I said as I let the book fall closed with an exhausted sound.
"I knew you would appreciate its beauty," said Steve.
"I don't think anyone could look at it and NOT appreciate it," I said thoughtfully, "It is a work of art."
Time suddenly seemed of the essence to Steve and he rushed around like a headless chicken before setting off towards the Priory, leaving me alone. I imagined Craig had the identical feeling I was sensing. I felt like Craig in his 'toy shop'. I wanted EVERYTHING!
This was the cottage I thought about in my dreams, and it was odd … yet wonderful. It wasn't the fairy-story I expected, but open the pages and the mystery and the magic would sparkle out like fireworks. It was a religious shrine to St Cuthbert, and boy do they love a hero around these parts.
Some of the artifacts in that room, and I assume they were originals, must outdate 90% of the kings and queens who have sat on the throne in this fair land. There was a carved stone that dominated the floor space in one of the rooms that was (according to a silver placard on the base) tenth century. Wind-battered and bruised but the original design was still there to see. The centre piece of this remarkable item of masonry was a carved child with a halo. Not above its head, as we see in objects of saintly virtue today, but around the face. I assume that to be the baby Jesus, accompanied with a carving of a priest or Holy figure in each corner praying. A significant piece of history, so why wasn't it in a museum? But the more I nosed around the house I suddenly realized this was a museum! Hidden away

like some private collection put together by an eccentric billionaire.

In an ancient looking wooden cabinet-cum-bookcase I came across a gold chalice goblet that was so highly decorated it must have been designed for some sort of religious ceremony. Probably the Eucharist in some grand church. Every piece in that cabinet seemed unique. None of those artefacts could have been mass produced. There was a smaller goblet that out-shone all the rest but was probably as old as every other item in there. Gold is what it is, metal cannot be carbon dated, so the age of those items could only be determined by the context by which they were found. Everything in that house would be mind-blowingly expensive if it was put on the open market.

There were old coins too, probably nothing unusual about that because Roman coins can be picked up in flea markets and on websites online these days. But these were Knights Templar coins, labelled Italian, French and British. Why were they in a collection of religious items? I wouldn't know.

As I mentioned earlier, two large broadswords decorated the north facing wall. I've come across decorative swords many times, but these were the real deal. The leather handle grips were so worn you could almost make out the hand that held them. It probably took two hands to swing one above head height, but I would need two hands and a fork truck to get one of them off the ground! Never mind the modern artillery of today, back 600 years, in the right hands those would have been weapons of 'mass destruction'.

Then I came across a majestic glass frame that displayed weapons and armour from numerous battles against the Picts and the Vikings. Each having a story to tell, I'm sure, but silenced by the sands of time. Seeing them was just half the tale. I wanted to know more.

Time passed so quickly, and it was only when I thought I heard a noise outside the front door that I looked at my watch. It was 11.12pm and Steve had been away more than two hours.

Then I heard that noise once again. A key was slipped into the lock and I looked anxiously towards the partitioning door. The key was turned, the door was free to open, but no-one walked in. Seconds dragged by like minutes and I stood looking and waiting. The light was low and it had formed a lovely atmospheric ambience to wander round this beautiful home, but now it only added to the tension. Peace and tranquility was now fear and trepidation. Do I move towards the door or do I run and hide? I couldn't decide, I just froze and stared at the door handle. It didn't move.

The clock ticked and nothing else made a sound, as the shadows on the floor turned the aura from welcoming to ghostly. Shadows moved across the floor and I knew I wasn't alone. Perhaps the door was the safest place to be. At least I could run away. I felt more anxious about what was behind me rather than watching for the handle to turn, so I decided to count to three and make a positive move, one way or another.

"One … two ..." then I stepped forward to grab the handle. It wouldn't open. Whoever had turned the key had locked me in.

I stood there petrified, knee-deep in silence.

"Oh my God!" I whisper to myself several times, as if punctuating the seconds. Each passing moment only led to the next, heightening my anxiety, before I heard the back door clunk open. Then I knew I'm trapped. I was not

familiar with every room in the cottage but I assumed there was only a back door and a front door, and one of them was going to open. I stood with my back against the wall, my eyes locked on the kitchen door.
"Sorry girl, but we are on the move again," bellowed a voice before the door opened.
Steve, walked in briskly, throwing his black coat onto a chair next to an oak cabinet housing even more ancient memorabilia. My heart skipped a beat.
"Someone locked the front door! I thought I was trapped." I said, pulling on the handle to prove my point.
"Yeah, it was me," he said. "Then I walked around the back to check the garden. I locked it because we will be leaving by the back door. Give me two minutes to pack a case."
"Not again Steve! Why are we leaving? I'm tired, smelly and I feel as though my head has been hit by a truck. I thought this would be the end of it all."
A voice from the bedroom made its way in my direction, "We are not going far, but far enough. I will just get a few things together. The causeway is open again. I'm expecting trouble, so let's make tracks ... quickly."
I looked out of the window towards the village.
"So I take it your meeting didn't go to plan, then?" I said in a resonating voice.
"It probably went the way I expected," he replied. "But we are dealing with fanatics."
"So that is why we are we still running around like blue-arsed-flies, because they have caught up with us," I reasoned.
"Not yet," he said as he returned to the room clasping a large suitcase.
"How long are you going away for? A month?" I mocked.

He didn't reply. He grabbed what he could and we left by the tradesman's entrance.

"What is the mode of transport this time? Trains, planes or automobiles?" I said flippantly, not understanding how dire our circumstances were.

I was in desperate need of sleep. Within two minutes, I was sat in the passenger seat of an old battered Fiat Punto clutching a glass of water in one hand and headache tablets in the other. Even in a moment of crisis he was considerate, I will give him credit for that.

I didn't ask him where he was taking me because I didn't particularly care.

I drifted in and out of sleep for several minutes. The windscreen was a blur of darkness, so we couldn't have been traveling on any major roads. Random images seemed to float aimlessly by. The flash of a car headlight and then the odd street light, then darkness again. I could feel somebody trying to look at me, staring into my eyes, but I couldn't keep focus. The whole moment felt in low resolution like a bad quality play.

"Come on girl, wake up," said Steve.

"Oh no," I groaned, "All I want to do is put my head onto a soft fluffy pillow and say goodnight." Thankfully, that wasn't too far away. He certainly pushed out the boat to keep a girl happy – this was a caravan on a holiday site – but I couldn't care less. There was a bed.

Waking up was an unusual pleasure. There was a fleeting moment when I feared my gentleman-friend was under the bedclothes with me, but he had the decency to give me my own space. I had to appreciate his manners, and he never crossed any line at any point in the short time I had known him.

The sun shone on a beautiful summer's morning. Rabbits played on the freshly cut lawn outside my window and a pair of magpies scolded each other in the tree above.
I was down to my underwear, but I could remember taking off my own stinking clothes myself, which was a relief. I looked at my watch. It showed 9.24 and I was just about to wonder where my camping partner was when he burst through the main door. Now I was awake, hiding my modesty, and he threw a couple of plastic shopping bags onto my bed.
"I've been over to the shop and bought you a few things to tide you over," said Mr Prince Charming. "Nothing much – more sporty than feminine – but they are clean and new."
I opened the bags and thanked him for his generosity and his thoughtfulness, and I was rather surprised at his good taste in women's clothes. Everything was there, from jogging trousers to t-shirts; socks to underwear. I had never ever had a man buy me a 'job lot' of clothes before. I'd rather pick my own, but under the circumstances, he did very well.
"I will pop out to let you shower and dress," he said, "and meet you over at the cafe for coffee and breakfast when you are ready. It's directly opposite this door, about 100 meters. There's no hurry, take your time."
I was so wide awake I felt like I was hooked up to the mains. No sleepiness, no slow burning warming up. I had a shower and felt on top form and ready for 'Carry On Camping'. I was even refreshed and primed for a few Barbra Windsor chest exercises. Yes, I was feeling THAT good. But then I decided it was probably best to keep my bra on and not distress the campers, so I headed over to the cafe.

We chatted over breakfast and the idle chatter turned to personal matters and I got to find out more about his private life. Sadly, the more I got to know the more I felt a little bit sorry for him. He was a man who never seemed to get close to anyone. He gave the impression that he kept his feelings under lock and key, and I don't think anyone in his entire life had broken his heart ... because they couldn't get anywhere near it!

He was hardly a family man, so I was curious to know who owned the caravan.

"I bought it for my mother," he replied, showing a compassionate side of him that I hadn't seen before. "She loves the countryside and I bring her down here once a month or so, when she wants a break."

It took me back to my youth: "I used to go on camping holidays with my parents when I was a child. The smell of bacon often makes me think of those days. And cow muck of course. There was always a lot of cow muck."

Back at the caravan we talked like children on a school outing. We covered a lot of ground in a short time: families; relationships; holidays; what we liked; and what we didn't like.

For the first time since I had known this man, it was 'shoes off and chill', and I kind of liked that. He was opening up to me and I was starting to look at him from a new angle. Not just his personality, but his features, too. His face had a peculiarity that I hadn't noticed before, as though he suited middle-age. I didn't know him but I assumed that with every passing year more of his inner beauty showed on his face. Or was I just fabricating all that because I was starting to grow fond of the man?

Corrie, a self-confessed authority on the male sex, claims men don't age as fast as women. She upholds that we – the pair of us - were over the hill at twenty six, although I'd like to think I made it into my thirties without parts of me dropping off.
"Although we are the same age, I look significantly older than Derek," she would often proclaim. "When I look in the mirror everyday I see the signs of aging staring back at me."
"Well, don't look in the mirror!" I would say, always getting a laugh from her.
Perhaps the main difference between men and women is arguably just that women fear getting older more than men do.
Although we were enjoying that particular moment of relaxation, I still didn't know if our problems were behind us or even what plans he had for the rest of the day.
"We left your cottage in a hurry," I remarked. "Why are we still on the run? You returned the Gospel, wasn't that the plan in the first place?"
"I don't think you are running from anything," he said.
"Well I do!" I retorted, even shocking myself at how forceful I had become. "We are hid out here in the wilds of no-place for a reason, Steve. Can we expect visitors? Will you be returning to your home? How will I get home? There's three questions to suggest we are not a willing campers."
"The cottage is not really my home," he replied. "And I got the impression last night that my tenancy has expired."
"So it's the camping life from now on," I replied. "Boiling your own water and cleaning out the toilet."
He laughed, "For the time being, perhaps."

It was then that he approached me with his business proposition. The 'Get Rich Quick' scheme that would give us so much money we wouldn't know how to spend it all.
"Oh, I am always up for any craic that involves paying off my mortgage," I smiled.
"You will be able to do that, without a problem" he said, and he wasn't smiling.

Steve had me captivated, and this was his story:-
"For years historians from the mainland have wanted to find the original monastery that Cuthbert built. Archaeologists believe the first monastery was build in the centre of the island but we could have saved them the time and the money because the Elders know exactly where the monastery is. And it isn't in the centre of the island.
"St Cuthbert died in 687 and his corpse became legend. His coffin, that lay in Durham Cathedral, was opened three times up until 1539 and his body remained as incorrupt as the day he died. The Cathedral grew rich because of donations from pilgrims, and his shrine became more lavish. Where Cuthbert lay – money flooded in. However, King Henry VIII broke from the Roman Catholic Church and religious buildings up and down the country were robbed of all their riches, and many were destroyed.
"But at Durham Cathedral, they were warned of the intended robbery and told that Cuthbert's shrine would be destroyed. That is exactly what happened, and in December 1539 the deed was done. But when his tomb was opened there was catastrophic deterioration to the body. They raided all the gold that was in the coffin, but although the golden-garnet cross (that is the symbol of Durham) was there, it was later found to be a replica.
"Unknown to the rest of the world, Cuthbert's body, and the original Durham cross, were returned secretly to

Lindisfarne a month before Henry's men arrived. That is where they lie today. The body in the coffin in Durham Cathedral was a nobleman who had died years earlier. Cuthbert now lies on Holy Island where, on his death bed, he asked to be placed. He lies at the original monastery, along with the plaque that was placed on Jesus' cross.

"Supposedly, Cuthbert's famous cross of Durham is in a long lost shaft, along with three chests of Emperor Hadrian's gold placed there by the Invisible College when Cuthbert's body was returned. Treasure was hidden away for centuries, and it's not that they don't know where it is, The Elders know the exact spot, they simply cannot get to it!

"Then comes the twist in the tale. It was kept secret until 1793 when a 16 year old local kid called Robert Bowman paddled his boat across from the Northumbrian headland to look for birds eggs on the north side of the island to sell at Bamburgh market. In those days Sandham Bay and Coves Beach were difficult to reach on foot as The Elders bricked off the entire stretch of the North Shore to keep away strangers. It was officially farmland but nothing grew there and there was no livestock. It was just a blank spot on the map of the island. The only approach was by sea, and even then you were trespassing on private land, and the farmer was prone to filling your backside with buckshot if you got within range of his blunderbuss. Young Robert was a foolhardy kid who seemed to enjoy risking life and limb for the few pence he would get poaching the eggs. But this particular day he beached his little boat and wandered inland, and stumbled upon a large rock from the island's sea defence that was a quarter of a mile out of place. He noticed marks on the rock, as though it had been scored by a rope and tackle. Next to it he found a rotting wooden trellis, covered in moss and heather, that had long been discarded. Robert tugged away at it for a couple of minutes before he was able to pull it away from the undergrowth and drag it a few feet, to find a depression in the ground about 6 feet in diameter. He looked down into the darkness, and with a head full of magic, he decided he was onto something that only kids could imagine. This was a pirate's horde. To this boy it could even be Black Beard's treasure! Sadly, the guy with the blunderbuss was patrolling his kingdom, and Robert decided to head home and return the next day with tools and help from a couple of friends.

"Back on land Robert shared his discovery with his two friends – Chris Hocking, aged 16, and Billy Swift, aged 13. The following morning the three treasure seekers rowed off in search of adventure and their fortune, armed with picks, shovels and a length of rope.

"After a four feet drop into the shaft they started digging and they soon realized they were gradually working their way down in a circular pit with walls of hard clay that clearly bore the marks of a previous dig. This was man-made, and their excitement reached fever pitch when ten feet down their picks hit a flagstone that could perhaps be the roof of an underground building. They removed it and found a 20 feet drop into a larger shaft with a floor of oak logs. But with the tools available, and rope that was now at its full length, they could go no further. They returned home to the village of Belford to seek help, but that proved a lot more difficult than they expected.

"In 1793 Holy Island was still a place of pilgrimage, as it had been for a thousand years previous. Babies; the ill; the infirm; and the dying were brought to be blessed. But with religion comes fear, with most of it conjured up by the monks themselves. The people on the mainland believed, most sincerely, that ghosts roamed the beaches of Holy Island at night. It was well documented that the head of St Oswald lay with St Cuthbert in a shrine in Durham Cathedral, but the monks spread the word that his headless body could be seen wandering the island on moon-kissed evenings hoping to find his head. Not only that, but another saint, Bede, was believed to watch over the causeway every evening ready to inflict a curse on any intruder. The Monks had all avenues covered. Not only that, but at night strange lights and fires had been seen by villagers. A few years previous a curious fisherman had rowed out to investigate the fires but never returned, and the story of hauntings was made even more real by locals who swear they could hear his screams. Robert and his pals were warned not to meddle with anything that was found on holy ground.

"But the thought of treasure drew them back, and when they returned to the pit they removed many platforms, and at 90 feet they came across a peculiar rectangular stone with faded wording engraved into the face. It was in Latin, and the kids paid little attention to what could have been a valuable clue in their quest for gold, simply because they couldn't understand a word of it. They removed it from the shaft with great difficulty, hauling it to the top with their three-man pull rope, and placed it in their boat. But the clay below was packed like cement and they convinced themselves their adventure was at an end. No gold or treasure, just a weird rock to take home as a souvenir.

"Robert kept the stone in his parent's garden for a number of years before cementing it into a rock wall he built on his own property in Belford when he married. It remained on show in the main street until 1817 when a monk from Holy Island spotted the Lindisfarne coat of arms and the Latin language. He asked Robert, who was now 40 years of age, where he obtained it. Rather reluctant to admit to stealing religious relics, the former treasure hunter waffled a tall story, but the monk offered him money for the story. He asked Robert if he could pin-point the exact location it was found, and after a financial arrangement was completed, the pair set out to the very spot. Robert rowed his boat ashore for the last time and took the monk to the shaft, where he explained in detail how they had dug down to find it. He returned home, content he had done right and the good Lord would forgive him for his sins, and the treasure became someone else's dream.

"The monk employed friends to dig the shaft but they found that the bottom of the pit was so waterlogged that they had to remove one cask of water to every two casks of earth. Then someone swung a pickaxe and struck something hard and unyielding that shuddered underfoot. All present agreed it was metal screwed onto wood, and excitement grew because they were convinced it must be a form of chest.

"However, the shaft flooded with water. Not only did it hamper the progress of the dig, but it demonstrated how dangerous the venture was. They bailed out the muddy water with buckets but no matter how much they removed, the level of water remained constant. The monks would have to come up with another idea, because they were getting nowhere pretty fast.

"A pump was obtained and lowered into the shaft but it couldn't handle the volume of water and broke on the second day. Work was suspended for eight months until the spring of 1818 when the monks returned with Plan 'B' – to dig a second shaft alongside the original, to drain the water. It looked a good idea on paper, but in practice it was a disaster! At 90 feet they tunneled sideways to link the two shafts, but suddenly there was a thunderous roar as a surge of water overwhelmed them so rapidly that two workers were killed and four were lucky to escape with their lives. "The old shaft had collapsed and it took decades before the Invisible College took up the task again.

"In 1842 they made another attempt but still the flooding continued. It was then that someone realized the flooding in the tunnel corresponded with the rising of the tide. The 60 feet of water leveled out at the hight of the sea so they changed their work structure to fit in with low tide.

"Then they brought in a horse-driven drill known as 'pod auger' which brought to the surface samples of whatever material passed through it. The auger brought up a tiny piece of gold necklace which proved difficult to date but thought to be Roman, and to the Invisible College, this was a monster of a find. Emperor Hadrian built his famous wall as a defensive fortification to keep out the Picts, and it was known that Hadrian, himself, travelled to Rome to meet the Pope. He brought back a wealth of gold that miraculously disappeared out of the annals of history, plus a Gospel that ended up in Lindisfarne. Could that gold possibly be down that well?

"Another bore brought up splinters of varnished wood and metal pieces, suggesting it may have caught the edge of two oak chests, one on top of the other. The last boring was the most confusing because the owner of the auger was seen taking something out of the drill, studying it closely, then putting it in his pocket. When asked to produce it he refused and said it was a coin he had dropped. Surprisingly, no attempt was made to search him, although tradition has it the item was a jewel.

"Over the following years those three treasure chests became a quest that always seemed just out of reach. Then in 1897 they drilled down to an incredible depth of 150 feet and found the chests once again. A three-inch pipe was lowered down and at last the monks believed that they were on the verge of learning what lay below. But that was the most the Invisible College got, because the treasure dropped even further down into some natural cavity and possibly a limestone sinkhole. Greater understanding of the geological formation of the island shows that area is littered with them."

I sat and listened and I hung on every word that Steve had to say. He made everything sound so plausible, and why shouldn't it all be true?

"Where are the shafts on Holy Island?" I asked.

"Coves Beach."

"So you know where the pit is?" I think it was perfectly obvious he knew, but I asked him all the same.

"Yes, I know where the pit is," he smiled, "but that isn't important. Nobody creates a masterpiece of engineering like that without being able to access it again. That has been fooling people for centuries. The design isn't to protect the treasure; it's the decoy. The guy who designed it had no intention of going back down there to recover what is there. It's the 'broken wing' theory. It's like the lapwing – the bird that pretends it has a broken wing to lure foxes away from its chicks. The gullible fall for the obvious. Yes the gold was buried there – but that was not the way they were going to get it out!"

I could imagine Steve being the perfect schoolteacher. Quick, bright, and a teacher the kids could never get the better of. When he talked it was with the passion of someone who lived to inspire. Some of his stories pushed the boundaries, but whatever he said … I believed.

CHAPTER TWELVE

The old house seemed to have collapsed inwardly on itself, like a loaf of bread taken out of the oven too soon. The roof sagged and the dirty garage windows seem to have been cracked or smashed a long time ago. The lean-to shed on the side of the building leant a little too much, giving the impression – open the door and the whole bloody lot would fall down. But this, apparently, was going to be our hide out in our quest for Emperor Hadrian's treasure.
I sat in the car looking at the run-down dwelling, trying to work out which room (if any) was capable of keeping out the rain, before asking myself: "What the hell is this all about?"
Meanwhile Steve, who was sat next to me knowing I was far from happy, tried to sell me the idea that this structure was "the answer to our prayers."
"I certainly haven't 'prayed' for a place like this, Steve. It may have popped up in a nightmare once or twice. Does it even have electricity?"
"That can be sorted, don't worry about that. This was my Dad's old house. Let's take a look inside." And off he went, scrambling about in his coat pockets looking for the door key.
I expected the door to creak as it opened, but even that moment of fun was taken away from me because it wouldn't open at all! We trudged our way through unkempt grass around the back of the building and saw tracks probably made by the local children. It had been visited recently, judging by the footprints, and quite often if the tracks were anything to go by.
"I see someone has been sniffing around here," said Steve.

"Yeah, 'sniffing' could be the operative word," I said as I looked for evidence in the grass. "Druggies probably."
"It is supposed to be haunted," he said in jest, looking for an expression on my face as I looked up at the bedroom windows.
"I can believe that," I replied. "So you HAVE got a sense of humour," I said, putting my arm around him. I was starting to see another side to this man.
The house we were trying to enter was in the woods about half a mile from Bamburgh Castle. Chop down a few trees and I would have been able to see Holy Island out of the living room windows ... after I'd cleaned them of course. Ideally situated for Long John Silver, Captain Dan and Billy Bones to go treasure hunting.
We finally got inside with the aid of a screwdriver and a heavy shoulder, but the place was far from what I expected. Judging from the decaying outside appearance I never for one second expect it to be a palace. Not even a run-down council house. But this was like going back in a weird and wonderful time-warp. It was a home, and a very proud one too.
"Oh my God, this is charming." I said as we walked into the living room.
I thought opening that door was going to be a choker. How wrong I was.
The electricity wasn't turned on so Steve obviously didn't have immediate plans for the place. But as he walked through to the kitchen I heard him mumble, "I will phone the electricity company this afternoon."
So perhaps we WERE going to move in immediately.
I felt sadness as I walked from room to room. The house was littered with personal items, and it was as though this poor old guy had died but the family didn't have the heart

to tear apart his 'home'. Or, on the other hand, perhaps they didn't care.
It wasn't as though the seasons had performed irreversible deeds upon this once proud and mighty house, because it could be restored. Everything was locked in a time and a space. I say 'home' in genuine appreciation, because I could almost picture the fellow sat by the large fireplace or perched at the large table having a meal. He lived alone but there was a happy vibe about the place, and the only negative aura came from the fact he was no longer there.
We wandered outside and Steve pointed out a secret cellar from the days of smuggling, and he told me it was so well concealed it would probably remain undiscovered even in a police raid. Well that was reassuring.
"Are you expecting a police raid?" I said in shock. "This just gets better and better. Do we hide down there?"
Under a flagstone (that looked just like all the others) was a shaft leading directly to an abandoned tunnel that Steve said led all the way down to the sea. 98 steps apparently. He said he had counted them when he was a child.
"One hundred and fifty years ago it would have been perfect for moving the 'merchandise' in and out," he explained. "And with a house as grand as this, I suspect it never came under suspicion."
I'm sure he was right. The driveway was obscured from the road by a tall rock wall, and that in itself added to its anonymity.
"It was left to me in my dad's Will. It wasn't run-down then. But he hadn't lived in it for years. I considered refurbishing the outside but I put the idea on the back burner. I'm sure someone with time on their hands could transform it to its past glory."
He wasn't wrong.

He then investigated the tunnel, making a makeshift light with his phone.

"Was it actually used for smuggling?" I asked.

"Yes," he answered in a booming voice from down in the passage. "It was big business around these parts. The boats on this coast made more profit from smuggling than catching fish."

"What's it like down there?" I shouted into the darkness.

"It's rat-infested and smelly," he shouted back. "There's a problem with water seeping in through the roof. The water runs down the steps from top to bottom. It seems to have eroded into a drainage system over the years."

"Are you intending to use it?" I asked, hoping I wasn't expected to venture down into that darkness.

"Probably," he boomed back.

Becoming rich was only going to happen at a cost.

I left him in the blackness and I went upstairs in the house to check out the rest of the building. I saunted across the landing floor to find a very peculiar bedroom. It was as though someone had pulled back the bedclothes of a massive double bed and walked out – about fifty years ago. A cup was still sat on the bedside table, and slippers lay on the floor. I couldn't help but wondering why such a place was abandoned so quickly. Clothes filled the wardrobe, stacked neatly on coat-hangers. 1950-style suits, about a score of them, all slightly different to each other. Beautiful starched white shirts lined up in military order as though they had never been worn.

There were many framed photographs on top of cupboards and tables, as well as being scattered on all of the walls. But they were all of only one subject – a beautiful lady. No family photos of any description, of the home owner or

anyone else, just that one person. A staggering amount of them – thirty or more.
I was just about to enter the second bedroom when Steve appeared up the stairs.
"What have you found?" he asked.
"Who is this woman in these photos?" I replied, expecting him to say his mother.
"We don't talk about her," he said without explanation, leading me away from the bedroom towards the stairs.
It probably wasn't my place to pry and I accepted his answer, but it just made me even more curious.
"You said this was your dad's house." I said, before pushing for answers. "He was the last person to live here, wasn't he?"
"Errr yeah, he was the last person here."
Steve wasn't comfortable with the questions so I backed away. Perhaps it wasn't the time or the place for an interrogation, but I'd return to it at a later date. And before we left the house I took a photo of the lady in question with my phone when Steve was otherwise occupied. I was intrigued. If he disliked the lady so much, why in twenty years had he not removed her photographs? After all, it was now his house.

We returned to the caravan and Steve laid out the plan of how we would approach the treasure hunt. I say "we", but at this point I was merely listening to what he had to put on the table. I was ready to return home to a normal life, and he said he would do the 'spade work' and I would get a call when I was required.
I suppose I had nothing to lose but I still wasn't totally convinced the plan would work. Was there treasure out there? If others had been trying (and failing) since 1793,

there was a reason. Persuasion was Steve's strongest talent, but it didn't always work. I did believe Cuthbert's remains were back where they truly belonged, and I understood perfectly the cause behind it and the need for the secrecy. But buried treasure is a literary theme, best saved for the flamboyance of the Hollywood big screen. I was convinced that the only treasure maps ever produced were fakes. Nobody ever created a map that took someone to find their fortune where 'X' marked the spot. But, Steve could be convincing, and I just knew he was going to produce one.

"There is a map of some sorts," he said. "The Invisible College do have a record of where they buried Cuthbert's gold, but it's not in geographical form. It's a series of numbers, carved out on the ceiling of the Priory on Holy Island. It is there for all to see. Visitors assume they are passages from the bible, although delve deeper and it becomes apparent they lead you nowhere."

I didn't want to sound negative but didn't the College know exactly where the three chests were, they simply couldn't get to them? So ... in the cold light of day ... what could we do that would be any different to what others had tried?

"But how can we dig to that depth when a massive drill couldn't manage it?" I asked. Where was the logic?

"When the monk found the stone with the Latin inscription," he replied, "and Robert Bowman took him to the pit, it was assumed the code was pin-pointing that very spot. It wasn't. The code locates the way to the treasure from the sea. The point where they would have recovered it, bypassing the death-trap they created. There must be another way, or they wouldn't have designed it as they did. It is a master-plan, and there HAS to be a back door."

Then Steve explained the mathematics and why we could succeed when others failed.

"I tried most of my life to decipher the code but what can you learn from a collection of numbers? Were they yards or footsteps in a certain direction, but from which starting point? The most logical explanation would be a word count, but that failed too because most of the numbers were higher than the 26 letters in our alphabet. Then I tried Latin, but the Romans only used 23 letters in their alphabet, so that wasn't the answer either."

"Then I looked at the author of the code," he explained. "I thought perhaps he used a book as a word count. The treasure was buried in 1539 and obviously the elaborate pit was devised at that date. The obvious books at that period would be the Bible or the Lindisfarne Gospels, but the code didn't work on either. A philosopher called Dr Howard Numasio wrote the code and after years of delving and analysis I found out that he had published a book in 1536 called 'The Synoptic Gospels'. It pointed out that the gospels of Matthew, Mark and Luke were not shared by the writings of John. I tried to get a copy of his book but the only one still in existence is in Florence, and it took me until two months ago to get the authority to get a photocopy. But it was worth all the effort because that gave away the secrets."

But knowing the spot still didn't guarantee success.

"There is a formation of caves on Emmanuel Head on the north side of the island that can only be approached by the sea," he defined. "According to Dr Howard Numasio's writings, the entrance is concealed by a wall of rocks 'but one looks as though it shouldn't be there,' suggesting it wasn't a sea rock. Considering the blockade has been untouched for centuries and the cliffs have subsided, I can imagine the rocks are welded together like cement with hardened clay. We will need heavy duty tools; and a boat that can motor pretty fast. Other than that, I suggest we get there at sunrise one morning."

There were many reasons to feel excited about this venture, but I didn't fancy the idea of bobbing up and down on a little sailing vessel on the North Sea (again), then moving a mountain of boulders.

"You do know that I'm not built to be a hod-carrier," I said, and I meant every word. "And I'm not built to be a sailor, either."

"Well you're probably not built to be a millionaire either," he replied with a smug look on his face. "The choice is yours. You can walk away now. We have covered our tracks well and, once we returned the Gospel to the Priory, the College lost interest in you. They want me … and in time they will probably succeed … but you can walk away a free woman. I am offering you an opportunity. All you have to do is say 'yes' or 'no'."

I was starting to smell the salty air and feel the nauseating seasickness. But I couldn't turn this down, could I?

My father always believed I was destined to become rich and famous, although I never gave him any reason. I don't have any special talents and I'm hardly intelligent. But fathers tend to be led by blind faith when they look at their offspring. We all know it's hope rather than belief, but I always dreamt one day I would prove him right. That too was blind faith.

Steve had scanned the area of coast-line in a fishing boat and he had this venture planned down to every minute detail. But the one failing was finding the wall that hid the tunnel to the treasure. "Although there is a stretch of 100 yards where it is sure to be," he explained, "100 yards is the length of a football pitch, and rocks cover its entirety. As for that special rock that 'looks as though it shouldn't be there', well that could prove to be as elusive as the treasure itself. There must have been scores of landslides over the years. That coast-line changes shape every decade, and that rock could well be at the bottom of the sea."

However Steve said there was a key to opening the puzzle. He explained: "Several years ago I wrote a book about the Viking invasions that saw St Cuthbert's body moved away from Lindisfarne, and I was approached by a Danish guy who claimed I had made mistakes with days and dates. He was a lecturer at University College London and I met him a couple of times. An odd fellow who must be in his late 80's now. He knew about the treasure pit, which was not ... and still isn't ... common knowledge, yet he claimed he knew the point to get to the treasure. He knew because of a symbol, although he wouldn't disclose what that symbol was. The guy is called Preben Kahlenberg. Obviously he wouldn't disclose where he got his information from, and I wasn't convinced it was as precise as he claimed. After all, why would he trust me? I lost contact with him for years but he got in touch recently and told me he now lives in Edinburgh and he wants to meet me."

"Perhaps he wants a collaboration to make you both wealthy men," I suggested, thinking it was the most palpable answer.

Steve thought otherwise, "Could be but he is a very wealthy man. And it's the timing that is my concern. He only got in touch when the Gospel couldn't be found. I was tipped off he was a senior figure in the Invisible College about thirty years ago. That could explain a lot."

"Do you know that for sure?" I asked.

"Nobody knows who they are. But I suspect he is ... or was."

I thought about this very carefully, "Let's figure this out logically. He contacted you at a time when the Invisible College had you on their radar. And things haven't exactly gone swimmingly since. You've killed two of them! So he could be a bit pissed off about that. Does he have a genuine reason to meet you? Or are they after your scalp?"

Steve pondered for a long time. Steve was going to treasure hunting whether I was interested or not. But suddenly I could bring something to the party.

"What can you give him that he doesn't know already?" I asked.

"He knows the 'sign', whatever that is, but I know the treasure is located from the sea. He doesn't know that, he still thinks it can be drilled out."

"Shall I meet him then?" I asked.

"Once these people assume you are involved with me - treasure hunting – you put your life on the line. Think very carefully what you want to do with your life."

Decisions, decisions.

CHAPTER THIRTEEN

I think the majority of us have an unashamed desire for wealth, and I'm sure it doesn't make us bad people. But, could my conscience handle taking something that was not rightfully mine? And that thought was starting to take over my life.

I decided that I should return home and take my time before committing myself to anything. Here was the opportunity to profit from all the madness I had been embroiled in. But was I really entitled to anything? Using the term 'compensation' in connection with a family death is another painful guilt trip I didn't want to face. That was

putting a price on a life. Also, if you have to go undercover to profit from something, I think there is a big doubt about your legal right to owning it.
I needed my home and the space to experiment with my own conscience before I spoke to Steve again, and a few day's grace would get me back to a sensible routine. A weight had been lifted and I didn't fear anyone anymore. My mind had been pickled for a few days. I just wanted the freedom to roam in my own space without the fear of getting lost.
Back in Seaham I walked through the door and all I wanted to do was to belong. But this time it was different. I understood for the first time that home is a state of mind. The rooms were cold, but that was irrelevant. My house had always been more than the sum of its parts, but on this particular evening, it didn't give me a welcome. Was there someone hiding in the shadows? Could I sleep in my bed without constantly fearing that the windows could be unlocked? Had someone already visited? Those are not homely thoughts.
But I got through it, and next morning I arranged a meeting with Corrie and we headed off to Newcastle for a day of coffee, shopping and a 'catch up'. But I had changed. Nothing much changes in Corrie's world, and our conversations that particular day weren't exactly invigorating either. She didn't have much to say and I was no better. I told her nothing of what I had accomplished (if that is the right word) in recent days, even though she asked. She had an excuse – she genuinely had nothing new to tell me. While I had my head up my own backside. After twenty minutes or so she didn't seem particularly interested anyway. And I don't blame her.

Why am I so judgemental? Why should I ruin her day because I was having a difficult time myself?
I nodded at (what seemed) the appropriate times and laughed when she laughed, but I blanked out her voice and instead all I could hear were the two sides of my brain giving me advice. The negative side was shouting at me "you are entering dangerous territory; don't take the risk; you could end up on a mortuary slab". While the other voice was calm and soothing, "Hey, it's a beautiful day, and you've got the ability to make it even better. Grab the opportunity of a lifetime. I'll see you in the winner's circle."
I don't like being shouted out. And I love a calming influence.
I returned home and those feelings of fear returned. Was it loneliness or was it anxiety? That night I was even terrified to open the toilet door because I had to walk three steps into darkness before I reached the light switch. I was petrified.
I could feel my life changing. It had been going through a gradual transition for weeks. My hopes had deflated to such a level I wanted out. And it was time to grow up and do something about it. I wasn't the one six foot under. Why should I live my life in a whirlpool of misery and depression, scared of what lies behind every door?
I phoned Steve later that evening to say I was on board, no matter what port his ship was sailing from.
My life in that house could be placed in a nutshell. I felt as though I was cooped up in a room full old clocks that didn't have the energy to tick ... and all I wanted was the window to suddenly burst open and time actually meant something. I wanted to be energized once more.

I hardly knew the guy, but Steve had a way of lifting me off the floor. A kind word, his enthusiastic manner, he had a gift that allowed him to re-evaluate anything negative and address it head-on.
He said he had started to get the ball rolling with the old house and pronounced it would be "habitable within two days."
It takes me two days to get round to picking up the phone to get things started when I'm planning a refit, yet he had everything in hand. I suppose it depended what he meant by habitable. Was he intending to move in and actually live there - or was he talking about our plans to use it as a temporary base?
As for the meeting with Kahlenberg, Steve felt we should go to Edinburgh together. I felt another holiday coming on. Or at least a day away. We booked it for the Friday of that week.

I caught the 8.10am train out of Newcastle Central station and met Steve when he boarded at Alnmouth. He looked as smart as always, "well turned out" as my mother would say, neat but comfortable. I, as always, seemed to over do it. I know that you need to be a Sherpa to climb (or stagger your way) up the Royal Mile proficiently. So what on Earth convinced me high heels made sense?
"You are looking beautiful," were Steve's first words. That was the massaging my ego wanted. So perhaps I had chosen wisely after all.
Is there a more beautiful city in Britain than 'Auld Reekie'? Vibrant, magnetic, and so captivating. Edinburgh sets my heart alight. Easily the most cosmopolitan city north of the border, and despite the crowds of people, I don't think we

heard a Scottish accent for twenty minutes after we left the train at Waverley Station. Is that too cosmopolitan?

Steve and I had coffee in a quaint little cafe that had a date above the door showing that the building was over 400 years old, which probably made it the ideal place to talk about a sunken treasure from the same era.

"Where do we meet the old gentleman?" I asked.

"An hour's time over the road at a place called 'Restaurant 100'. The table is booked for four people. He's bringing a friend with him."

"Are you nervous?" I inquired.

"No, why should I be? Are you?" he said with a large smile on his face. "Just regard it as a meal with an old friend."

He seemed perky enough, but that soon changed when we got to the restaurant. We were there early and took our seats in a beautiful room half full with customers. During the long wait I noticed Steve was getting more and more agitated. The holiday feeling evaporated very quickly as we both looked towards the door every time it opened.

"What's keeping them?" I asked.

Steve fumbled for an excuse, "Perhaps they couldn't get the car parked."

The longer we waited the more embarrassing it was becoming because we had to stall the waitress who was wanting to take our order. After twenty minutes I wanted to leave but Steve was convinced they would show.

"Let's give them another ten minutes," he said, looking at his watch.

Then the antiquated wooden door opened one more time and finally in walked our supposed business associates. The old man looked noble but he seemed to struggle to take in his surroundings and find us. I was annoyed because

Steve didn't give him any help by indicating where we were sat. He seemed happy to let him struggle. The old guy had a weather-worn face, with a thick groomed moustache of sliver-white. His back was slightly hunched and he walked with the aid of a black cane, but that didn't take anything away from his steely presence. I can only describe him as being of Churchill-ian demeanour. If he had creaking bones, and I'm sure he had many, he wouldn't want to show the weakness.

Steve finally walked towards him and ushered the old gentleman and his friend towards our seats, and I felt guilty for earlier suggesting we leave. The poor man must have summoned up all of his strength to walk up the Royal Mile to get there.

His associate could be, and probably was, his grandson although no introduction (apart from his name) was made. He had a strong, chiselled chin that made me think of Desperate Dan the cartoon character. Dress the guy in red shirt, black waistcoat and hand him a cow pie, and there was your man.

They both apologised earnestly for being late, putting the blame on the traffic congestion in the city, and we settled down for an hour or so of lunch and conversation.

Mr Kahlenberg's voice was slow and he stumbled on his words at times. But once he had a thought in his head he would battle on until he had made his point. Sometimes he was overtaken by forgetfulness and he would have to pause, knowing that what he was about to say was most important. He would seem excited to tell us a tale, while other times he seemed like he was honouring a solemn duty to keep his secrets. The gentleman was honourable, there was no question about that, but to me he had the resigned look of one who knew that at his age, life had stopped

giving - it was only taking away. Did he want to give away secrets for no profit? I doubted it. There must have been a deal involved because I was convinced there was a significant reason behind all of this.
The conversation was edgy at first. Steve in particular seemed unyielding in his quest for the information he didn't have. Both were cautious and I sensed Mr Kahlenberg seemed to fear the consequences should anyone find out they had been collaborating. For a novice like me, I felt like I was being party to something quite sensational. The more Preben glanced around checking to see who was watching us, the more he drew attention. I would smile at everyone as though I was protecting my dithery old grandfather.
The most engaging conversation was Preben giving Steve a history lesson: "When medieval cartographers produced maps, they wrote 'HERE be dragons' over the areas they hadn't explored. It wasn't written as fiction, the mapmakers honestly believed it to be a statement of fact. Everybody believed that monsters lurked beyond the walls of civilization. I have drawn out a map of Holy Island with the symbol you are looking for. Everywhere there is a camera on the stretch of coast I have marked 'HERE be dragons', because if the Invisibles get one sniff that you are close to the treasure, they will have you rot in Hell."
Isn't it refreshing to have light conversation when you are just finishing off a meal?
"Yes I know about the cameras," said Steve. "You said you could help me. We have both broken the code. The only people to have done so, as far as I know. What do you know that I don't, and what do you want from me?"

He surprised us both by saying: "I was going to exchange information with you. But I don't want to know anymore. I leave it all to you Mr Campbell."
Was there a catch? Had I missed something?
"What I believe you missed was the symbol," explained Kahlenberg. "It refers to a ley-line. It mentions the sun, as you know. But its significance is its alignment with a man-made structure - the Priory - at sunrise. That created the ley-line and everything on Holy Island is structured around it. It's not obvious now, but it was then. The Elders believed it was a spiritual and mystical alignment to the sun. Forget the treasure pit, that is a hoax and a death-trap, the riches are buried somewhere on that ley-line. Perhaps you know where, I don't know, and I don't want to know. The problem is now yours, and yours alone."
Steve knew the entrance was from the coast – not a tunnel down - and that was the clue he had been waiting for. The map was handed over and, with a quick message of "thank you", it disappeared down Steve's inside pocket before I had time to blink.
"What have you done to upset the College, Mr Campbell?" asked the Dane. "Why are you engrossed in fighting a battle you have no chance of winning? It is your own personal Armageddon. You do realise that, don't you?"
Steve didn't give much away. While Mr Kahlenberg was generous in what he had to give, Steve kept his powder dry. But he replied to that: "It's their battle against me. The Gospel was stolen on my watch, and they think I planned it."
"Did you?" he asked.
"No I didn't, sir, I tried to get it back. And I did get it back."

I could sense Steve cowering in his own defence, but the Dane finished him off with his 'coup de gras'.
Mr Kahlenberg added: "What you are doing now is for your own personal gain Mr Campbell. Not for history, nor God, nor country. It's on YOUR conscience. The world's history is the world's judgement. No matter how it ends, you won't come out of this looking good."
"That is utter rubbish Mr Kahlenberg, and you know it," ranted Steve in return. "That treasure was plundered by the Romans. Nobody knows exactly what the treasure consists of ... but we both know how it ended up on the Island. Hadrian did some deal with the Elders, probably to keep the Romans off the island. Nobody knows why The College buried it, but if you are so conscientious about it, why have you given me the key to find it? Why me?"
The Dane replied equally forcefully: "It was plundered, I agree, but that doesn't give you any right to it. The only way to find out its history is to dig it up and see what's there. Who it belongs to is irrelevant to me. The world needs to appreciate its beauty. It has been lost for too long."
"Are you a man of honesty Mr Kahlenberg?" said Steve going into unchartered waters. "Why are you here? What do you REALLY want from me?"
"You cannot fight them!" raged the Dane. "They are the 'Great Untouchable'! There is a price to pay for greatness – but the great never pay it themselves."
Steve had found his answer to the obvious question, the entrance to the treasure, but he still wondered which side the Dane was on.
"The College is not an organisation you step out of Mr Kahlenberg, is it?" he asked, looking the man straight in his eyes, creating an incredibly tense atmosphere.

It seemed to take an eternity for the Dane to reply and he did it like firing a machine-gun: "No you don't walk away, they won't let you. But I'm no use to them now. I have served my time. I am a past generation. A fossil."
I'm not psychic or clairvoyant, and I looked at the pair of them and I still didn't know if their meeting had gone well, even though I had sat through its entirety. They shook hands and gave one another a glimmer of respect. Steve was almost smiling - as if something good was about to happen. Perhaps a smile that suggested the hint of victory, and the joy of the conquest that you only feel after the battle has been won.
I'm not suggesting the Dane lost the battle, but he had more to give away, and he seemed to give it rather too freely for my liking.

We had seven hours to kill before our 9pm train home and we decided to call for a drink in a traditional Scottish bar. We picked 'The World's End', a place I have frequented countless times on my trips to Scotland's capital city. A quaint little bar with all the trimmings you would expect for the tourist. You can imagine what I mean - tartan carpet and curtains; two large battle axes placed above the bar; and Walter Scott's poem "A Tale Of Flodden Field" transcribed on the wall. Another bonus for the day-tripper is the painting of the 'unknown murderer' that has a tale as gruesome and ghastly as anything Edinburgh has to offer. Apparently the murderer was strung up on that very spot and left to hang for years, and (as the story goes) if ever the painting is taken down "the world will end". Who would have thought it would be that simple?

We sat by the window, hoping no-one would pinch the painting, and tried to sum up what was achieved by our little get-together with Kahlenberg.
"Would you say it was a success?" I asked.
"Well you were there. It had it's moments, didn't it?"
"What have you learnt? Are we any nearer finding our fortune?" I laughed.
He pulled out the map from his pocket and laid it on the pub table. It was actually a map ripped out from a guide book, with scribbles, drawings and the text "Here be dragons", as the man said. Steve took a pen from his pocket and marked two 'X's' where he believed the cave was.
"It's somewhere between a stretch of cliff face about 100 yards, from here to here," he said, pointing to the map.
"And according to Preben we are looking for a ley line that links the Priory to the sea. But it's not on this map."
After ten minutes we decided to check on Google Maps on Steve's phone to see if that could shed any light on our darkness, and low-and-behold, there was the ley line. There is a massive crater that must have been a strike from an asteroid centuries ago, and it showed up like a beacon on the photo. Just to the right of it was the line. Everything in the village fell into place, streets, fields and pathways, as though someone had placed a ruler, drew a line, and cut the island in half. It actually cut right between the two 'X's' Steve had marked on the map on the East cliff.
"Kahlenberg and myself both broke the code, and we must have come up with something very similar. I thought we were looking for a symbol, some kind of landmark viewed from the sea, not from the land looking out to sea. He believes the entrance is on land."
A special moment deserves a special celebration – and he returned from the bar with a bottle of Moet champagne.

Two glasses later and he held my hand. Was it the thrill of the moment, or a genuine affection for me? He leaned in a little closer and his lips brushed mine, not innocently like a tease, but sensual and passionate. Initially I felt I wanted to pull away before I lost myself, but who was I kidding? I didn't want him to pull away at all.

"Linda," he whispered slowly. "You make me a very happy man."

I didn't reply, but I admit he had my heart fluttering at his soft voice. And then he clasped my hand.

He kissed me again. It was slow and soft. I could feel the beating of his heart. Something I will never ever forget.

After the champagne had been drunk, he decided we should do a little a mini-tour of the city in the time we had left, and we strolled out of the tavern holding hands like two lovesmitten teenagers. I know there had been signs before, but I was completely unprepared for that moment. Was it the thrill of the adventure, or was he just fooling around? That man of mystery always showed me respect, but I never thought for one second I could take his heart.

We got absorbed in the bustling crowd of tourists, which grew continually as locals headed home after work. Struck by backpacks and briefcases, we got jostled as we wove our way down past Assembly Hall towards The Mound. The crowd parted around a newspaper dispenser and I lost Steve for a moment as I tried to keep my high heels on my feet. I looked around, and I couldn't spot him anywhere. People streamed past but I couldn't see his black leather coat.

Then, as I turn towards Market Street, I saw him slumped against a wall, slowly sinking to the pavement.

He stumbled forward and I felt an indescribable pain flowing through me as I tried to hold him up. It hit me – this man was about to die! I felt his heart throbbing as I

squeezed him and we both fell over. He lay in agony as blood flooded from his shirt and gushed down his trousers. Together we lay on the pavement and I cried and screamed for help. He stuttered an apology, saying "I'm sorry, I'm sorry," while I tried to steady his head.
"There's nothing to be sorry about," I told him. "What's caused this Steve? Please tell me."
He had the courage to cry, but they were hardened tears, as they rolled slowly - one at a time - down his face.
Onlookers were screaming, but two kind gentlemen took him from my arms and one tried to stop the flow of blood. I stood above them, crying, screaming, holding my red stained hands out in front of me.
A lady came to support me, telling me everything would be alright, as she led me away. I heard people talking, and I could see eyes staring at me. Scores of eyes staring.
"Keep fighting," I heard a lady shout at Steve. Then I heard no more.

CHAPTER FOURTEEN

I woke up on a hospital trolley that seemed to be bumping into just about every wall in the corridor, hardly sympathetic to my needs, but I suppose I should have appreciated the man's urgency.
"I cannot have been asleep for very long," I recall thinking to myself, but I had no concept of time so that was not based on anything valid. I was confused, extremely sleepy so I was obviously pulling around from being sedated.
The hospital corridor was stuffy and I remember the air had an undertone of bleach. I tried to sit up but double doors lay ahead, and the person in charge of my 'vehicle' was hardly

the safest 'driver.' But I glanced at my blood soaked clothes and hands and that gave me a reality check.
Was Steve still alive? Who had done this dreadful thing? I was obviously in an emergency ward and before any length of time I was asked a barrage of questions about my own well-being. But on close examination there were no wounds to myself, and that took away the seriousness from the doctors and nurses. All the blood was Steve's, and all I could find out was that he was "still in surgery."
I was taken to a private ward where I was washed and given temporary clothing. I looked around and I could see vases of flowers and a water dispenser, and if I listened very hard I could hear the noise of a television coming from a room down the corridor. The atmosphere was completely different from the pandemonium outside. The bed was clean and comfortable, and the nurses were calm and unhurried as they tried to keep me relaxed as best they could. But all I wanted to do was cry. Even that was no trouble to them. One held my hand, while another spoke lovely, caring words. My mind was all over the place and I constantly bombarded those poor nurses with "I need to know if he is alive."
They replied with a serene purposefulness that I would get my answers as soon as there was anything to know, but my tears still flowed. I was grasping at straws because I already knew he was gone. Nobody could lose that much blood and survive.
An hour went by, and I could see ambulances arriving outside my window. Another hour. More emergency cases, and I realised how bigger a priority they were than me. The shock had past and I was capable of walking out of the door and going home. I felt the guilt that I was taking up a bed that could be used by someone with actual needs.

I said to one of the nurses: "I'm not really a case at all, I'm perfectly fit and healthy. I am just wasting everyone's precious time."
Finally a doctor came in to take details and to tell me the shattering news that Steve was "dead on arrival." So obviously that meant he was dead hours ago, so why didn't they tell me? I was prepared for it.
"I am so sorry," he said in a most sympathetic voice. "He had four stab wounds, one to the heart. Do you know how it happened?"
The meeting with Kahlenberg was nothing more than a trap, and I'd expected it all along. I even offered to go alone to Edinburgh because they wouldn't have harmed me. They weren't after me. What was I to them? A dumb blonde with the intellect of a schoolchild. I could have got away with it. But Steve couldn't recognize the danger. He thought he was invincible, but they drew him in like a moth to a flame. They finally enticed him out into the open. That wasn't a crackhead or drunken lunatic carrying out a random killing in broad daylight on a city street. That was The College. The Invincibles serving out their retribution - an eye-for-eye.

Death is straightforward. It is not a gateway to immortality it's simply a departure from life.
It came to Steve with the slow rattling gasps that had taken my father years before. He died in my arms, as I'm convinced Steve did too. That would leave a scar on anyone.
It's ghostly and rather grotesque how bereavement takes away everything from you. For a moment Steve was sitting beside me – kissing my lips and holding my hand – and that in itself was a wonder. He had never done that before. A

few seconds of hope and trust. It was almost a "goodbye" gesture. Minutes later, he was a pale body covered with blood, and everything left me.

I won't talk about love because we weren't at that point in either of our lives. I don't even think the seeds were sown, and what would be the point of dwelling on something so hypothetical? One thing is certain, I cannot blame myself for his passing. He lived in the fast lane, for sure, and he knew the speed limit. Before my father died, he had a sever heart-attack that he just survived. The nurses said his heart machine 'flat-lined' and later he claimed – well he even "bragged" - that the incident made him clinically dead for a few seconds. He often told the story: "Many say that when you die you will meet the Grim Reaper, or go to Heaven or Hell. You could be reincarnated in someone else's body or turn into a ghost. But all you do is sleep for eternity. That's the bottom line. I never met the Grim Reaper or stood outside the pearly white gates of Heaven. I never went to Hell for my sins nor was I a ghost. Instead, I felt nothing. There was no emotion, just the feeling of floating. I felt rather happy." I had to remind him that at that time he wasn't really dead. But he is now. And like Steve, I hope the pair of them feel "rather happy."

I never told the police about our meeting with Preben Kahlenberg, and I didn't feel it necessary to delve into things I didn't understand. I played ignorant of motive and suspects. The police had a job to do, they are the experts, let them do what they do best. There are numerous CCTV cameras on the Royal Mile, but, unfortunately none by the Assembly Rooms where the murder took place. No-one to

date has ever been prosecuted, and I suspect nobody ever will. After all, aren't we talking about 'the silent untouchables'? They do what they want.
Steve summed them up when he told me prior to our meeting with Kahlenberg: "The College are out to get me, but I don't want to get to the end before I'm finished." He didn't even get to the starting gun!
Kahlenberg was still one of them, and I don't think it's an organisation you leave because you haven't renewed your cards or paid your annual fees. You are in that fraternity for life ... or until they decide to pull the plug.

I returned home and walking through that door I felt sadness, but a wave of relief washed over me. After a steaming hot bath I sank into the couch and made myself comfortable. My initial thoughts were "it's over" and I can return to my life. The police investigations were on-going, but I'd written my statement and I felt someone else would mop up the details and my involvement would be minimal. That's how they work it, I suppose. There would be someone with an imaginary brush to sweep everything under the fictitious carpet.
Then I looked back at the last few weeks. A whirlwind of fear, happiness, tears and every emotion a body could endure. But I locked it all away in a little make-believe box, and only I had the key.
I took a trip to Chester-le-Street to see if Steve's car was still there, but there was no sign of it. It could have been towed away by the police, or had the College 'caretaker' pushed that under the carpet too? I don't know.
My life was back to normal, and that could only be a good thing for my own wellbeing, but I had to attend the funeral

to bring it all to a close. I don't like goodbyes, and I wasn't going to 'like' this one either.

Kahlenberg was at Steve's funeral, which was organised by the good people of Holy Island Priory. But I kept my distance from him, and everybody else for that matter. I was the mysterious lady in black, stood a few yards behind the rest, with a veil covering my feelings. I'm not sure I hid my identity, but who was bothered about me anyway?
The funeral service was slower than a country bus, taking just as many detours. Everyone wanted to speak, but few had a memory of Steve or a kind word to share. It was contrived, meticulously planned, but very sad. Not for his passing, but for such a loveless life.
Whoever arranged the sermon had religion first and foremost in their mind. Steve's coffin just happened to be there at the time. I didn't know if any relatives were there, and it was strange because I couldn't pick out his mother. Mother's always show the most grief because nobody should see the day when they have to bury their offspring. But there was no grief from anyone. Did nobody - friend or acquaintance - have a happy tale to tell about this man? I ask because nobody gave one.
Outside the congregation moved to the burial plot. The sun shone brilliantly and the beautiful colours of the trees were a perfect backdrop for an event, but probably morally too bright and cheerful for this occasion. Even offensive.
I struggled to hold back the grief, not so much for Steve but for the pure sadness of this heartless scene. I felt I should have been walking behind that mahogany coffin. I didn't really have any right to be there, other than as a friend, but I was the person he trusted most of all in his final days. That must account for something.

Words from the minister, speeches from dignitaries, then we watched the casket lowered into the grave.
"Goodbye my dear friend."

Kahlenberg left with a group of church people, and everyone else drifted away in their twos and threes, leaving me to bring to a close this sad occasion. I noticed another lady standing a few yards away looking in my direction. I gave my acknowledgement, and wondered where I had seen her face before. She wasn't beautiful in the classical way. No flowing golden curls or ivory skin; no piercing eyes of blue. However, in her ordinariness she was stunning. This was the lady in the photos in Steve's father's old house. She hadn't aged at all.
She walked over to me and offered me her hand.
"Hello, I am Jacqueline Campbell. Jaq for short … obviously," she said in pleasant, bubbly tone of voice. "Can I ask you, how do you know Steve?"
"Hello, I'm Linda ... Linda Wilson. I haven't known Steve long, just a few weeks. We are barely friends. I met him here on Lindisfarne."
Her smile turned into a dainty laugh, then she gave an unusual reply: "A lucky escape, then."
I wasn't sure where to go with that comment.
"I think I recognise you from some photographs. Obviously with the name Campbell you are part of his family. Your face is everywhere in Steve's father's house. I have a photo here on my phone."
It was the last photo I had taken so it didn't take much finding. I enlarged it on the screen and passed it to her.
"Dear me, that brings back memories. Corfu, about three years ago. That is one of the better ones. Why is it on your

phone? Why are there pictures of me in his Dad's house? I never met his dad."

I found it all as strange as she did.

"What relation are you to Steve?" I replied, as Jaq handed me back my phone.

She smiled, but that didn't mask the tone of her voice, "I'm his ex-wife. I'm only here for one reason. To make sure the bastard is really dead. I'd open that coffin if I was allowed to, just to double check."

"Oh he is dead, I can promise you that," I said, rather shocked at her reply. "He died in my arms. So you have it from good authority."

There was so much I wanted to ask this woman.

"Would you like to go for a drink somewhere?" I asked. "Perhaps we could have a coffee somewhere on the island or wherever you would like to go?"

She glanced at her watch, sent a quick text to someone, and said: "OK, I have half-an-hour, but if you want the truth I won't be sugar-coating it. You get warts too."

Perhaps the warts would be the most interesting of it all.

We went to the coffee shop where Steve and I first met, and found it just as busy, filled with a lot of people who had just been to the funeral. However, there was a spare table outside in the garden and we sat ourselves down in the sun.

"Before you ask me questions," said Jaq in an uncompromising manner, "you have asked me what I think of him, but what do YOU know about Steve?"

"Well, he had the cottage that my husband and I wanted to buy …" however, she cut me off mid-sentence.

"He didn't own that cottage, you know," she butted in to make her point. "It wasn't his."

"Yes, he did point that out."

I stopped talking, giving her room to add more of whatever she wanted to say, but she went quiet.

"He was always charming to me and I kind of liked him." I added. "A gentleman, respectful and fun to be with. He loves his mother, who he takes to a caravan once a month, and his Dad died about twenty years ago. And that is just about all I know."

Jaq shook her head with a disapproving look of disgust, then lit up a cigarette and sucked the life out of it before replying. I sensed I was going to get the watered-down version when she finally spoke, but she must have thought "sod it, I'm going in with both barrels blazing."

"I get the feeling you and Steve didn't get on," I said, knowing that if someone goes to a funeral simply to confirm someone is dead ... well ... it wasn't a good relationship.

"Where do I start?" she chuckled, blowing stale smoke into the blue sky. "His mother is in the grave right next to his, and the poor lady has been in that plot since 1997. His Dad, well they never did find his body, but I'm sure someone will stumble upon his shallow grave sometime in the future. I was determined to unearth the truth about that and I've covered most of Bamburgh looking for his body over the years. I have probably walked over it at some point. But he is out there somewhere."

"Oh my God," I said in total shock. "How did his mother die?"

"Suicide, if you believe the coroner, but nobody does believe a word of it."

It was all too familiar to me.

"Are you getting the picture, now? It was quite a dysfunctional family." she said with a hint of "you know what I mean" in her facial expression.

"Oh it's been a regular thing since I met Steve," I said. "My husband, his best friend. What an idiot I have been. What am I doing being involved in this? He dresses up murder as a suicide and he gets away with it! Are you suggesting he killed his own mother? Oh my God!"
"I don't know for certain – nobody does. Not many on this island go along with that story. But there is far more to it than that, Linda," she said, paving the way for a spine-chilling explanation: "I was Steve's wife. I don't think he murdered his mother, but I'm sure he murdered his father. However, you need a body to prove it. And for that I'd suggest someone look in the woods in Bamburgh, because he lies in there somewhere."
This was like a bad dream. None of this made any sense.
"Why suicide?" I asked. "Why does it look as though the victims have killed themselves?"
Ask this lady a question and she wasn't shy giving an answer.
"Everything on this island is based on religion, and Steve has been indoctrinated with it since the first day he could form a sentence. It's in his blood. He has known nothing else. Suicide is objectively a sin which violates the commandment 'though shalt not kill.' And they invent their own rules here on Lindisfarne. Here they view suicide as the road to Hell's damnation. So if you are going to murder someone, you may as well send them to Hell while you do it."
I was starting to think I got away from it all at the right time. Not only was he a murderer but there were serious doubts about his mental state. Who had I been dealing with? If this woman was telling the truth, I was probably lucky to get away with my life.

She had more to add: "It's only in recent years that the Roman Catholic Church has allowed the bodies of suicide victims to be buried on sacred land. But, even now, they don't allow it here. But Steve's mother is buried in that graveyard because the Elders didn't believe the coroner's verdict." "Jaq, the photographs in the old house. They are everywhere. On tables, window sills, every wall. Why are they in his father's house? He wouldn't talk about you. He wouldn't even say who the photographs were of."
"As I said earlier, I didn't know his father. If there are photos in that house - Steve put them there!"
"He must have been infatuated with you," I said, looking into her eyes, looking for a reaction, but she refused to look back at me. She was not winning me over with her charm and innocence, and suddenly I wasn't believing everything she was saying. However, I couldn't detect the face of a liar, either, although I searched deep enough. Was she trying too hard to be convincing?
"If you don't mind me asking," I asked, "how long was the relationship and was he ever violent to you?"
"It wasn't a proper marriage," she said. "You cannot love him, because he wouldn't let you. The only violence was when we made love. Did you have sex with him? I don't mind, you can tell me."
"No! Certainly not," I replied, making it plain that our relationship never got beyond friendship.
"I say 'when we made love' but love never came into it. He made the bedroom a war zone. You chose your weapons and 'let battle commence'. It was intimidating to the point it was repugnant. I had never been degraded like that, before or since. He was messed up beyond belief."
"Why did you put up with it?" I asked.

"Three years we lived together, but after the first week I wanted 'out'. But I couldn't summon up the strength to go. I was petrified of him. He would look at me as though he was going to rip me apart. He would go from being a rational, lovely human being, into a raving madman. You knew when to shut up; when to give yourself; when to beg."
Were we talking about the same man?
I recalled Steve's words when we first met - in that very same coffee shop: "Yeah I married once, but she left me. Nothing more, nothing less. She gave a thousand reasons for leaving, but it takes a very strange kind of person to live here. Very strange. Trust me."
Well ... both of them were certainly that!

CHAPTER FIFTEEN

I appreciate a friendly and amiable conversation with anyone, but I couldn't help feeling there was a hidden agenda with Jaq. It was unnerving the way she wanted to dismantle a guy's identity piece by piece ... at his own funeral! I couldn't help but feel that it was not so much a show for my benefit, but for her gain. What was she gaining?
My questions flowed, one after the other, and if I was going to get the juicy bits I may as well get fill a bucket.
"What do you know of his childhood?"
Jaq didn't disappoint: "He had a very disturbed upbringing. Learning difficulties, and he told me he spent time in hospital suffering from meningitis when he was six. He was in a coma for four months and, when he came out of it, he didn't know his parents at all. He went through many years of counselling. That was probably why he became so

detached from them. He told me many times that he didn't believe they were his true family, and that was how he went through life, as a loner and an outsider."

That intrigued me because he was a very intelligent guy. That came with the territory. He was a successful author, after all.

"How do you mean 'loner'?" I asked.

"Steve struggled to retain information. His mind was never focused on one particular thing at any particular time. He would wander, and I could never hold his attention. Most people couldn't."

That was difficult to believe because Steve had a memory like a computer. What she said could possibly be true of his early days, but when I met him he had an astounding retention for facts. He would rhyme off days and dates of historical events because they were embedded in his memory. This woman was trying to push against me like a gale, trying to reverse everything I knew about him. One step forward - two back.

"What problem did he have with his parents?" I asked, and added "He spoke very fondly about his mother. He even bought her a caravan."

"He blamed his parents for his unconventional upbringing. There is no school here and he was taught by the Priests from the Priory. That meant he didn't have any school friends, as such, just the kids who came for holidays with their parents in their holiday homes. He wanted to socialize, but he had nobody to socialize with ... just a set of brain-washed priests who lived their lives by the holy book 'twenty-four-seven'. The caravan wasn't for his mother. Yeah, we visited it many times, but never with his mother. She was not around when he bought it. She was long gone. So I can't understand why he told you he still sees her. That's just plain weird. And the photographs disturb me, too. Normal people don't act like that, do they?"

EVERYTHING was too "weird" for my liking! He never came across as eccentric, in any shape or form, but Jaq was starting to paint a very peculiar picture.

"Did he ever mention stories of treasure?" I had to quiz, if only to see the reaction on her face.

She laughed out loud, then started smiling to herself like a Cheshire cat. "Did he ever mention it? Oh he mentioned it alright, every day for the entire time I knew him. Do you believe it's there?"

"I wouldn't know." I answered.

"He must have said something about it," she said.

"Little bits and pieces, nothing more."

"Do you know where it is?" she asked, growing more intense by the second.

"I don't believe there is a treasure."

"Steve believed the story and he knew where it was," she said.

I didn't reply, and that made her even more uneasy. She was wrong, he had a rough idea where it was but he didn't know the exact location until we got to Edinburgh, and I was starting to think she knew that already.

She wouldn't let the subject drop ... "Did he know the spot?"

"He said he didn't, but if he did he wouldn't tell me. Would he?"

The less I gave away, the more she was convinced that I knew the location ... "He would tell you, I'm sure of that. You know the spot. You're just not saying."

I was starting to feel a little uncomfortable. The tables had turned, she was now grilling me, and I didn't particularly

like it. So I made my excuse for leaving and I was glad when I was back in my car.
Why would Steve fill his father's house with photographs of his ex-wife? She obviously despised the very ground he walked on. She even admitted herself that Steve never loved her, or certainly not in the conventional manner. It was hardly a marriage built on trust and affection - more like tolerance and abuse. And if ever there was an argument for hearing two sides of a story, this was it. But we were too late for that. One of them had led me down the garden path, filling my head with utter nonsense, but I couldn't work out which one it was – and for why. Why would she lie? What was she gaining?
I pulled the car into a lay-by just south of Seahouses and I opened my phone and flicked through the photo album. There were four images of Steve's grave, shot from a variety of angles, but NONE showed a grave next to it. Just as I thought. But what did Jaq say: "His mother is in the grave next to his, and the poor lady has been in that plot for years."
Well, 'The camera never lies,' and there was the concrete evidence. Buried next to him? No she bloody well wasn't!

In my mind, rich people belonged to an exclusive club. I wasn't part of it, so I could only imagine what it must be like. I didn't think I had the intelligence to be a member, because in my mind's eye those people could spot the opportunities to make a better life for themselves, while I plodded on.
But now I had a treasure map with an 'X', just as I had predicted earlier. I had the key to unlock the greatest treasure horde since Howard Carter and Lord Carnarvon

discovered Tutankhamun's tomb in the Valley of the Kings in 1922.
But I couldn't do it alone, that spoke for itself.
Allegedly, only one other person (other than myself) knew about Steve's plans to go searching for Hadrian's treasure. The jolly sailor with the boat, Steve's life-long pal, Tommy Kirby. I hadn't met him but he was the man Steve tried to contact in Blyth when we returned the Gospel by boat. So I knew where he lived, and Steve had already briefed him about our plans many weeks earlier. I assumed he was just waiting for an update on the plans and a starting date. I didn't know what sort of financial cut he was expecting, but due to the circumstances, it was going to be a lot higher because there were only two of us. Would he would still be interested after losing the man with the master-plan?
What better time to ask him than on my journey home from the funeral? His home was on my route so I headed down the A1.
Blyth is a town with a one-way system that must have been designed by the council to discourage tourists, because I spent half an hour driving around in circles. I could see the area I wanted to be in, many times, but no road would take me there. In the end I gave up, parked the car, and walked. Soon his house was in sight and the nearer I got I could hear music coming from inside. At least someone was at home. A teenage girl, dressed in a flamboyant t-shirt and black leggings came to the door.
"Hello, I'm Linda Wilson, I'm here to see Mr Kirby on behalf of a gentleman called Steve Campbell. Is he home?"
The girl looked me up and down, more than once, then said: "Does my dad know you are coming?"
"No, he doesn't. I don't have his phone number. I was hoping I would catch him in."

She continued to stare and that was starting to irritate me. Finally she seemed to accept that I wasn't a threat to 'man nor beast' and summoned her father with a bellowing: "Dad! There's a woman to see you!"
If the music didn't annoy the neighbours, her voice certainly would. He obviously didn't hear her the first time because of the din, but her screams the second time would have woken the dead!
A rugged bearded gentleman appeared at the door, introducing himself, but still little Madam Muck would not be moved.
"Who is she dad?" she asked in a patronising fashion, as though I had no right to be there.
"Go back inside Millie and turn that bloody music down!" I finally had his attention.
"I'm Linda, Steve Campbell's friend. I'm so sorry to trouble you but I don't have your phone number and, as I was passing, I thought I would call in."
He looked a really likeable guy, with such a big beaming friendly face.
"Oh you are Linda, I'm pleased to meet you," he said, then he shook my pitifully thin hand with his giant sized 'sausage fingered' paw. He was being gentle but I could still feel the power in his grip.
"I'd ask you in but the house is in no fit state to invite a lady," he said, pointing towards the living room. I couldn't see inside, but that was probably for the best, as all I could see was dirty clothes scattered up the stairs.
"Listen," he said, "I think I know why you are here. And perhaps today isn't the day to talk."
I was surprised. Who could possibly hear our conversation?
"Oh, OK then," I replied. "Shall I phone you?"

"I'd prefer not to talk on the phone either, if you don't mind, because you never know who could be listening. Could we meet in town some day and go for a coffee?"
"Yes, that would suit me fine," I replied. "You mean Blyth?"
"If Blyth is too far, anywhere will do," he said.
"What about half way, how about Whitley Bay? That's about half way." I suggested.
We agreed to meet the next Tuesday at the Rendezvous Cafe on the northern promenade at 11am. But he dashed my hopes somewhat by saying: "I know about Steve's sad death, Linda, and I don't think I want to be involved in this."
"Yeah I understand," I replied. "I'm not sure what I want to do myself, but I want to do something. I've made my mind up."
He took a deep breath, looked around the streets, then said: "How do you know you are not being followed now? Your car could be tagged."
"What threat am I to them?" I asked.
He put me in my place, "Don't underestimate what they are capable of doing."
"So, to cut out all the bullshit Tommy, you don't want any part of it any more? I understand, just say."
"What I'm saying is that we can't go into this without Steve," he replied. "The man did the brain work and he had the outlet to sell whatever we recovered. We are like two amateur treasure hunters with a boat and a shovel. He knew more about the security and the daily workings of the island than anybody. When to dig, when to stay silent, and most important of all, when not to be seen."
I don't agree," I said, standing my ground. "He was a wanted man. There was never going to be a time when it

was acceptable for him to be seen. They knew what he was after. That was how they sucked him into their trap. They dangled a carrot and he went for it."
But still he didn't look interested. Not even curious. And despite his huge frame and monstrous hands, he just looked plain scared.
"I know where it is, Tommy, and I know how to get it. I really do. If you don't want to be involved I don't blame you one bit. But let me just say one thing, I will go to the Rendezvous Cafe on Tuesday regardless, and if you aren't there I will understand why. Think about it. The choice is yours. But if you aren't interested - don't lead me on."
"You really know where it is?" he smiled. "The College wouldn't give Steve the final piece of the jigsaw. Give me one reason why they would do that? They conned him to get at him."
That left me wondering.

As I mentioned earlier I had three very special friends in Grace, Joe and Emily, and thankfully, all three were back on the scene following various breaks in their routine. Grace had spent four weeks on holiday in Florida with her husband and the kids, visiting her parents who had emigrated to the sun ten years previous. I grew up with Grace and Joe from our school days. Her jet black hair made her mysterious, even to a kid like me. I had pig-tails swishing left and right, and floppy socks around my ankles, meanwhile Grace was true to her name. She had the elegance of a ballet dancer and the poise of a swan. You either have style … or you don't. Every girl wanted to be like her, but none of us ever got within a country mile. Some teachers regarded her as "stuck up", and I remember a couple of them gave her a hard time because of it, but that was far from the case. Some said her shyness, and overpowering parents, made her that way. I wondered many times in our school years what it would be like to live in her head, fearful of letting her parents down.

Single and unattached Joe had been transferred to Frankfurt in Germany on a six month work exchange plan and he was now back at his parent company in Newcastle. Joe had a crush on Grace from around the age of 14, but he never got beyond first base. Personally I'd have cast them together because they were made for each other. He was a lovely kid, with a laugh so infectious the teachers would punish him even when he giggled, because he would have the whole class sniggering into their maths books. When Joe laughed – the world laughed with him. He was 'cool' without even knowing it. He never set out intending to be the unfazed, unruffled rebel without a cause. He could have been a revolutionary fighter like Fidel Castro, because he had that look about him, but he wouldn't have the heart to fire a bullet.

Finally, poor Emily had just returned from London where she had been called to her mother's bedside. Following a sharp deterioration in health, her mother died the day Emily arrived. Is there anything more soul-searching than a family bereavement? Emily is like a fragile piece of porcelain even when she is on top, and her mother's death was catastrophic to her. A girl who is as confusing as she is gentile. When she holds a conversation it is usually to put the world to right. Not in a bad way, that is simply how her mind works. She is simply a little bit mixed up. Emily is prone to shedding a lot of tears for a lot of different reasons. I will explain later.

The four of us were back home and I felt a lot more happiness was about to enter into my life.

Emily was given the 'hostess with the mostest' duties, because she was the one who needed it most, to keep her mind off recent events. But entertaining was what she was best at, anyway, and although Joe's solution to party food - ordering a take-away for everybody - got my vote, Emily thought it was a "cop out." Grace was just happy to go with an evening away from the kids.

The girls made the effort to dress, while Joe sat at the dining table in a faded t-shirt that looked as though it was ready for the bin. His jeans weren't much better, and are odd socks the fashion these days?

"You've done something with your hair," Joe said to Grace, then gave it a rethink "or maybe it's your eyes."

Grace chuckled, "It's the same style I've had for five years, Joe, and I haven't changed my eyes, unless it happened when I was asleep."

Laughter filled the room and the stories brought back memories of my fresher days at university. I loved those people then, just as I love them now. Each had plenty of tales to tell, although Joe (like Craig) could spin a yarn and embellish it to such an extent it probably never even happened at all. I don't think either of them could repeat a tale and tell it the same way twice.

Unfortunately, Emily's was a tale of tragedy. I don't think that girl has ever been at ease with herself all the years we have known her. Two marriages, both disasters, leaving her penniless, embarrassed, and childless. All she ever wanted was children and a loving home, and she got neither.

Then it was my turn to help raise up the now deflated atmosphere, with tales of suicide, murder, religious feuds, a Gospel, buried treasure, more murder … and a partridge in a pear tree. It had it all.

They all sat and listened, with gasps of shock and displeasure, but nobody stopped my flow. Emily's jaw dropped on the first chapter and she sat open-mouthed throughout. Grace seemed somewhat disbelieving, while Joe sat like some wide-eyed kid at a movie matinee. Joe would believe anything, that wasn't a problem, but he was probably more flabbergasted that my story was even more absurd than his!

I ended with "watch this space – I'm not finished yet."

Joe was so animated and excited I think he wanted to applaud. Emily just kept mumbling to herself, "Oh my God!" and Grace didn't feel it necessary to form an opinion just yet. She was working on it.

Emily was first to speak, "Did you say Corrie knows about this?"

"Not really," I replied. "She knows about Craig and my house being visited, but I've played everything else down. She doesn't want to get involved and I'm perfectly happy with that. I don't want her knowing any more than she knows already."

Joe, in his own little world of fairies and Goblins, seemed more impressed with the storyline than actually believing human beings had been killed.

"Man, that is AWESOME!" he shouted, then he really did burst into applause. Meanwhile Grace shook her head as she looked at him, her stare putting him in his place, "For God's sake Joe, this is serious."

Joe's strength was always his ability to shrug off anything negative, particularly anything Grace had to say to dampen his moment. "I'm telling you … that is AWESOME Grace, baby!"

Looking at Joe, I drifted back to my childhood when a school friend of ours drowned in a pool over the Meadow where we played. We were fishing for minnows with children's fishing nets, catching them and putting them in jam jars. Then someone shouted out that our friend Paula had slipped down the muddy bank and was in difficulties. Joe dived in to try and save her as the rest of us looked on in shock. Nobody else made the effort, not that we could do anything, we were only about ten years old. The water was dirty and murky, but Joe tried his hardest to get to her. It was all so quiet, her movements were subtle, and she didn't make any noise at all. One second her head was bobbing above the water, and then it sank to the bottom one last time. I was there when they pulled her lifeless body up to the sand-bank, all water-logged and blue. Only Joe cried. He sobbed because he couldn't save her. The rest of us stood at the bank side like cardboard cut-out figures. I will never ever forget that moment.

I felt relieved that I had shared my story with my friends and I was no longer carrying the burden alone.
"How do you feel about Craig being murdered?" asked Emily, looking as though she wasn't sure if she should raise the question.
"He's gone, Emily, there's nothing I can do about it," I answered, "But it's strange in a way because I think I was more upset when I heard he had hung himself. I couldn't believe that he would leave me that way. We weren't together, but I never thought it was the end of us."
Meanwhile, Joe had "£" signs in his eyes. "How are you going to get the treasure?" he asked.
"As I told you, Steve's mate has a boat, and I was pinning all my hopes on him. But he won't show up on Tuesday, I know that for a fact."
"What if he does?" asked Joe. "Will you trust him?"

"Probably not," I replied. "He's a nervous wreck and he would make me nervous too. But what else is there? Any other suggestions?"

"Yeah, I do have a suggestion," said Joe, always a man full of self-belief and faith in the cards the Lord dealt him. "I will help you!"

"How can you help me?"

"I can sail a boat; I can use a spade; I can help a friend in need. Which one of those applies to you, babe?"

I considered it for a moment and looked at that beautiful beaming smile of his. He wasn't pulling my leg, he really meant it. And what's more, I remembered he used to have part-share in a fishing boat when he lived in Australia for a couple of years. He really can sail a boat.

My knight in shining armour? Perhaps.

CHAPTER SIXTEEN

The date in my diary was: Tuesday 11am the Rendezvous Cafe, and I arrived there 15 minutes early.

I visited the cafe, with my family, many times in my childhood on day-trips to Whitley Bay. The "Geordie Costa Del Sol" my mother used to call that town, "Benidorm without the weather." Everywhere has 'weather,' but unless the sun was peeling her face, my mother didn't think it counted. So that particular day wouldn't have counted either. Dull and dreary.

I was early but I couldn't be bothered to wander around in the damp, killing time, so I went inside and ordered a cappuccino and took my seat.

I have no idea what year the building was constructed but it has a very 1920's feel to it with a bold and proud front that faces the sea, a flat roof, and arched windows. If it is authentic, it has stood the test of time rather well, and it had me musing over moonshine and speakeasies. I could imagine girls back in the day wearing the wonderful flapper dresses, dancing the Charleston, and sipping from elegant champagne glasses. I bought a Charleston dress for a fancy dress party when I was a teenager, and I adored it. Shimmering with lace, tassels and bursting with over-the-top glitz. Mine had a high scalloped hemline and low back. Sexy and chic. But my father disapproved saying, "It gives too much away," and I only wore it that once. Oh dad ... you old fool ... I loved it and you broke my heart.

11 o'clock suddenly became 11.20 and Mr Kirby was nowhere to be seen. I remember thinking to myself, "Why the hell does everyone keep me waiting?"
Joe gave him a 50-50 evens chance of turning up, but I knew, when he wasn't there at 11am, that I was wasting my time. The guy wasn't particularly cultured, but I did hope he would have shown a bit respect.
"Hello, are you Mrs Wilson?" asked a young waitress.
"Who's asking?" I asked, scanning the room looking for someone I may recognise.
"There is a gentleman on the phone for you," she said, pointing to the bar, "The phone is over there."
I picked up the receiver and asked, "Hello, who is this?"
"It's Tommy Kirby, Linda."
"I take it you can't make it today, Tommy." I said. "I probably guessed that anyway."
"I can't take the chance Linda. But I've got a proposition for you, as a sort of token gesture for Steve. I bought an old fishing boat that could be a help to you. It has been a regular sight off Holy Island for decades, doing fishing trips, so it nothing that will arouse suspicion. It's not

registered in my name and the guy who owned it passed-away, so it cannot be traced to anyone. It's old but it's still sea-worthy and I take it off the coast most days. You can borrow it. I won't ask any questions. Do with it what you want."

"How can I get in touch with you?" I asked.

"When you want the boat, phone me a day in advance from a call box and I will have it ready for you. My phone number is ..."

"OK Tommy, I will do that. I have things to sort first, but I will be in touch soon."

I had no excuses. I had the map, a phone number, a boat and a skipper. Happy days.

If a fragrance is particularly unusual, I tend to remember it and link it with that person. During our school days, Grace always smelt of peaches. As for Joe, even at the age of 14 he always sprayed himself with his father's aftershave. I don't think he even shaved at that age but he would woo the girls (usually Grace) with the smell of Kouros. His father must have gone through bottles of the stuff, wondering how it was disappearing so quickly. I loved the smell but I hadn't come across it for years, until I walked through Newcastle's Eldon Square shopping centre and I was stopped by a guy on a sales-pitch selling internet broadband and he smelt as though he had been swimming in the stuff. I stopped to talk to him (even though I didn't need broadband) just for the memories that the smell brought with it. Then I spun around to head back in the direction I had just come from and I came face-to-face with a strange man I remembered from Steve's funeral. I thought back to the day and I also remember seeing him in the coffee shop garden when I was talking to Jaq.

I caught this guy on the hop and it showed by the shock on his face as he tried to recalculate where he was going. He was following me. There was no doubt.

We were a yard apart, eye-to-eye, and he didn't know what to do with himself. So I stepped into his private space and put him out of his misery.

"I know you, don't I?" I quizzed with a determined tone of voice. He wasn't going to walk away so easily, although he tried.

He fumbled and mumbled, and tried to squeeze past me, but I grabbed his coat.

"Who the hell are you?" I growled. "You had better tell me or I'm going to shout at the top of my voice that you tried to assault me. So make your mind up, very quickly!"

"I'm just on my way from work," he said, trying to get away.

"I'm not kidding, I will shout. Don't for one second call my bluff! You knew Steve Campbell didn't you?"

This guy was a bald, skeletal little creature, who reminded me of Gollum, the strange character in the film 'Lord of the Rings' who called himself "Smeagol."

"I don't … errr ... think I can recall the name Campbell," he stuttered.

"You were at his funeral last week, try recalling that!"

"You have the wrong man, excuse me please," he pleaded.

"Why are you following me?" I said, raising my voice so others could hear and draw attention to us.

I felt like squeezing his scrawny little neck. But he made his getaway, pushing his way past shoppers as he ran towards Northumberland Street. I could have shouted, and looking back I think I probably should have, but he made enough commotion on his 'escape' to be tracked on CCTV should it ever be needed.

Later that night Joe asked me: "Are you certain it was the man you saw at the funeral? There couldn't be a case of mistaken identity?"
"I'm sure Joe, he was there. Ugly little cretin."
"You know what this means, don't you?" said my trusty friend. "It means they aren't going to let you walk away, Linda. They won't know what you are planning, but they intend to find out. If we are going to do this, we do this alone. Forget Kirby and his boat. The man could be as true as his word, but he is another cog in the machine. We don't need cogs and we certainly don't need a machine."
"But we need a boat from somewhere," I added. "And Kirby made sense when he said his fishing boat wouldn't be noticed."
Joe was not convinced: "I'm not so sure. Let's look at it from a different perspective. What if that boat was a 'set up' and it WOULD be noticed? We may as well paint it pink and hang a sign from the crow's nest saying 'Here We Are!' Do we need a boat at all? If it's a cliff I could abseil down it? I've seen the map, Lindisfarne isn't even an island. We can go whenever we want, we don't need a boat."
But I remembered Steve's words: "You would abseil into the sea, there is no beach on that cove."
"OK, let's go there tomorrow and I will swim to it from the beach," he suggested. "At least we will get the lie of the land and see if I can find the tunnel. It's another step forward. Probably the most significant step forward."
I couldn't disagree. We had a plan.

The next day we were back at the seaside, shingle underfoot, fishing boats glistening in the morning sun, and both of us hyped up, but cautious at the same time.

It was very strange going back so soon after Steve's funeral, and I actually wanted to visit his grave to see if anyone had left flowers. But that made no sense at all. I didn't even mention it to Joe because I knew what his reaction would be. I was terrified of being noticed. Going to the church yard would be putting everything on the line. I wouldn't even walk the streets of this beautiful island without a scarf hiding my face. I seemed to be cowering from anyone who walked in my direction, before Joe pointed out that I was drawing attention to myself and he told me to "get a grip girl!"
We got to the beach and Joe, unlike myself, was already prepared, mentally and physically. He probably wanted to get this over and done with and get back on the motorway before I gave the game away.
He knew the exact spot to locate (as shown on the map), and within seconds he was off with his trousers and shirt and into the North Sea wearing only his swimming shorts. The ocean looked like a divine painting, but the sun was not doing its day job. The sea was like the Arctic Ocean. Joe splashed around for a few minutes, pretending to be a proper holiday maker, happy to get hypothermia all in the good cause of a day by the sea. But soon he swam towards the cliffs on the East coast.
Joe researched the waters on the internet and told me on the journey up that the hazard in those waters is a layer of Whinsill rock that (apparently) is like swimming over razor blades. 'No Swimming' flags and signs were displayed right up that east coast, because there wasn't a coast guard on duty. For that reason alone, Joe was drawing attention to himself. They are some of the most dangerous waters around the British Isles, not only because of the sharp rocks, but from the tidal currents that hit the swimmer from

all directions. The fast changing currents race around the rocky bottom disturbing the coal slurry making visibility almost zero in some places. Joe was a very strong swimmer, so I was sure he was strong enough to get to the cove, but coming back he would be fighting the currents that pull from three different directions, none the way he wanted to go.

He slipped out of sight, and all I could do was wait.

After half an hour I could barely formulate a thought. The breeze grew stronger and the sun disappeared. I was absolutely frozen to the marrow, so God only knows how Joe was feeling. He was was an adrenaline junkie, always had been, so it was obvious he was going to take up this challenge. To everyone else there was a pit full of treasure to be found, but to Joe it was a pit full of adventure! "To hell with the treasure … let's have some fun."

I looked out at the ocean and I watched an incoming fishing boat bounce across the waves, being pulled about like a plastic toy. Poor Joe could be drifting halfway to the Farne Islands.

None of this was a price worth paying.

An hour passed and I was growing more impatient, even more so as I was being eaten alive by a swarm of sand flies. Then I felt a tug on my arm. I turned around and there was Joe, having crept up from behind, looking frozen, with blood running down his thigh and left arm.

"Oh my God, are you alright?" I asked, trying to clean up the blood with a towel. How did you get out of the sea, I was watching for you?"

"I couldn't fight the tide. I had to swim towards the castle, then walk back round. But the good news is, I've found the entrance. It's there alright."

"Have you seen the treasure?" I asked in a fit of excitement.

"Nope, it's all bricked up and caked with clay, as I expected. But it's man-made and it leads somewhere. I don't know where, obviously, but someone put in a hell of a lot of effort to hide something. The problem is it's a death trap out there. Steve planned to get to the cliffs by boat but you wouldn't get any sailing vessel within 200yds of that cove, and he must have known that. No boat has ever been there at low tide. It's impossible. No matter what century that hole was bricked up, they wouldn't risk their lives by going by boat. I will tell you now, Tommy Kirby has worked these waters all of his life, and he knows that too. If Steve is a con ... that guy is too!"

"Joe, the blood is pouring down your leg," I grew more and more concerned. "That needs stitches."

"No, I will be fine," he said, covering the wound with a handkerchief. "Let's get out of here. I'm drawing attention to myself."

CHAPTER SEVENTEEN

I had to drive us home because Joe was in no fit state to take the wheel because his badly injured leg was seeping blood at an alarming rate. But he could not give one jot!

"You are going to need stitches, Joe. You have lost a lot of blood."

"It's just a scratch."

"Scratch? It's a laceration!" I replied harshly. "Shall I take you to the hospital?"

"No way. The dried blood makes it look worse than it actually is."

His mind was on the entrance to the treasure, and I was starting to wonder if I'd unleashed the devil in him because I was not liking what I was seeing.
"I never thought it was going to be easy, babe" he said, "but it doesn't seem as challenging as I imagined."
"Joe we haven't even started this bloody caper yet and you're going to be hospitalized!"
He laughed to the point he seemed giddy on drugs: "It's not as though we have to clear the whole wall, just make a hole big enough to crawl through. The major concern is the weather because the forecast isn't good. The season is changing and soon the sea will be even more unpredictable than it is now. I still say we should abseil off the top of the cliff. A rope ladder would do."
"We?" I said sounding a bit resentful.
"I can't do it by myself Linda. Honestly, babe. And I can't swim there carrying tools. It's going to take two of us, dropping in from above. The cove itself is tidal, but it's sheltered, and there is a rock we can abseil down to. We will both have to swim, but not far."
"I can't swim that well, you know that Joe. And I'm not risking my life on any 'cock and bull' story that is only hearsay. If you look where the pit is, the original dig, we are miles away from it. What makes you think we are right and those were wrong?"
He explained: "It's not miles away, at all. Fifty or sixty yards maximum. We may not be right, but they were wrong! They got nothing Linda. A gold chain, and that was their lot."
I couldn't argue.
"OK," said Joe, "What we need is a camouflage dinghy. No bright colours, something the army would use that inflates itself. Once inflated we can leave it in the cove and use it

when we need it. Then you won't have to swim. You can do that Linda."
I had to show willing, so I agreed, because I wasn't in any position to back out. It was either 'do it' or call the whole thing off, because involving someone else was another mouth to keep quiet, and perhaps too many people knew about it already.
Joe was starting to think we were being stitched up by Kirby, and he wouldn't let it drop.
"I cannot understand the logic that Steve and Kirby were working to. That guy is a sailor, and he knows the perils of approaching the East cliff by boat. Things don't add up. Perhaps your visit to Kirby's house set alarm bells ringing. Your proposed meeting in Whitley Bay give someone the opportunity to tag your car while you were in the restaurant. Then, perhaps the same guy followed you around Newcastle. That's when you spotted him."
I admit, paranoia was setting in. I was neurotic about every person I passed in the street. I turned corners then stalled for a few seconds to see if anyone was following behind. I dreaded the evenings because I imagined spooky noises and I jumped out of my skin at the sight of my own shadow. It was a very difficult time for me.

The following day after work I called to see Corrie, which was an eye-opening experience. If I was classified 'unstable' in medical terms, Corrie was on the brink of 'disintegration'. I knew she was suffering financial problems but not to the extent they had become.
"Nothing has changed since I last saw you Linda, nothing in material terms, anyway. We're still up to our eyeballs in debt. The dog is digging holes in a backyard that I guess now belongs to the bank, and I feel like digging a hole for

myself. Our financial advisor says he can't see us staying in this house much longer."

It is sad to admit to it, but there are times when it helps to meet someone in a less stable condition than yourself, if only to bring about a reality check in your own life. I'm not suggesting Corrie's sad predicament helped ease my own. But then again, being perfectly honest, it probably did! Just imagine what a quick injection of cash would do for her. I was looking to tick a few boxes in the 'I should not feel guilty' section of this treasure hunting adventure. There was one. I could help her.

Emily phoned to say she was on her way over to my house with "a rope-ladder and a pick-axe", which was a sentence I never thought I would ever hear her say. Emily - rope ladder – pick-axe?

Joe had dropped those items off at her place while on his travels to get everything sorted for our trip back to Holy Island the next day. He had briefed her on all the details and she sounded pretty excited to be involved. And I was delighted to see her.

Emily has two moods. This day her dial was set to 'good.' That meant nothing could possibly go wrong (in her world). She had come up for air, and the world looked pretty darn good. That was wonderful, because the alternative was usually so bad I wanted to donate my ears to charity.

"Why does Joe want this stuff here?" I asked. "We're taking his car tomorrow so why couldn't he keep it all together?"

"No idea Linda. Something about a trailer and a dinghy. You probably know more about it than me."

"Well we're certainly going to arrive inconspicuous then, aren't we?" I laughed. "Like Hannibal with all his friggin elephants!"
"Are you excited?" she said, giving me a smile that was so genuinely sweet.
"Have you ever climbed down a rope ladder on a cliff face before?" I laughed.
"It will be fun, Joe will take care of you." she replied. "I wish I was doing it. I could do with an adrenalin rush. Although I've got a date for Friday which is a bit exciting."
"Wooo!" I replied. "Who is the lucky man? That comes out of the blue."
"I met him in Sunderland yesterday. He was lost, asked directions, then charmed me off my feet. We went for a coffee in the Bridges Shopping Centre and he asked me out."
Little Emily on the road to romance.

Joe phoned to say he had been thinking about Tommy Kirby and our dilemma over his boat: "Phone him and put him off the scent. Cancel everything. Tell him you have changed your mind and you won't be needing his boat. Say you have decided to forget about the whole project, and hopefully that will be the end of it."
It was a difficult call to make. I used a public phone box, as he had suggested, but I wasn't sure I was as persuasive as I wanted to be.
"So you don't need the boat?" he asked in a very slow response.
"No I won't be needing it Tommy. Thank you for your kind offer but I'm finished with all this hair-brained stuff."
He didn't reply at all. I said "goodbye" and he didn't reply to that either.

Perhaps he was grief-stricken to be told he was stuck with his old rust bucket of a boat. Or maybe ... just maybe ... he didn't believe a word I said.

Back on the trail of Hadrian's lost treasure and I suggested we call in at Bamburgh to run the rule over Steve's old house. Steve made me aware that no-one (other than myself) knew that he owned it, so it could prove useful as a home-from-home when we were waiting for tide changes. It was more convenient to travel 15 miles to Bamburgh than 70 miles back to Seaham. I didn't have a key to the door but it wouldn't take a master safe-cracker to get in. Driving through the woods towards the house Joe noticed fresh tyre tracks from cars and wagons on the muddy road which made us cautious as we turned into the makeshift drive. A wagon was outside the house, plus two cars, and workmen were transforming the property from top to bottom. I wanted to turn around and drive away but Joe was intent on investigating.

"Come with me, let's see if we can bluff our way through this," he said as he stepped out of the car. I followed.

We approached one of the workers who was plastering the hall way at the entrance.

"You're doing a good job son. How's the house coming on?" Joe asked.

The young gentleman stopped what he was doing and looked around the room.

"I think you need the foreman," he answered in a broad Irish accent. "He's kicking around somewhere. I think he is working on the bathroom."

"Brian!" he shouted. "Some folks come to see you."

Brian appeared at the door, covered from head to foot in plaster. Did he actually put any plaster on the walls, or just roll around in it?

"Hello Brian, I was just wondering how the job was going?" said Joe, but I was starting to wonder if we were getting anything constructive out of this.

"Well it's going according to plan, although the plumbing is the problem," said the foreman pointing here, there and everywhere. "I'd rip the whole lot out upstairs, and in the kitchen, and put in new pipes. I take it you are Mr Campbell's business parter?"

"Yes, that's me," said Joe in such a convincing manner he almost had me convinced. "Just checking everything is in hand. Were you paid up front?"

"You're asking the wrong person. I'm just the foreman. The gaffa sorts that out. It's usually half before the job starts and the other half at the end. I know Mr Campbell put the money up at the beginning, and he pops in every now and again to check the work."

"Mr Campbell?" I asked, probably speaking out of turn, and the foreman was quick to realize it.

"Yes," he said cautiously, "is there a problem with that? It is his house!"

"OK, give my regards to Mr Campbell when you next see him," said Joe, and we headed towards the door trying to avoid the debris scattered everywhere.

"I will do," said Brian, "In fact you just missed him. He was here an hour ago."

That stopped us in our tracks.

"An hour ago?" quizzed Joe. "Are you sure?"

"Yeah. He came with the boss. They had a look around."

We returned to the car and the inquest began.

"I don't think you were the only one to know about this house," said Joe as he reversed the car out of the drive. "Is Campbell's father still alive? Does he have brothers?"
I had to think for a moment: "I don't know about brothers, but his father went missing twenty years ago. It's his father's house. I don't know of any other family members apart from his ex-wife, and she must have known about the house because she said she had searched these woods looking for the father's body. I'm sure Steve told me he was the only one – no brothers or sisters. But, if his ex-wife is to believed, he lied about everything else. That was always the problem with him, I never knew when he was telling the truth but I could never prove him wrong."
"What about his ex-wife? You didn't trust her, either, did you?"
"I got the same vibe from her as I did from him," I joked, "I'd take both of them with a pinch of salt. They were probably perfectly matched, spending evenings alone talking utter bullshit to each other."
"I'm afraid someone has gatecrashed 'Old Dad's' home," said Joe, "and we can rule out using it as a 'safe house' because that ain't gonna happen. And I have the strangest feeling that Daddy is still alive and kicking."

Joe's strategy on this trip was all about two objectives:-
1) Getting the dinghy in the water and inflating it without being noticed. A task in itself.
2) Putting the tools inside the corridor in the cliff face.
It was more preparation than hard graft, or so he lead me to believe. But he did want me to see the cove and show me what work needed to be done.

When we were apart, communication was done by phone text only, in a sort of primitive code that we worked out between ourselves.

The weather was turning sower and it was going to be a long day for us both.

Getting the tools and the dinghy to the cliff was not as bad as we feared. We drove to the Castle, which was as far as we could go by car, then unloaded a box (with the dinghy inside) onto a heavy duty two-wheel sack trolley. Joe, dressed in council weather-proof work gear, ferried it to a spot close to the beach heading in the direction towards Emmanuel Head. I stood watch over the car. He didn't rush nor panic and he genuinely looked like a man doing a day's work at a leisurely pace, which was probably a give-a-way because the council workers rarely get past 'start,' and 'leisurely' is normally a gear too far. I couldn't detect anyone giving him a second glance, and I was becoming an expert 'spotter' in those situations. There had been council workers refurbishing the Castle in those recent weeks, which was still on-going, so he was nothing out of the ordinary. However, I was. And I couldn't move the car until he came back for the box carrying the tools, and a bag with the rope-ladder and pins.

Within ten minutes, a genuine council van arrived, and one of the workers asked me to drive away because I was blocking the fence gate. I had to go, and that was not in the script. I pulled the car over at St Cuthbert's Square and sent a text to Joe, which we agreed NOT to do.

"Moved on – text me when you are ready." I didn't expect him to reply, but he did, with a simple "OK."

I waited another 30 minutes at least, watching tourists going about their business, doing what tourists do.

Finally the text arrived and I was back on the dirt track leading to the Castle. Joe was waiting, hands on the wooden gate, checking out the state of play with the workers. I had to park by the gate, there was nothing else for it, but immediately one of the labourers came over.
"I told you before," he bellowed, "we need this pathway clear!"
Joe interrupted him: "It's OK, fella. It's all in hand. Just a minute to unload this weather equipment we are setting up at Broad Stones over there on the crag. Shipping forecast for the Met office. You know the stuff ... Viking, Cromarty, Doggar, Fisher, that sort of shit."
The worker obviously didn't have the authority to say much else. He nodded, waved his hand, then got back to his job. I gave a long sigh of relief and opened the boot of the car. Joe took out a box and bag and placed them on the trolley, as two of the guys watched on. This was hardly undercover. We may as well have advertised what we were doing. I just wished I could carry it off like Joe, who remained as cool as a Rasta sucking on a spliff.

CHAPTER EIGHTEEN

We were still proceeding as to plan, although along the way we had to convince the Holy Island Parish Council we were legitimate weather equipment installers. How successful we were with that project would presumably depend on whether blue lights were flashing in the next half-hour or so.
It was only 10.15am, in dull and raining conditions, but we were doing OK. I took the car back to St Cuthbert's Square then hurried to meet up with Joe to watch him hammer two large spikes into the weedy ground to hold the rope ladder.

The cliff edge was off the beaten track, probably twenty yards or so from the path, and we were concealed by long grass.

"You seem as though you know what you're doing, Joe, which is reassuring," I said in jest.

"I learnt that you never take anything for granted after that fall I had in the 'Death Zone' when I climbed Everest," he replied. "I didn't secure the rope right."

"Oh my God ... you are joking!"

"Yep, it was a joke," he laughed. "I've never secured a rope-ladder on a cliff face before. How difficult can it be?"

On the one hand I was pleased he hadn't fallen, but not so pleased that this was his first attempt.

We waited for a couple of tourists to pass, then the coast was clear. We could see them but I don't think they saw us. The weather was getting more gloomy by the minute and there were very few people about. Then, like a soldier going over the top, Joe descended out of sight. He looked so confident, as though he was just stepping off the top of a bunk-bed, but I cringed at the thought that I would be doing the same soon. I was nowhere near as fit as Joe. That guy was in superb physical shape, with the mindset to overcome any fear. I was a fat(ish), out of condition nervous wreck. He clamoured back up and said, "There's nothing wrong with that ladder, I'd stake my life on it."

Looking at it objectively, I was the one staking my life on it ... because I was the one going down it!

We looked for fishing boats off the coast because we would be noticeable from the sea, but nothing was happening. We were in the clear.

Joe walked further up the coast to inflate his army-surplus dinghy, filled it with tools, then set off to the cove. That was the most hazardous part of the whole operation. We knew it was out of the question to expect a clear run and nobody see him floating out of sight at Emmanuel Head. But it was essential that those who did see him were tourists and didn't question what he was up to. Thankfully, the Council workers were well out of view, as were most people, but six or seven ageing walkers (further up the headland) must have clocked him sailing beyond the cliff face. We had to assume they weren't curious.

I returned to the ladder and watched from the cliff top as Joe sailed majestically (of sorts) into the cove. This was a monumental step for us, meaning we could dig without fear of intrusion. This made us the latest in a long line of starry-eyed treasure seekers to continue the work of young Robert Bowman who started it all back in 1793. He came across a shaft, founded the dream, and created the fantasy.

It was at this point I realized why the ladder was there. I was expected to climb down it.

"I'm frightened Joe, I'm frightened for you down there, and I'm petrified for me up here!"

"Just take your time," he replied. "Don't worry girl."

This was the time - now or never. I hung onto the top of the ladder and lowered myself over the cliff top but I couldn't find my footing. I was hanging onto the rope but where were the wooden rungs? The wind was blowing the rope sideways and all that was stopping me from falling was the strength in my arms, and I couldn't keep that up for much longer. I was shaking, my fingers were white, and the last thing I needed was a panic attack, but I felt one coming on. Then I thought about the rock down below that I was supposed to step onto when I reached my descent. It wasn't as though I would fall straight into the sea, which was bad enough, I would hit the rock. That escalated the anxiety and I was now reaching a point of hysteria.

Suddenly, the wind dropped and, down below me, Joe grabbed hold of the rope and swung it outwards so it was at my feet. Finally I could put my weight onto the wooden steps and the relief rushed through my body. I clung on and caught my breath.

"There you go," said Joe. "No problem, was it?"

If I was in a more secure position I'd have told him what I thought, but now was not a good time for an argument. I took deep breaths and thought about what to do next. Upwards and back to the car did cross my mind, but I don't think I had the strength to pull myself over the cliff ledge. Downwards was actually easier, and at that time all I wanted was my feet on firm ground – I would worry about getting my tired body up the ladder later.

"That was good," said Joe, and I wondered for a second if he was winding me up.

"GOOD! I nearly died! What the hell do you mean 'good'?"

"Well I thought you did very well."

"I was hanging on for dear life!" I replied.

"OK, we are going to have to rethink a couple of things," he said. "Tweek a few knobs."

Then he burst out laughing. And you know what ... I did too. I couldn't help it.

"Tweek a few knobs?" I laughed.

I don't know what it is about that guy. He was positive in every thing he did and nothing put him off his stride. He was an inspiration to me, and always had been.

"I need some motivation, Joe. Why are we going to make a success of this, Joe, when nobody else has?"

Joe's reply: "Wisdom, my friend. The fountain of knowledge. We happen to know more than the others did. Give us a point of support and we will lift the world!"

I hadn't the foggiest idea what he was rambling on about, I just nodded and pretended I did.

I believed in him, and even more important, this was the most exhilarating time of my life and he had me convinced we were going to succeed.

All I wanted was to feel the emotion that ran through Howard Carter when he found Tutankhamun's tomb. I had been brought up on that story. Never mind Treasure Island, that was for wimps, Carter made the ultimate treasure discovery and it was for real. When asked: "Can you see anything?" he replied, "Yes, wonderful things!"

I wanted to look through a hole into that chamber on Holy Island and say those very words.

The little dinghy ride to the entrance of the tunnel was no more than a few yards and suddenly this experience became an adventure. The nerves flew away, and as fear left my body I felt daring ... even courageous. Little Miss Lionheart.

Down there we were out of the rain in such a tranquil environment and I knew nothing could harm us in the shelter of the cove. I felt like a 17th century pirate come to collect my hidden bounty. Just like the Count of Monte Cristo in Alexandre Dumas' classic novel, when he leaves the Château d'If prison to go in search of hidden riches left to him by the old priest. That was ME ... and Joe of course. Let's not forget the captain of this gallant little dinghy.

We slipped out onto a sort of platform rock edge in this underground chamber that had been hidden away for centuries. We must have been the first people to set foot in that time-warp since the monks of a long lost past.

I could see the work that Joe had done previously, and there was no question about it, this was a man-made wall of rock.

He handed me a large flat-nosed screwdriver and told me to chisel away at the cement-like mortar that held the boulders in place.

"It doesn't seem as difficult as I feared," he explained. "It's designed to keep the wall watertight rather than act as cement. It comes away quite willingly."

We picked our target and clawed at it with great vigour, like two beavers gnawing at the bark of a tree. It was hard work, but it was fun.

"Why did you pick the boulders at the top of the wall?" I asked. "It would have been easier starting at the middle, make a hole then we could climb through."

"See these lines on the wall here," Joe said, rubbing his hand across the muddy contour. "That's how high the tide gets. If we take away the rocks below that, the tide will flood the cavity and we could lose the treasure when the tide recedes … if there is treasure."

"Good thinking Einstein," I laughed. "We don't want to be losing treasure."

"No we don't, babe," he agreed.

The clay came away easily but moving the rocks was a different story, and I started to doubt if I was the right person for the job. No way could I budge rocks that big, and I wondered if I was starting to become a hinderance. Joe would never criticise, but I know my own lack of ability. He didn't need to tell me.

It took us just less than an hour to pull away the first boulder, and then it became apparent there was at least a second lair of rock behind that. This was not going to be easy. That shattered my illusion of just walking into the cove and walking out a millionaire. OK, I didn't think it would be that straight forward, but I didn't think I would have to move Kilimanjaro, either.

The causeway would close at 3.05pm so we did what we could in the time we had, but it wasn't that much. Four rocks moved, and that hardly made an impression. But Joe still kept the momentum going, telling me I was doing "remarkably well" when obviously I wasn't. But the planning was coming together. The dinghy and tools were in place, easy to hide, and the rope-ladder was something we could conceal in the bushes on the top of the cliff. It was a very productive day. Not only had I come close to death, but I became educated in the art of climbing ladders. Well, sophisticated enough to learn that it is far easier when you put your feet in the right places. But that's what experience does for you.

Heading back to the car, Joe explained that to stop salt water decaying a cliff face it is customary to place boulders in the sea to deflect crushing waves.

"It's a sea defence called a 'breakwater,'" he told me. "It's normally built off shore to break up the waves, but in small coastal ridges like the one we are working on, they build them against the cliff. What I'm trying to say is that our wall could be nothing more than a breakwater. There is no guarantee there is anything other than a cliff wall beyond the rocks. I'm not trying to shatter your dreams, just being logical. Everything is going to schedule as regards the exploration, but all we have is the word of a Danish gentleman and a few drawn lines on a map. It is as uncomplicated as that. We probably have less to work with than the kid who found the shaft back in the 18th century."

"So you have doubts now?" I asked.

"No, I have the same belief as that kid. It's there, I know it is. Whether we are approaching it from the right direction is open to debate, but it sure isn't in the place they have

195

been digging for the last two hundred and odd years. I think we are as close as anyone has ever been to recovering it."
He asked me if I was OK to continue, but I knew something was troubling him.
"What's up?" I asked.
"I can't explain it. I had a weird feeling in there. It's as though I feel a presence when I go into that cove. Something very strange."
"I felt it too, Joe," I replied, and I didn't feel comfortable talking about it because it scared me.
"What did you feel?" he asked.
"As though we were being watched."
"Did you see anything?" he quizzed, and turned to see my reaction.
"No, I didn't see anything, but it was there. I tried to be brave because you were with me, and I thought it was probably fear for fear's sake. But the unease of darkness always spooks me. Then something whispered in my ear. I couldn't make out any of the words because the tone was very low … more a grumble than an actual sentence."
Then I asked Joe what he had seen or heard.
"Oh I remember every word as clear as day," he said. "The torch dimmed for a few seconds as though the power was drained from the batteries. There was a faltering light before someone spoke in a low monotone voice. The words were: 'This is a place for the dead. A place of rest. Go!'"
"Bloody Hell!" I shouted. The whole episode was starting to un-nerve me.
"I wouldn't say I was frightened," he laughed. "But what the hell ... being frightened keeps you on your toes. That can be a good thing, right?"
"Rubbish!" I replied. "Being frightened is NOT a good thing, Joe. Don't try and con me into thinking it is."

He chuckled: "I wasn't particularly frightened because I couldn't see him. Then for some defiant reason I wanted to reply to him.'"

"So what did you say?" I said, hanging onto his reply.

"Nothing at all. I bottled it. Whatever it was, didn't seem as though it wanted to get into conversation. Or perhaps it couldn't. It seemed a statement, no reply would be acceptable."

That confused me. "How do you mean?"

"It was like the re-run of a video tape," he answered. "More a declaration than an exchange of words. The matter wasn't up for discussion."

I knew what was going on in Joe's mind. The last thing he wanted to do was unnerve me, and he knew I was on the borderline. But he was going to plough on regardless of threats, whether I was there with him or not. He suggested he spend the next day by himself digging out the rock, giving me a rest. But it was as though he didn't want me there for my own safety.

"I've checked the crossing times," he said, "and from 9.05 tonight, until 3.55 tomorrow afternoon, I can work. I'm going to stay here tonight, book in at the hotel, and get a start before daybreak. You take the car, go home and have some rest. Could you pick me up around 3.30 tomorrow afternoon?"

I felt I was copping out of the work but it made a lot of sense. The adrenaline rush I suffered on the ladder had sapped my energy, and the strange sensation in the cove had me very unsettled. A day's grace would probably help us both.

"Yeah Joe, that's no bother. I think I will call at Seahouses for lunch tomorrow and pick you up later."

CHAPTER NINETEEN

I returned to Seaham and I thought long and hard about my future. Some folks just aren't built to withstand stress, and that includes me. I decided there and then I was going to put the house up for sale. No matter what happened about treasure, my life or my business ... my future was not in that place. I phoned the estate agents and put the wheels in motion.

I was starting to think there was more than just treasure lurking behind that cliff wall. Whatever it was, it had the ability to be heard but not be seen. Steve said Cuthbert's tomb was buried somewhere very close to the treasure on the island and I was starting to believe we were about to stumble upon it.

I wanted to know more about the guy. I knew Craig had a whole library of books on Cuthbert that I boxed up after his death. They were packed away under the stairs, ready to be taken to a charity shop.

I pulled open the first box and one book included a chapter entitled 'The Mysterious Story of St Cuthbert's Mist.' Apparently, during the dark days of World War II the German Luftwaffe decided to bomb English cities with buildings of great historical importance to deflate the morale of the British people. Durham Cathedral was on the list, and in April 1942 the Germans sent over Dornier bombers for a raid. However, witnesses claim a dark cloud blotted out, what was, a "beautiful brilliant silver moonlit night" and the bombers couldn't find their target. Some religious folk considered it to be the action of St Cuthbert protecting "his Cathedral, his city, his people."

It's a good story, granted, but to credit St Cuthbert with saving the city is probably pushing even his magical powers just a little too far. The saint was mentioned again in the book, this time at the Battle of Neville's Cross in 1346. The Scots had their sights on Durham city and made their way over from Cumbria, crossing the Tyne and regrouped on the outskirts of Durham at Bearpark. The English army set up camp three miles away at Ferryhill. On the night preceding the battle, St Cuthbert appeared in a vision to both armies, telling the Scots they would lose the campaign even though they outnumbered the English by more than three-to-one. Allegedly, he told the English troops they would win, but only if they went into battle carrying his coat of arms. They did just that and, sure enough, won the war.

The following day I arrived at Seahouses at lunchtime. Soon after I arrived I had one of the strangest physical sensations I had ever experienced. I decided to call into The Schooner Inn for some food, and sat comfortably looking out of the window at the day shoppers. Then out of the blue I felt physically shaken and my balance went wayward. I wasn't particularly ill at that stage, but as I sat by the window drinking coffee, I tried to get my eyes to focus, feeling grateful that this bout of sickness didn't happen when I was driving. Then ten minutes later, a weird feeling came over me as though I could not feel the inside of my body - just my skin. I stayed still, too frightened to get to my feet, and then I pictured Joe standing in front of me asking me if I was alright. I wanted to answer, but I felt the eyes of everyone on me and I feared I was going to collapse. I turned towards the door and Steve was standing there, arms folded, his face stern and focused, his eyes piercing me. Then he turned and walked away. He frightened me.

I had a ridiculous feeling that my skin was peeling off me, showing muscle tissue and veins. It was dreadful. This all lasted for little more than a few minutes, as though I was high on drugs. An old gentleman approached me to ask if I was OK. I don't know what I replied, but he walked back to his wife and both of them watched me like parents looking over a child.

My body was dragging me into a swirling shadowy world of dreams. I felt this blackness come over me. Like a blanket, but not a blanket of warmth but a blanket of coldness making me shiver. My thoughts became nonsense, and I realised I had to pull myself together … quickly. The old gentleman returned and took hold of my hand, talking to me constantly in a soothing manner. Then Steve appeared once more, taking hold of my face with both hands, looking into my eyes. Then nothing!

I don't know how long I was unconscious but it can't have been long. The old man was still holding my hand but there was no sign of Steve or Joe, not that either of them had been there in the first place. I felt drugged up to the eyeballs. Either that or I needed a trauma therapist because I was having a breakdown.

I looked around and people seemed to be looking at me as though they thought I was drunk. I felt a deep distrust of everyone. What about the barman? Had he phoned for the police? Oh my God, they were going to take me to a police station. I had to get out. I got to my feet, picked up my handbag, and thanked the old man for his concern, then walked to the door concentrating fully on putting one leg in front of the other. I opened the door without falling flat on my face and it was so refreshing to feel the salty drizzly

wind on my face. I was still confused but I'd rather face the indignity of a tumble in a quiet side street rather than in a public bar.
I strolled along to the harbour in a slapstick sort of manner, taking whatever direction my feet were pointing, but trying to go seaward.
Time ticked away, I pulled myself together and the strange sensation finally disappeared. Everything, from start to finish, lasted no more than 30 minutes. The dizziness disappeared as quickly as it started, and I felt I was sane and rational to drive my car. I motored up the A1 to rescue my dear friend from his hidden cave.

We had a new code for texting, which probably could be deciphered within seconds by anyone with an IQ in double figures. The plan was to do the opposite of whatever the text said. For example "yes" would mean "no", "stop" would mean "go." However, I couldn't find my phone in my bag. I knew it wasn't on the table when I left the pub because I always look behind me to check I don't leave anything. I was semi-conscious when I left, but I distinctly remember doing that.
I remember Joe saying the crossing time was 3.55pm and he would meet me at the car park, but we had to text and confirm it. Well, that wasn't going to happen.
I got to the Castle at 3.15pm hoping to catch him walking towards the village, but he had already gone to the car park. It was like a Laurel and Hardy script. Finally I saw him walking down Church Lane looking like a coal-miner, carrying a hold-all and a bunch of flowers. What was the plan again? "Whatever you do, don't act conspicuous."
I pulled over by the pavement and manoeuvred down the car window: "All dressed up with nowhere to go, I see. I'm

pleased this is your car, Joe, because I wouldn't let you in mine. You look like the chimney sweep in Mary Poppins."
Joe came to the car with a beaming smile saying, "These flowers are for you, beautiful lady. A present from Bert the chimney sweep, 'Chim chim cher-ee'."
That man could charm the birds down from the trees.
"I seem to have lost my phone Joe. Sorry about that. Well, what's happened? How did it go today?" I asked.
"We are almost there, Linda. We are inches away. The boulders are three deep from what I can see, a wall about 12ft x 10ft, but all we need is a hole that we can squeeze through. I have shifted six large boulders and, if there is a chamber, another three or four should get us through."
We set off home in the car and Joe toyed with the idea of returning to the cave.
"I'm tempted to go back. I really am. We are so close. The causeway reopens at around 9.30 tonight. I could be through the wall by the morning."
"Come on Joe, you told me to stay focused. To take no chances. You would be using a flash light in the dark, and we both said we would never take that risk. It would be spotted by fishermen from as far away as the Scottish borders to the Farne Islands!"
He agreed. Why spoil it all?
"Did you feel a presence?" I asked."Did you hear anything?"
"Yes, in the chamber," he replied. "Strange voices again."
"Saying what?" I asked.
"Same tone, same words. Then 'don't walk in dead men's shoes'."
"That's MY saying!" I replied. "That's what I said to myself when I first returned to the island. Oh my God, Joe. Were you frightened?"

Joe looked at me and smiled that big beaming smile: "Frightened? Me? No way! Do you want the truth? I was friggin petrified!"
I told him about the stories I had gathered about Cuthbert from Craig's old books, and Joe was actually starting to become a fan of the great man.
"Is he the man whispering?" he asked, "I don't know. All I DO know is that we are on the brink of something very big and very special. But someone, or something, doesn't want us in that cave. Is it Cuthbert's ghost? I've never been a believer of ghosts or spirits. But the voices are coming from someone. Let's see what he throws at us next."
When Joe and I first started out treasure hunting, the thrill of it all was exhilarating. It still was, because we were so close to But now it was starting to become fearful. Fearful because I knew Joe was up for a fight, and that troubled me greatly. Because this scrap wasn't going to have any rules.

We got to Joe's house in Washington and he invited me to go out for a drink that evening and stay over. Not so much a celebration, more a chance to talk about what we had been through to get this far. Joe phoned Grace, but she had made plans, however Emily was up for a party. Joe picked her up and brought her back to his house. We dumped the car and took a taxi to the Havelock in North Biddick. A decent enough place with good food and a pleasurable atmosphere. We were looking forward to a fun evening.
"You said you were going to Seahouses today," quizzed Emily. "How was it?"
"I was just killing time, Emily," I replied. "Not much fun by yourself. I took a dizzy spell in the Schooner. I think I need to make an appointment at the doctors."
"Are you coming down with flu?" asked Emily.

"No, I don't think so. I can't explain it. If I didn't know better I would say someone spiked my drink. I felt as though I had been to an acid party!"

Joe laughed but Emily didn't. She grew very animated: "I felt exactly the same last night! For about twenty minutes I didn't know where I was. I was out with that guy that I told you about, the one who wanted to take me out on a date. What a waste of time that was. He took me to Bar 38 on the Quayside, and it was OK at first, but all he wanted to do was talk about you!"

"Talk about ME?" I asked.

"Who is he?" asked Joe.

"Well, that is a good question," Emily smiled. "He said he was called Mark, but I called him that twice when he was looking elsewhere, and he didn't respond to it. He was weird. He asked about my friends, I mentioned you two and Grace, but he started bombarding me questions about Linda."

"What sort of questions? Does he know me?" I asked.

"I'm not sure if he knows you personally but I got the feeling he knows ABOUT you. He asked where you lived but I got the feeling he knew that anyway. He asked about your family, Craig, where you worked, your weekend routine, were you dating anyone? That sort of stuff."

"What did you tell him?" I asked, growing more disturbed by the second.

"I took ill at that point. I got confused and felt dizzy. He said he would take care of me but I kept pushing him away. More and more questions that I struggled to answer. I went to the toilet and I blacked out. A couple of girls rescued me and got me to my feet. I felt ill. I don't know how long I had been unconscious for, but when I pulled myself around I went back in the room and he had gone!"

Joe said the words that I was just about to say: "You were set up, Emily. He didn't take your handbag, did he?"
"No, I took it with me to the toilet. But he did try and pick it up earlier in the night and I snatched it back off him. At some point I lost my phone. That was why I contacted you on the landline tonight. Unbelievable. That phone cost me a fortune, it's top of the range. Yet another claim on the insurance."
The three of us ended up at Newcastle, dancing well past midnight. But I couldn't get Emily's comments out of my head all evening. Were 'those people', whoever they were, closing in on us?

Next morning Joe and I talked in depth about what lay ahead. Everything was going to schedule as regards the exploration, but there were many other things that concerned him.
"There's something not right about this," he kept repeating. He would point a finger as though he was just about to make a speech, then take a deep breath and think again. A philosophy so simple "don't speak until you know what you are talking about."
He scribbled on a wire-bound notebook asking me names and places; facts and details; analysing every specific component.
"I've made a list of the points I don't understand. Things that don't make sense. Let's go through them and you tell me what you think, one by one. First of all – why were Campbell and the Invisible College both trying to find the Gospel but were so willing to kill each other? Why were they on different sides?"
"Steve had told me The College thought he stage-managed the theft and they believed he wanted to make his fortune

from it," I replied. "That was why he wanted it returned as soon as possible. The longer it was missing the more danger he was in. Particularly when it appeared on the open market."

"Number two," said Joe, working down his list. "If Craig was murdered, who did it, Campbell or The College?"

That was a question I couldn't answer, "I don't even know if he was murdered, that came from Steve, and he insisted he wasn't involved. He even suggested the husband of his ex-mistress could have done it. I don't believe that."

"Number three – did you see Steve hand back the Gospel to the priests in the Priory?"

"No," I answered, "But he left the cottage carrying it and he didn't have it when he returned."

Joe added: "So he could have kept it himself?"

I wouldn't go along with that, "It's possible. He may have hid it, but why would he go to all the trouble of returning it to Holy Island? I believe he took it to the Priory hoping it's safe return would pacify the College. But they still didn't trust him. I'm not saying that is a fact, but that is what I believe."

"Number four - who is following you Linda? The small guy in Newcastle who you got a good look at - who is he? Emily's date - what was that all about? You have your phone stolen, then the same happens to Emily. There is a lot of information on a phone. How close are they to us? Because, in your case, I think you can almost feel them breathing down your neck. What's your thoughts?"

"I don't know, Joe. I can only assume someone is protecting what they have been protecting for four hundred years – Cuthbert's body, the Gospel, the treasure. Am I a threat? Are WE a threat? I don't think they know about you yet. But, in the cold light of day, we are trying to rob them! And we reap what we sow."

"Finally question number five - and the right answer would be pivotal to everything we are working towards. Did you actually see Steve dead?"

"Dead?" I answered, "He died in my arms. I told you."

Joe continued, "You held him but you collapsed. Was that through trauma, or was it the same feeling you had in Seahouses when you thought your drink had been spiked? The same feeling Emily had two nights ago when her drink was spiked? Because you had been drinking champagne just before the murder took place. Was your drink spiked, because there was that opportunity? How sure are you that he died? Did you see a knife? Did you see Steve's dead body in hospital?"

"Oh my God!" Everything was starting to come together now.

"Can I borrow your phone Joe?" I asked.

He typed in his personal code then passed it to me. I phoned Emily.

"Emily, hi, it's Linda. I know it's Joe's phone, but I'm just using it to ask you a couple of questions. You know that date you had with that weird guy a couple of nights ago? Did he have any distinguishing features?"

Emily thought carefully, "Good looking, dark hair, nothing that stands out. Why?"

"Did you notice his hands?"

"Yeah, I looked for a wedding ring but he wasn't wearing one. Come to think of it, he wore a very big old-fashioned ring on his right hand. Something a Goth would wear."

"With a large ruby?" I asked.

"Yeah, it was a ruby. Do you know him?"

"I know him alright, Emily. That's the ghost of a guy I once knew. Can I ask you one final question? Did you tell him I was going to Seahouses the following day? I'm not cross, I'm only asking ... for my own sanity. Did you tell him?"
"I think I did, Linda. I'm so sorry. I really am."
"Don't you worry girl. It confirms that I DID see the bastard in the pub. He did spike my drink! And he did take my phone, as well as yours. Thank you Emily. Take care girl."
I handed back the phone. Joe heard everything of the conversation.
"I started to wonder when we visited his house a couple of days ago," said Joe. "When the foreman said Mr Cambell had been there that morning. Yeah it could have been his dad or his brother, but something was not right. Even his meeting with the Dane in Edinburgh. That sounded like a set up too. His 'death' happened in Edinburgh because he wanted The College to KNOW he was dead!"
"You're right," I replied, "It was all stage-managed. I honestly thought Kahlenberg set him up, but it was the other way round. It was all a hoax."
Joe had every angle covered: "That was meticulously planned down to the finest detail, and he couldn't have carried it off by himself. The ambulance; the hospital; getting a doctor to sign the death certificate; the funeral. It must have taken unbelievable groundwork to carry it off involving a lot of people. All for what? Who is he fooling? He was on Death Row with The College, make no mistake. Now he starts a new life for himself with a new identity far away from the madding crowd."
I thought for a second, "You nailed it. He feared The College would get him sometime and he even expected it. He was a dead-man-walking, just waiting for the moment

someone pulled away his life-support machine. But, actually BEING dead ends the chase."
I thought Steve was the perfect rebel. Too unlikely to be taken seriously until it was too late. The College must have been astounded when he took out two of their top men when they fought over the Gospel in Chester-le-Street. I think they misjudged him then, but what about now? How involved is Kahlenberg? Is he friend or foe to Steve?
Joe had his own theory: "A lot of people went to a lot of trouble to protect Campbell. He can come back to life and re-invent himself and I'm sure a passport is already in place. Whoever backed him will already believe he is out of their hair, and his name was buried in that coffin when it was covered in soil. So why hasn't he gone? Because he wants the treasure that he has waited all his life to own. He understands he can't set foot on the island again, so he wants us to get it. That's his plan. He's hiding under a rock waiting for his moment."

CHAPTER TWENTY

We made plans for our next trip to Holy Island and we decided we would travel up on the Monday as the tide times were reasonable for a 'stop over.' We had all morning to arrive, up until 12.45pm, and the causeway re-opened at 7.25pm. That gave us well over eight hours to do what we wanted to do. All the equipment was in place, we just had to climb down the ladder. Little Emily was put in charge of ladder duties, God bless her little cotton socks, and Grace was doing some research from her home checking out odds and sods that Joe had given her.
We named ourselves the 'Three Musketeers and Joe' – Athos (myself), Porthos (Grace), Aramis (Emily) and the

one and only Joe as D'Artagnan. A phoenix rising from the ashes, born again from university delinquents. We had brains; we had potential; self-confidence and brawn (just a little bit). Oh yes, and we had Emily.

I was still smarting from the betrayal of someone I had grown to trust, and the humiliation of how I had been part of Steve's elaborate hoax. To top it all off, he even stole from me!

There was a similar thought foremost in Joe's mind, too: "IF we get the treasure and IF we get it home, at what point is Campbell going to turn up? He won't be on the island, that is certain, but he wants his treasure, and we know what he is capable of."

We travelled up in Emily's Range Rover, a motor that had never crossed the causeway before, so there was that little added insurance policy that we wouldn't be tracked.

I bought another phone, so they (whoever they were) couldn't trace us in any way. The plan was for Emily to go with us to the cliff and pull up the ladder after we had descended down to the dinghy, then return at 7.30 that evening. The ladder was a giveaway that we were active in the vicinity, so that had to be pulled up. The phone codes were different – perhaps ones that worked this time. We knew there was nothing Emily could do if we were in trouble. She had a new phone too, but we weren't too concerned about sending messages apart from when we wanted the ladder. If something did happen we told her to scarper as quick as possible. We took this burden upon ourselves, so we were our own responsibility.

Autumn was almost upon us now, and although the weather had been unpredictable all weekend, there was nothing erratic about that rainy sultry day. It was constant and set in for the entire duration.

Joe gave me orders of what NOT to do in a crisis, and that was the first bit of anxiety I felt because I wasn't used to him being so controlling. The excess caffeine didn't help either. Four cups of coffee would hardly reduce my stress levels.

Joe went over-the-top first, and when he reached the rock he held the ladder for me. We agreed not to talk or make a noise for fear we attracted onlookers, but Emily wouldn't shut up.

"Be careful, Linda," she jabbered, and her constant chatter was not helping. I needed words of encouragement, not "if you fall, that's it, you do know that don't you?"

Of course I knew it.

"Step by step, move down, hold on tight," then repeat. I was glad when I got out of earshot of Emily, and I became even more aware of that when Joe's comforting words were getting louder and louder.

"You are doing well girl," said Joe as he took hold of my shaking legs. "This is the difficult bit, as you know, going up is far easier."

"I didn't know we had established that," I snapped.

Then I realized how horrid I could be. That was a nasty attitude and I regretted it. I touched base and I felt such a rush of adrenalin I almost cried. Joe hugged me and I felt all the better for it.

"I'm sorry Joe," I said, "I'm in a bad place at the moment. I didn't mean to shout at you. I'm so stressed. I think Emily is getting to me."

He laughed, we cuddled, and my world was back in order. The dinghy ride was just a watery stepping stone to the cove, and once more we were back in our little cave. I could see the work Joe had done, and it was remarkable what he had done alone.

"How the hell have you moved those rocks by yourself?" I asked.

"Don't feel guilty," he replied.

"Oh I don't feel guilty at all," I laughed. "I couldn't budge them!"

We set about our work clearing the top layer of clay, trying to release rocks and boulders as we chipped away. It was challenging work for a lady who gets a 'cob on' just when I snap a nail. And three were broken the last time I got my hands dirty doing that work.

We moved two rocks in the first hour, which was good going, paving the way to a third layer that we assumed would take us to another chamber. The rocks seemed even bigger, but removing one would be the equivalent to opening the door. This had to be the breakthrough.

We made conversation as we toiled away, and I asked Joe about our legal rights to whatever we found.

"I've looked into it, and we don't really have any guarantee to claim anything we find. That is the downside."

"That's some downside, Joe," I said. "What's the upside."

There actually WAS an upside (of sorts) and like an officer of the law, he read out our rights: "We don't know what we are going to find, but if an ancient artefact is discovered, such as a coin, brooch or pot, it is the property of the person who owns the land where it is found. In our case I'm not sure what a coastline constitutes. Are we on a beach or on dry land? Because that makes a difference. This cove is tidal. The water comes in, it rises, it drops, and that is a grey area in terms of the law."

I understood his meaning, but whatever was hidden behind the rock wall was placed there, the tide didn't bring it in.
"So, in the eyes of the law, we are doing this work without authority?" I said dejectedly.
Joe wasn't so sure: "Yes, you have a point. However, there is a catch. The law says the legal owner of all finds discovered on dry land ABOVE the coastal tide-line is the property of the owner of the land. If there is gold and riches beyond this wall, they are below the coastal tide-line when the tide is in. Will that stand up in a court of law? I'm not sure. But that could come under the terms of another law called the 'Treasure Act of 1996'. That says that anything over 300 years old counts as 'treasure'. Treasure then becomes the responsibility of the state, and landowners and the finders may be paid a proportion of its value. If the treasure is as large as Campbell says, that could be a substantial amount."
Joe singled out one boulder on that third lair and it looked to be the one that would leave a hole big enough to crawl through. Sadly, the one he picked was the biggest he had faced, and it was not going to budge without a monster effort from us both, and I wasn't sure I was capable of being much help. The mortar came away relatively easily and the preparation was done in no time, but the tide was rising up the wall very quickly making it very difficult to manoeuvre to lever the boulder out. We had not even thought about the tide. Obviously when the causeway was closed the sea-level was at its highest. So that made it double the danger for us both.
Within minutes we were thigh-high in North Sea salty water and it was freezing! But we got the rock to shift ever so slightly by rocking it with a crowbar, building up a rhythm. However, a rock in the second layer toppled

forward. It had become unstuck with the rocking movement and freed itself. Joe had the sense to get out of the way, but I slipped on the slimy seaweed that covered the platform and I landed in the water. The rock follow me down, splashed into the water, and it landed directly onto my leg. The sea water cushioned it's weight as it plummeted downwards, saving my leg from serious injury, but I realised I was trapped by my foot and shin bone. Nothing seemed broken, but no matter how hard I struggled, I was going nowhere. I was snared like a badger in a gin-trap. Joe had a glazed expression on his face as he waited for my reaction.
"Oh God, Linda, are you OK?"
"I'm trapped Joe. I'm pinned to the bottom. You are going to have to do something."
I could not move a muscle. To make matters worse, I was now bent at such an acute angle the freezing cold water was up to my chest and the pain was penetrating my legs. I looked up at the wall around me and immediately realised we were battling against time. The tide was rising and we needed to address that problem very quickly.
"What time is high tide?" I asked.
"What are you on about?" he replied.
"The causeway closed at 12.45 until 7.25pm, OK?" I said, "That makes high tide around 4 o'clock. Look at the tide mark around this wall, my head is about ten inches below it. You've got about 20 minutes to get me out of this f***ing mess!"
Joe tried to push the rock but each time I couldn't stand the pain. I was crying, sobbing, wishing I was a million miles away from that place. I always said I would trust Joe with my life, but I never once meant it literally.

Joe tried just about everything while I was having a full-on panic attack. It begin like a cluster of spark plugs in my abdomen. My breathing became more rapid, more shallow, and I was trembling throughout my body. The water was up to my neck and each time Joe made any effort he had to dive underwater. Minutes flew by and I knew what was going through his mind every time he came up for breath. I thought of poor Paula Raine being dragged from the Meadow pond that fateful day, and Joe sobbing. My head was pounding, every cell in my body was screaming for oxygen. But I kept fighting desperate to take a breath. Black began to seep in at the edge of my vision. I tried to open my mouth to breathe, but I only got salty water. I was breathing through my nose and time was ticking by. Then, ever so slowly, painfully and quietly, everything started to fade away.

Joe found a rock about twice the size of a house brick and placed it as far under the boulder as he could, wedging it by kicking it with his steel toe-capped boots. Then he took off his leather belt and wrapped it around the peak of the boulder, and pulled the belt with all his might, using the small rock as the fulcrum. Nothing moved. So he tried again, trying to time it as the tidal wave pulled back. The tide must have added a few extra pounds pulling strength and the boulder finally rocked forward about six inches, giving me enough room to pull out my foot. I went under the water for a few seconds and took in a few gulps of the North Sea's finest waste and refuse. But Joe grabbed me and dragged me up the rock face away from the water. He pushed hard on my chest as I drifted way, trying to make me cough up the refuse in my lungs. Harder and harder, until finally I spewed out the filthy water out onto the rocks. He tilted back my head, pinched my nose and placed his mouth on mine, before giving me more chest compressions.

For many minutes we sat there, and Joe didn't say a word. He sat cradling me, and I looked up and saw the face of a sad little lost child, just like that day on the Meadow. He stroked my face, then kissed my forehead, and did it allover again several times. Then he cried.

I gained my strength, and spoke in some incoherent language that was a mixture of peculiar noises. Words spoken in fear, and finally in relief.

Joe's face turned from passive to serious. He listened intently and then held out his hand to silence me.

We sat for several minutes, then I composed myself and told him, "I know what you are thinking, Joe. Paula Raine." He didn't reply. But I knew.

CHAPTER TWENTY ONE

On an inclement day, in the darkness of a hole in a cliff-face, I met an angel.

He was dressed in muddy clothes, there was stubble on his chin, and he sat there waiting patiently with the serenity of a saint.

"You need to get out of those wet clothes Linda," he said, and handed me a rucksack that held everything I needed.

"Do you always carry a bag with the whole caboodle?" I asked.

"Today is different, we cannot get across the causeway, so we are stuck here. We need dry clothes, food and drinks, so I bring the lot. Dry off and change your clothes," he said, "Before you catch pneumonia."

"You saved my life, Joe. How can I ever repay you for what you did?"

He is a guy who can embellish tall stories to give people the full effect and draw an even bigger laugh. But I knew this latest tale of adventure would fall under the radar. I bet he never tells a soul about the day he saved me from the might of the North Sea. That's Joe for you.

We had a challenge to complete.

"What do we do now?" Joe asked. "Do you still want the happy ending? We can move out if you've had enough. The choice is yours."

"I'm not broken yet," I smiled. "It just means being more careful in future. Warn me when there's a falling rock and I'll get out of the way next time."

"Ok, your decision, babe. Don't let that spark of hope become extinguished. We are so close to achieving this."

"I'm sorry Joe," I said, rising to my feet and grabbing my trowel. "It was a shock. I was not expecting what happened. I didn't want to put you through that. Anybody but you."

He gave out a sigh and a shrug of the shoulders: "I'm pleased it was me. That will exorcise a few ghosts. Don't feel bad about it."

I felt more pain in my fingertips than my leg, having spent a couple of hours scratting and scratching at rocks, and I understood how lucky I was to even be able to walk. I was fine, a little bit wounded, but not disheartened. So we continued.

We had cut through two layers of rock. The final one would give us all the answers.

Joe tapped on the rock with his trowel: "This is the canary in the coalmine. Shifting this boulder will tell us everything. If there is another rock face behind it I think we can assume it's a hoax. It's not blocking up a cove, it's a breaker for the tide."

We sweated on that stone for over two hours. It would move, slightly, but remained in place. Trying to pull it away from that massive rock barrier proved futile. Joe even tried to break it open with a hammer and chisel, but it wouldn't shatter. That rock wasn't sandstone, it had been transported from some hillside far away specially for a purpose. But Joe came up with the idea of using ropes. He drilled two holes and inserting two metal hooks screwed into rawl-plugs. We attached two ropes and we fought with all our strength to wrench it clear. The brightest ideas produce the most shining rewards, and we finally dragged it clear of the wall.

There was a hole, which was the most satisfying feeling I can ever remember experiencing, but what lay beyond? We looked at each other and Joe had a smile on his face as big as the hole itself. He handed me the flashlight and said: "This is your moment. Take a look. Tell me there are wonderful things."

I climbed up to the cavity and I tried to peer inside but I couldn't see six inches in front of me. The blackest of black. I pushed the torch inside and switched it on. We decided that we would only use a torch when we got inside the chamber. It was still light outside so we weren't giving the game away. The cavity inside was small in width and height, probably no bigger than eight feet square, but it was a tunnel that stretched into the darkness. How far, I had no idea.

There stood our dream - one large wooden box settled on a sort of podium of sea stones. That was all I could see. The chamber was certainly man-made, chiselled out of pure rock, with another compartment in the roof leading somewhere else.

"There's a wooden box, Joe. That's all I can see."

Joe took the torch and scanned the chamber.

"It looks as though the box has fallen down that shaft," he said.

I recounted the tale I was told: "Steve said there were at least two, maybe three, wooden chests in all. They sank down the shaft when The College tried to get to them with a massive drilling rig. Perhaps the other two are lodged up above."

Joe felt around the boulders in the wall and found one loose: "Let's knock this stone inwards and we can get inside the chamber."

The job was done in five minutes. The mortar was scraped away and he used the crowbar to force the boulder inwards.

"That's even better," said Joe, "we can use it as a stepping stone."

He threw the bag of tools through the hole and climbed in head-first, landing in a heap on the other side. I went in a more dignified fashion, feet-first, and he caught my fall at the other end. The wall had done a remarkable job of holding back the sea for hundreds of years, but the place was still damp from water seeping in through the shaft. We only had the one torch and Joe shone the light on the wooden box, but when he looked to find which way was 'up', he stumbled upon a bag of bones. It was the skeleton of some unfortunate guy who's soul had long gone. It seemed as though he had fallen down the shaft and couldn't find a way out, or maybe he was one of the two men who died in the explosive disaster back in the Victorian era.

I felt emotional as Joe lifted up the tattered clothes, or what was left of them, and said: "Well I hope he had a quick death."
But he pointed the torch at the wall and said: "It was slow. There's scratch marks on the stones where he tried to claw his way out. He may have fallen down the shaft, but I think he was locked in this place when the wall was built!"
"Why would someone do that?" I asked, cringing at the very thought.
He had scratched his name with a stone – Philip Woods – with the date - 1697. That alone was an achievement because he would have been sat in that hell hole in total darkness. Joe rummaged through his soggy, grimy clothes and found a silver half-crown coin that read 'William III 1694', as well as two sixpences and a shilling.
"That must have been a hell of a lot of money back in those days," said Joe. "Probably his month's wages for working on this job, poor fella. But for some reason, somebody buried him alive."
"Perhaps the workers didn't know the purpose behind the tunnelling," I replied. "And maybe this man found out, to his cost."
But, the sadness didn't last long. He was dead, had been for centuries, and there was nothing we could do about it. His moment had gone, while ours had arrived, and we stood looking at the box and almost hugged the life out of each other.
Joe explained he never had doubts about accepting Steve's story: "In the old black and white films I never swallowed the story of big, wooden treasure chests. But, for some reason, I believed this yarn right from the start. I don't know why, but I did. Right, let's get the top off this baby."

He patted the wooden chest then tried to move it, but it would not budge an inch.

"It's full of something, for sure," he proclaimed then picked up his crowbar and hammer. "And it's upright, which is a help. But what happens now, Linda? If this was an Indiana Jones film this box would be full of poisonous snakes or poison darts will come shooting out from holes in the wall. Do we take our chance?"

"Give me that hammer. I haven't gone through all this for nothing," I insisted, but in jest.

"Before I break into this," Joe smiled, "If the worst comes to the worst and it is full of rocks, at least you will go away with Philip's silver half-crown as a booby prize. I will take the sixpences."

He hammered the tip of the crowbar into the slit of the wooden casket and tried to prise it open but it came to nothing. The chisel worked so much better, and when we heard the crack of the lock breaking as he drove the metal through it's mechanics, our moment was upon us. The cask was open.

The seal was broken and he raised the lid with an almighty thrust. I shone the torch and the whole tunnel lit up with the reflective sparkle of gold and jewels. Wonderful, magnificent objects. Joe squeezed me with an affectionate bear-hug and we could have waltzed around in the darkness because we were so happy..

"Beautiful things, Joe, beautiful things!" I shouted.

"We've found it babe, we've finally got our hands on it."

There were so many objects - gold coins; drinking vessels; two golden hawk's heads; a golden collar covered in the finest jewels; many head-pieces; jewellery; trinkets and gold embalming oil jars.

"Where did all this come from?" asked Joe. Picking up one of the gold necklaces: "This looks Roman to me."
"A mixture of places, but I suspect it was all plundered," I replied. "Steve said Emperor Hadrian brought it here from Rome, at a time when the Roman's ruled most of the civilised world. So they could have come from anywhere, Alexandria, Jerusalem, Carthage, God only knows. Steve said The College added to it, so once again, that could have come from anywhere."
Joe selected one of the gold embalming oil jars and shone his torch on it.
"This has to be Egyptian," said Joe, "It must come from the Valley of the Kings. It's breathtaking. Have you any idea what we have here?"
I looked at Joe and I would swear I saw a figure stood behind him. The only glow was the light from his torch reflecting back from the gold embalming jar he was holding, but there was someone stood in the darkness. Make no mistake.
There was a chill in the air, or maybe that was just the hairs on my arms standing to attention, but I could see a shimmer of mist surrounding a shape ... a form ... a man.
"Joe, behind you," I said in a slow, determined, stuttering voice.
"What?" he replied.
"There is a man behind you Joe, honestly, trust me."
He turned, but before he could shine a light, he dropped the torch. It cast a light in another direction but it reflected off anything bright and gave us a glimmer of illumination. There stood an apparition. Some ghostly figure dressed like a monk in a habit, covered by a scapular and cowl. He was burnt, no hair, no eyebrows, features melted and raw. The pair of us froze solid, staring, petrified.

Then this figure spoke in a voice that reverberated around the chamber, in a tone that was two octaves below any power of speech I had ever heard before.
"Have you come to play?" he growled.
That sound vibrated through my body, leaving me shaking and mortified.
His grin became a snarl, baring teeth, or what teeth he had left. And he let out a rasping laugh.
"Let's play," he said to Joe, and I could see my dear friend searching for words to respond with.
The monk started to clap but it was soundless, his hands clapping together but in total silence. Then he laughed as though he had never seen such a funny thing. The voice was there but his physical presence didn't seem to be. He was stood two yards away, as real as Joe, but then again … he wasn't. Don't ask me to explain that because I cannot.
He clapped, to the point of enjoying himself, and sang out: "Old King Cole was a merry old soul and a merry old soul was he."
Joe turned to me, gave a look of bewilderment, but immediately the monk edged forward, not too happy that he was being ignored. Joe stepped back, moved towards the torch, and just as he was bending down to pick it up, another figure stepped out of the darkness.
"Witchcraft!" bellowed this new creature, even louder and deeper than the previous spirit.
"Joe!" I shouted, "Be very careful what you do."
Neither of them looked in my direction or acknowledged what I said. As though I wasn't there.
Then a third figure appeared, dressed like the other two, and once again none of them noticed me. All eyes were on Joe.

"The torch is losing battery life and starting to dim," I said.
"We have to get out Joe. We can't stay here."
"Yeah," he replied. "I'm going to pick up the torch. You walk to the hole and get out."
That immediately upset our visitors.
"You lurk … under a veil … of black!" said the first monk. Joe tried to reach the torch but some force of wind and light whipped him off his feet and propelled him ferociously against the rock wall, clashing him, arms flaying, 3ft off the ground. He fell to the smelly, wet sand, slumped face down. I had to fight my fear and help him. I dashed over and pulled his face out of the puddle and turned him over.
"Joe, are you OK? Please talk to me."
The three figures stood, motionless, like waxwork dummies. I picked up the torch, pointed it at the nearest one to me, and tried to dazzle him with the light. But it hardly produced a flicker. He didn't move towards me or say a word, but I noticed he was levitating. His feet were an inch or so off the sand. He was actually in mid-air.
Joe was dazed and winded, gasping for breath.
"We have to get out Joe, please," I sobbed. "Get to your feet, I cannot carry you."
His head slumped down, but I grabbed his chin.
"Listen Joe! Get to your feet!"
I helped him up but he wanted to sit on the rock we had pulled from the wall. He was disorientated and breathless, too confused to sense the danger.
"Up Joe! Use your legs. We are going."
A white translucent figure slowly came into focus, shimmered with a hazy bright blue aura. It was as though I was looking through strange glasses and I couldn't quite get the focus right. At first a face appeared like a soft whisper. That is the only way I can describe it. Shimmering

like a soft wind blowing through the trees. It was beautiful. Wondrous. Indescribable.

Then the form became a man, dressed in a white robe with hands crossed. His gaunt soulless eyes didn't frighten me at all, although I was looking into the eyes of a dead man. He too was levitating. There didn't seem any life in his body, but he was wonderful. I have to say that because he truly was.

Joe opened his eyes and stared. I lay cuddling him and we both looked upon him in amazement. The monks had gone. Where? I have no idea. All our attention was on the light that was shimmering, radiant and so exquisite. I felt a moment of captivating peace. No danger, no fear, just beauty.

"We go now, Joe" I said, and I pulled him towards the exit hole. "Come on, let's go home."

CHAPTER TWENTY TWO

There are laws stopping amateur treasurer hunters (like ourselves) from plundering lost riches, and I was starting to understand why. After that harrowing experience I was starting to wonder what was right and what was wrong. What I saw, I couldn't begin to explain. We sat at the cove entrance and said nothing.

The plan was to take all we could carry on this trip, then think about the consequences later. But we took nothing. Not even so much as a single sixpence from Philip's aged and decrepit clothes.

Finally Joe spoke: "You never know how strong you are, until being strong is the ONLY option you have."

"And what does the mean in this context?" I asked.

"It means, if we try this again, we are not going to walk out of that cave as easily as we walked in. Whatever is in there is not going to give us freedom to take what we want. The dead guy – what's his story?"

"Dead guy?" I asked, reminding myself what we had just seen. "Which one? Was anything 'alive' in that cave? Do you mean the skeleton on the floor, or the precession of monks that appeared out of walls and hovered around like hummingbirds? None of that was real, was it?"

Joe had no answers, just questions: "I think the dead guy had been placed in that tomb, but by whom, or by WHAT, I don't know. Was he trying to take the gold? Is that a warning to us?"

Emily, always a punctual lady, arrived on queue. But the code she sent was not the one we were expecting. In layman's terms it meant, "I'm in trouble".

"Just phone her, Joe," I said. "She's probably lost."

She wasn't lost - the rope ladder was missing. That meant one of two things. Someone was onto us; or the dizzy girl had not hid it properly and someone had walked off with it. It was irrelevant which, because it wouldn't help our cause.

"What happens now?" I asked.

"It's no big deal," said Joe, "We've got the dinghy. I will drop you off on the beach, return to the cove to dump the dinghy, and swim to meet you. We can easily get a new ladder, so don't be too hard on her."

That was the plan, that was how it happened, and soon we were back on the A1 heading south.

Emily was curious, and rightly so. But how could we explain what had just happened? I told her we had found the treasure and described what it consisted of, in as accurate detail as I could. Then I explained my brush with death and how Joe had been my hero. I mentioned ghosts but didn't go into too much detail because I didn't know how to! When I suggested the treasure could be 'cursed', which was something I firmly believed, Joe implied I was pushing the boundaries a little too much on that one. Emily was as excited as only Emily can be: "How much fun can you cram into one single day on Holy Island? Ghosts as well?" To her it was like a day trip to Disney World.

Our plan was to take a proportion of the treasure home with us that evening, if we found it of course, and Emily was choked that we didn't have something to show her. Joe told a good tale about skeletons and ghouls and, far from being discouraged, she wanted to be part of the crew on the next trip. Her attitude was so flippant I half expected her to suggest we take champagne and cakes and let's have a party down there!

We had thought of everything when it came to 'stashing the swag', including backpacks and fold-up sports bags. But we returned empty handed.

"You could have brought the small stuff," said our little friend. "Even a few coins."

"I'm on a guilt trip, Emily," I said, and I genuinely meant it. "Have we any right to take it?"

"Isn't it a bit late in the day to consider self-condemnation?" she queried. "Particularly now that it's in your power to take it. I'd have taken something, if only for a souvenir. You don't have to take Egyptian jars or Roman eagles, but enough gold to make you 'comfortable.' Pay off your mortgage, and have a few holidays. You can't just leave it in the ground."

I got home and battled with my demons (again), assessing whether I had the confidence to put myself in that position again. Has there ever been an instance when someone has been killed by a ghost? We were in unchartered waters because, whatever it was, it had the power to touch, pick up and throw.

The phone rang. It was Joe.

"What happened today, Linda? What the hell did we see?"

"I don't know, Joe. Whatever it was, it has a power we cannot match. It threw you 15ft across the cave, just because you wouldn't play nursery rhymes with it!"

"Would you go back in there again?" he asked.

"I've just been thinking about it. That 'something', whatever it is, doesn't want us in there."

Joe still couldn't get Steve out of his mind: "That's why he wanted someone else to recover the treasure. He knows there is a presence in there. And he knows what it is. I'm not saying he has experienced it, perhaps he has – perhaps he hasn't, but Campbell has the knowledge. He knows the history."

"Was that Saint Cuthbert we saw?" I asked. "The image in white? He is buried down there somewhere. We've established that."

"Is there such a thing as a dead ghost?" he asked. "That figure was dead, and the more we looked, the more I expected him to suddenly come to life. But he didn't. Pilgrims have been flocking to his shrine for 1,300 years to feel the presence of a dead man. To be part of his miracles. He was that special."

"So you think it was Cuthbert?" I asked.

"Do you? I don't know what it was. You cannot put logic to it. Did we witness a miracle? Or is that just too preposterous to even contemplate?"

Joe had checked out the nursery rhyme Old King Cole on the internet: "It was first put into print around 1700. And although there was much speculation about the identity of King Cole, he cannot be identified reliably as any historical figure. The date of of 1700 is interesting because it ties in perfectly with everything we know about the cave."

"Those monk figures were threatening you!" I said.

"I don't think reciting a nursery rhyme can be regarded as a threat," he laughed.

"You can read it anyway you want, Joe, but I beg to differ."

The Musketeers met the following night at Joe's pad for a social evening of wine and pizza and an update of all things involving treasure. Emily was still feeling "worthless" for losing the ladder, but at least she was now getting involved, and that was good. We accept the little lady for what she is, and I say that in a nice way.

Grace had been scanning the net for information on some of the characters involved with Steve's past, and she uncovered some gripping truths about Steve's ex-wife. "Jaqueline Campbell - formerly Nixon - formerly Jackson - formerly Kaye." said Grace. "Quite a character is Jaq. She has been around the block has this lady. Married three times and for the record, she has spent two stretches in prison. This girl is harder to shake than a broken hand. Her problem is she seems to want to have sex with men who presumably don't want to have sex with her. And that brings with it a few concerns and the bad reputation she obviously has."

I stepped in immediately, "She told me Steve sexually abused her to the point she had to 'beg'!"

"Well that doesn't seem to be the case with other men she has harassed," laughed Grace.

Grace produced a print-out of an article that involved Jaq being sentenced to six months in HM Holloway prison for stabbing a man.
The gentleman who was stabbed commented in a newspaper article: "Women like her can take over your life, and make you feel very unsafe. Your guard will constantly be up, because whilst it is easy for a man to physically defend himself against a woman, this is only true if he sees her coming. That woman has an illness. She told me she was a former child actor, who had apparently gone off the rails and developed a drug addiction in her teens. Despite not appearing to work, she was able to maintain a wealthy lifestyle, saying she had rich parents who bought her a luxury apartment. She approached me one day and initially I considered her strange, but definitely harmless. I found out later she was a high-class prostitute who worked in the city (London) with clients from the large banks. However, she soon began following me everywhere – to and from work, on my lunch break, to the gym – and she definitely wasn't subtle. A few times I came home late at night and I saw her waiting in her car. She would post me explicit photographs of herself, and after somehow finding my phone number, bombarded me with text messages. I told her to leave me alone or I would call the police, then she charged into my local bar and, after an argument, stuck a knife in my stomach!"
"How old is she?" asked Emily.
"Quite some age," I replied, "a lot older than Steve. I'd say early 50's."
Joe couldn't stop laughing.
"Oh there's a lot more where that came from," laughed Grace. "It was suggested in one court that she had: 'major mental and personality disorder' when she set fire to a

lover's car; posted nude photos of him to his entire list of e-mail addresses; and punched his new girlfriend. She got away with that one. The charges were dropped and she didn't serve any time in prison."
Joe was now in hysterics, "Nude photos of the guy? Please tell me he was 25 stone."
The article claimed she may have troubled even more men because women, in cases like this, are not regularly held accountable for their actions. Male stalkers are far more likely to be prosecuted than females."
I couldn't wait to find out what her second jail sentence was for.
Grace enlightened us: "She refused to pay a fine when she was charged with prostitution. I researched it and according to one feature in a magazine - 'can't pays' are separated from 'won't pays'. Those with a drug addiction don't have the money to pay the fines. But Jaq was raking in the money and the court demanded she was made to realise that breaking the law was a serious matter. She went back to Holloway and did two weeks."
But regardless of the convictions, I couldn't see any reason how she could be any danger to us: "She is a character but is she a threat to anyone? I remember her eyes lit up when I mentioned the treasure, although I didn't think she had the knowledge or ability to actually go and get it. As for the photos in the house, I noticed Steve was more annoyed than embarrassed by them. Without knowing the truth, I can only assume she put them there. She had a habit of leaving 'little presents' for other men, so why not Steve? Most of the photos seemed recent, probably no older than two years. She was no 'spring chicken' in the swimwear.
Next on Grace's investigation hot-list was Steve's mother.

"Elizabeth Campbell is a strange one," said Grace. "There is no record of her dying but there is no record of her living after she left her property in Berwick. She goes off the map at the same time as Steve's father. She lived in Berwick-upon-Tweed in a street called Sea View which is next to the Holiday Park. Then nothing! She was not buried on Holy Island, as Jaq says, or if she was it was in an unmarked grave because the Priory don't have any record of it."

I asked if she had done any research on Steve's dad.

"Yeah, Linda, I did," she replied, "but that is very much as Steve explained. There was an appeal made in the local newspaper at that time, saying police were 'growing increasingly concerned for Bamburgh man Norman Campbell'. They said his disappearance was 'out of character' and he was last seen in the Olive Tree Pub in Bamburgh on October 15th at 9.30pm twenty years ago. They never found his body."

Finally Grace had the lowdown on the main character himself, Steve Campbell.

"For a man who writes books he doesn't push his products very well," said Grace. "There is very little published about him. There is plenty of information about his books, but nothing at all about the author. He led a very secretive existence. Even his funeral, on the island itself, was not reported in the local newspaper. That is astounding these days. It's a custom every borough observes."

It was time to reveal the truth about our 'experience' in the chamber. We had skipped over things with Emily, giving her the kiddie's version, but now was the time to tell her (and Grace) the fear we went through that day. I let Joe do the honours. The reaction was one of shock, as we anticipated, and the atmosphere changed dramatically.

"Are you serious?" said Grace, with a jaw-dropping facial expression that made me chuckle.

"Oh we are serious," I replied, "to the point of being worryingly serious!"

After several questions, most of which we didn't know the answers to, Emily "found God". The dear girl got herself so wrapped up in the story she proclaimed: "I wasn't a religious person, but I am now. I think it was Jesus you saw!"

"It wasn't Jesus, Emily," laughed Joe, "I cannot tell you who it was, or who it was, but it was NOT Jesus."

"I want to go inside the cave and see him," insisted Emily.

I thought I would remind her there was a negative side to the story: "What about the monks, Emily? They were nasty and frightening," I added.

"Yeah," she said, "but I want to see the saint, and the treasure."

"OK," I replied, "you can take my place because I'm not going back in there. You can have my share of the treasure, too. Because I believe whoever tries to take that gold won't get out alive. That's how strongly I feel about it."

But it didn't discourage any of them. They all wanted to bring down the curtain on this adventure with a grand finale.

Emily had it all planned out: "The happy ending always comes on the last page. When I was little, I always dreamt of the last page of the story of my life. I wanted to write it myself, and keep it safe with me."

I couldn't get to grips with that: "That is just weird, Emily." But Joe didn't agree.

"That is beautiful, Emily," he said. "Everybody should have a happy ending."

CHAPTER TWENTY THREE

Joe was a born adventurer. Courageous, dashing, and perhaps too much of a 'chancer' for his own good. But he was no fool.
After all we had been through, I still thought we were dabbling in the 'unknown' with this final escapade. Were we starting to take our eye off the ball, because Steve Campbell hadn't shown his face up to this point? Was he even alive?
To Joe and Emily it was like 'Summit Fever', a disorder that climbers suffer when climbing Everest or any other high mountain. They see the peak and no matter how bad the conditions, they are going to get to the summit despite the dangers they face. No weather warning, or no threat of an avalanche was going to stop those two. Joe had reached that point where he could see the summit and come 'Hell or high water' he was going to stick his flag on it. I could read his mind.
Later that night when Emily and Grace had left to go home, Joe and I talked about the cavern.
"What's driving you on, Joe? It's not the money," I asked him. "Rich is never rich enough for you, so what is your motivation?"
After all the years of preparation and all the effort that people had put into the pursuit for the treasure, we were given our opportunity by slipping in through the back door. Yeah it was there, ripe for the picking, and Joe wanted it. But he wanted Steve out of the way first. Forget the ghosts in that chamber in the cliff, he feared Steve more. He talked about him often.
Joe said: "He takes me from one uncomfortable place to another. I feel I'm waiting to be called. I want him in front

of me where I can see him, not hiding in the shadows waiting for his moment."
It was starting to become an obsession, and Joe put together a plan to flush him out.
"Where can he be? He visits his father's house which is due to be habitable, so he could already be moved in there. What about the caravan? You said he takes his mother to it once a month, and I can believe he still does. That could be where we lay our hands on him. As for his mother, one way of finding out about her is asking in Berwick. Perhaps she still keeps in contact with the neighbours. Old people do those sort of things."
First he wanted to take a trip to the caravan site, but I didn't know where it was. We looked on the internet and pulled up all the holiday parks in the area.
"It was some place within 20 miles of Holy Island," I recalled. "It didn't take long to get there."
That gave us four holiday camps to choose from: Ord House Country Park; Waren Caravan Park; Riverside Country Park or Haggerston Castle. I immediately ruled out Haggerston as my grandparents took me there often as a child and I would have recognised it immediately. You can't miss a 14th century castle, now can you?
"Can you describe the place?" asked Grace as she pulled up information on all the camps.
"There was a play area with a wooden castle-like climbing frame that kids play on," I remembered. And Grace set about tracking it down on the internet. That wasn't too difficult and that play area popped up on photographs of the Wooler Riverside complex. That was the one!
We had a plan for Mr Campbell, and Joe was in a very self-assertive frame of mind: "Oh I've got his number. Believe me."

I stayed over that night, and next morning Joe was up bright and early, clanking pots, frying bacon, and projecting his voice even though I wasn't in the frame of mind to listen to it. The bed was warm and I didn't feel like moving. It was only 7.55, what was the rush? We didn't get to bed until well past 2am!

"OK Joe," I whispered to myself, "I have a bit-part to play with no lines. All I need to do is shower, dress myself, nod, eat, grab my bag, and get into the car. No smiling required. Can you cope with that?"

It almost worked, too. For twenty seconds. Then Joe came bounding into the room: "You have the chance to achieve more than you did yesterday ... if you get your arse out of bed and move now!"

The sun shone through the window but we stepped outside and the chilly wind hit us like a two-ton truck. That's the new morning for you, saint and sinner.

We set off on our journey and Joe wanted to go to Berwick first, saying it was the furthest trip so we may as well start there and work our way back.

The housing estate of Sea View sounds a lot more picturesque than it actually is. Large enough houses, granted, but pebbledash is usually put on a building for a reason - to hide the defects and shortcomings. I'm not saying that was the case here, but it certainly looked it on Elizabeth's ex-home. As for a view of the sea? Well, it's there OK, but it is like the old picture postcards showing a guy hanging out of the third floor window with a pair of binoculars. Just enough "sea view" so that you couldn't take the landlord to court for misrepresentation.

The sea was about a mile to the east and the train-line about 30 yards away, between the house and the beach.

"I hope she had good double-glazing when she lived there," I commented. We pulled up to the actual house Elizabeth used to live in, but we didn't expect to get much information from there because (according to Grace's research) the house had been sold three times since Elizabeth had left. But, thankfully, the neighbours either side had lived in the street when she was a resident.

The plan was to play the role of a long-lost daughter, looking to find her mother, and it worked to a certain extent with the first lady, but she soon became suspicious.

"Do you know where Elizabeth is living now?" I asked.

"We weren't that friendly, I'm afraid. She left a long time ago."

She didn't want to get involved. But there was more joy two doors along. The lady had sent Christmas cards to Elizabeth at an address in Seahouses, but she hadn't received one back for the last couple of years. The end of the road, perhaps, but it proved conclusively that the lady had been alive until recently. So much for Jaq's story about her being buried in the Priory cemetery. Had she made that up or did she actually believe it, because it wouldn't surprise me if that was what Jaq had been told. Nothing was conventional with the Campbells. All three of them were missing, assumed dead, and we weren't convinced that any of them were six feet under.

The lady kindly gave us the address that she corresponded to in Seahouses, giving us another piece to fit into this bizarre jigsaw. Another lead or a red herring?

Next we drove to Riverside, the holiday camp where Steve bought me the clothes after our rocky boat trip. The shop, the cafe, and the river all brought back happy memories of that day. If I'm honest, I couldn't wait to find the caravan.

After all, there was no concrete evidence that Steve was alive; yet there was a plot in the Priory cemetery that suggested the opposite. Nothing we were doing, the whole investigation, had any substance to it, only hearsay and supposition.

We parked the car some distance away, and as we approached the caravan we saw the door close. We didn't see a figure but someone was obviously staying there.

"What do we do now?" I asked Joe. "We can't wait here, he may spot us." I said, already concerned because campers were starting to watch us with suspicion.

"I want him to spot you!" said Joe very assertively. "You have nothing to hide. He's the one hiding."

I didn't see it that way, and I knew what Steve was capable of if he was put in a corner.

"Why the hell do you want him to see me? That puts my life on the line!"

I backed away and dragged Joe with me, and we hid behind one of the static homes. Hardly under-cover, as a family of holiday makers looked at us, probably concerned that we were about to break into someone's home. Let's admit it, we were rubbish at keeping a low profile!

"Joe, you don't understand do you?" I said, "If he is in there, I don't want you being one-on-one with that man. It doesn't matter who is in the right or who is in the wrong. What are you going to do when you see him?"

"We are in a unique situation," he replied. "The man is officially dead. Dead and buried with a certificate that proves it. I can do whatever I want to him, because, in the eyes of the law – he is already dead."

"You're going to kill him?" I replied. "On a holiday park full of kids? There's three kids looking at us right now. Have you got a gun?"

"You don't need to know," he said.
"The last time I asked someone that question he had just blown someone's brains out! Two people, actually. And that meant we were on the run like Bonny and Clyde. I don't want to go through that ever again."
"It's us or it's him, Linda," he replied, looking every inch as though he was about to go in that caravan with all guns blazing.
"Leave me out of this gunfight Joe. I've had enough. I'm going over there now and if he is there – ALIVE as you say - I'm going to tell him he can have the treasure. Every last piece of it. I don't want killings or murder, I've got out of this what I wanted, and I am finished with it all."
"You really mean that, don't you?"
"I do Joe. I have thought about this and I don't want anyone killed. Steve never did anything wrong to me. I can't explain why he staged his death or why he has had me followed, but I don't believe he is what you say. Just think about it, if he staged all this and he is living there with his mother, he is terrified. Terrified of being killed."
"Oh, he is a lovely man," grunted Joe sarcastically. "He drugged you and Emily, let's not forget that, and possibly killed your husband. Let's make a statue for him."
I had made my point and I did exactly what I said I would do, I walked over to the caravan and knocked on the door. I didn't really expect Steve to be there so I wasn't really being THAT brave, but there was always that chance he could be. Instead, an old lady opened the door, small in stature, looking as white as a porcelain doll.
"Hello, are you Mrs Campbell? I'm Linda Wilson." I said, putting on a smile and hoping she would do the same.
She looked at me, probably feeling (as I did) that it was time for some explanations.

"So you are Linda," she replied, and I knew there and then that she would be sociable. I was invited in but there was no sign of Steve, and I was thankful for that. I felt at home immediately. I looked at the bed I had slept in just a few weeks before. There was a warmth about the place that I spoke of earlier, and I was glad that I had returned.

"What can I do for you?" she asked, and I didn't know where to start.

She was charming to me, intelligent, I'm sure, and a very proud lady.

"I've been to your old house today at Berwick. I've been talking to your old neighbours."

"Why did you go there?" she asked. "I left there when Steve was just a teenager."

"I was told you were deceased, and I went looking, hoping you weren't."

"You heard I was dead? That brings you to the caravan?" she asked.

"I was here a short while ago, and Steve said he brought you here sometimes for a holiday. Someone was telling lies about you, and I didn't think it was Steve."

"You know," she said in a puzzling voice, "we all play dead sometimes. To keep us alive. That's a contradiction, I know, but you will understand one day."

"I think I understand already," I said.

We sipped tea from China cups and took biscuits from China plates, in a sophisticated and novel setting. Rabbits played in the field opposite, just as they had weeks earlier. This was so much better than having Joe running amok with his gun, a laughable picture I couldn't get out of my head. We covered a lot of subjects that I hoped I would get answers to, and she kindly obliged without once mentioning treasure; The College; or a death in Edinburgh.

A lot of nudging, and a lot of winking, if you understand what I'm saying.

Was Steve alive? Well she didn't answer either way, but she apologised for the "theft of two phones" that had to be "removed" because they had been "tracked". She was suggesting they were "taken" to stop us getting visitors at the cove, so we certainly had crossed-wires with those two incidents. We thought Steve was the one doing the tracking. All that was left was the mystery of Bamburgh woods. Is there a body in there?

"Your ex-husband," I asked, "is he still with us, Elizabeth? Did he pass away?"

"Oh he's not my ex-husband, we never divorced. He lives abroad. I forget where. Some country with a funny name. He lives with our son now."

That just about tied up all the loose ends. What a beautiful way of putting it. An intriguing lady.

"Your son is abroad?" I asked, hoping most sincerely that he was, before 'Sundance' Joe started gunslinging.

"Yes he went a couple of days ago," she answered. "He won't be back. That is his home now. I'm here to finalise the sale of the house in Bamburgh and I will be moving on. Do you like holidays, Linda?"

"I do, very much. I love the sun."

"I'm going away very soon," she smiled. "I forget where. It's old age, you know. I'm going away to retire."

"How lovely," I replied. "And you don't know where it is? I bet it's a country with a funny name?"

"Yes," she laughed, her brown eyes opening and closing with duress from the brightness of the sun peeping through the big front room window.

The conversation was 'peculiar,' every word demanding analysis before we moved on to the next. Never a straight question - never a straight answer.

"Is Steve having me followed, Elizabeth? I would love to know the truth."

"No, not as far as I know," she replied in a more serious tone of voice. "You need to be careful. If they are onto you, I'd suggest you stay squeaky clean and go about your business as normal. Don't think you can take from them and get away with it. It doesn't work that way."

"It's The College isn't it?" I asked, not expecting a reply, but I got one all the same.

"If you enter their world you do so at your own risk. They understand you were not party to anything. You were drawn in. They checked you out when they were looking for the Gospel."

I felt I was over-stepping a boundary, but I had to ask: "Is Steve still after the treasure?"

"I'd suggest you leave that alone," she said, turning those delicate chocolate brown eyes into a piercing stare. This woman was hardened to ways I could only imagine, but I had to delve a bit deeper.

"It comes to something when you have to die to live," I said, hoping she would respond.

"My husband knew the rules, Linda, as did my son. If you take from them you go to Hell, and they take you there in a handcart."

I left her on good terms, which was rather nice considering the ground we covered, and I returned to 'Wild Bill Hickok' who was now back in the car. I gave Joe a summary of what was said and explained Steve was no longer a threat to us or our treasure hunt, because the man was out of the country. But he needed something more convincing to dump the idea entirely. He gave me the impression that every answer Elizabeth gave was a red mark in a ledger with a question mark next to it. Non-negotiable. Joe wasn't ready to accept her story. Suspicious is a term that sits comfortable in Joe's world, making it sound like a wise choice instead of a compulsion. He could be infuriating, but still the love of my life, in a bromance sort of way.

CHAPTER TWENTY FOUR

I tugged at the new dress that the store assistant swore made me look so flattering, but now I wondered if it was too short. With each tug the front went lower and that was another eyeful I wanted to stop. With no time to go home to change, I was just going to have to wing it.
Emily arrived looking ten times more beautiful than me, so at ease with herself that she could show up in the work jeans she wore all day, and still carry it off. No jeans this time, a short summer dress that looked sensational, and already she was turning heads.
This was going to be the Musketeer's last gathering of assembly to decide the outcome of our adventure, whether we go forward with the grace of God, or take a few steps back and count our blessings. The final council.
Newcastle's Silk Room Champagne Bar was the venue, nestled behind the Quayside only 30 yards or so from the river Tyne. I was treating my friends on this night of 'decision', although I preferred to call it a night of 'celebration', because we had achieved what we had set out to do. The only question on the table was do we tempt fate and go back for what we had found, or do we get on with our lives? My mind was already made up. I knew Joe's was

too. As for Emily, I suspected she wanted to experience the unknown rather than become a rich woman. Grace, on the other hand, had always been orderly and disciplined, and I knew she would take the minimum risk without even thinking of gain. I didn't expect her to go out on a limb to acquire anything that didn't come with a receipt and a warranty of return. Even if it was for free!
Joe was early of course, "I have to be," he laughed. "It's part of who I am. It would never look good to keep three beautiful ladies waiting. I have too much respect for you." Awww, always the darling.
For all his antics, Joe was still the smart one. He had a swagger, not everyone's cup of tea, granted, and shyness was never his gig. But he was never a poser. Joe could fit effortlessly into any company, rich or poor.
For twenty minutes we were a trio, until Grace made her … how shall I put it … unrefined entrance. She sauntered round the corner, hands in pockets, hair casually ruffled just as though she had just pulled up on a motorbike. And she STILL stole the show.
The evening was a success from a party perspective, and probably just as triumphant on a business front. Nobody waffled, everybody put their cards on the table, because Joe had told us all to be honest with ourselves and honest with him. And that was how it came across.
"We all know why we are here," said Joe. "You know what's at stake, the reward and the risk that goes with it. We've all had time to think, so I'm asking what you all want to do."
No-one was particularly eager to get the ball rolling, so I took centre stage: "Joe knows the legal side of things and apparently all treasure finds have to be reported. Being on Holy Island cannot be seen as trespassing, and I don't

believe we have broken any law, but if we take whatever we have found - we cross that boundary."

Grace and Emily wanted to hear more, so after pulling a piece of paper from his pocket, Joe put them in the picture. He read out The Treasure Act of 1996 and picked up on various pointers that could rob us of any entitlement to our reward.

Joe explained: "Treasure is gold or silver that is less than 300 years old. The treasure on Holy Island dates back to Hadrian so we are talking about items that are 2,000 years old. Whether that gives us more entitlement to a reward, or less, I don't know, and I can't seem find out. Then the Act goes on to explain about items that have been 'deliberately hidden with the intention of recovery' by owners or heirs unknown. We don't know why it was hidden but they have been trying to dig it for 300 years. That goes against us too. Then there is the right to dig. We didn't get permission, and the act stipulates that permission is a priority to a claim. Archaeological digs are rarely allowed on Holy Island. They are few and far between, and that is probably for the reason why we are sat here tonight. There are some things that are best hidden. But on the rare occasions they are allowed to poke around, they have no claim to whatever they find. They don't get a cut of anything that earns financial rewards."

"So we won't get a penny if we announce to the world what we have found?" asked Grace. Nobody knew for sure, but that seemed to be the bottom line. Nothing went in our favour.

Grace was first to back out: "I have a family and I cannot risk my job or the scandal of a court case. I'm sorry but I cannot go any further. In the eyes of the law I have done no wrong, so I will step aside now and leave you to whatever you intend doing."

Emily questioned Joe's official ruling: You may get a share of the reward if you are the finder and had permission to be on the land.

"You don't need permission to be on Holy Island," she said forcefully. "Who's to say the cliffs are owned by anybody?"

Joe replied: "All land is owned by someone, Emily. I don't think there is a square metre in England that remains unclaimed."

"So what are your plans, Joe?" I asked, knowing full well he couldn't resist the temptation to return to the cavern. But I had to ask all the same.

"It depends on you and Emily," he replied. "If you two go, I will too."

I don't think I was ever good at reading Emily's mind. I believed I was, but she was always capable of throwing a curved ball, probably just to shock. Initially, I didn't think she was aware of the consequences of what she was getting herself into. But that was doing her a big injustice. She knew the danger, alright. And that didn't intimidate her in the slightest.

"I want to go into the cave and see the treasure," she insisted without a hint of hesitancy. But she spoke inside the warm and snug Champagne Bar, not hanging off a rope ladder with the wind from the North Sea blowing up her kilt. I got the feeling it would be: "Let's see what happens on the day," from that girl.

My speech was very much "here's one I made earlier," prepared with deliberation and attention to detail. There were things I wanted to say to the gang, but I explained it

was an opinion rather than a judgement. It was my morale standing rather than criticizing anyone else.
"I got you all involved so I cannot walk away now. Emily wants to observe the weird phenomena that Joe and I experienced, and I wish you luck with that Em. It won't be anything like you imagine. Trust me. But I will be there if you want me. I won't take any treasure because I don't think it is right, but that is only my opinion. You 'try' and take what you want. I say 'try' because I don't think you will be allowed to get anything beyond the wall. Whatever is in there will stop you."
I could see Emily collecting her thoughts, but she was always a tough little cookie. I never had the ability to change her mind, unlike Joe. She would hang on his every word. Joe could sway her into believing anything he believed himself. He gives people hugs instead of cold stares; acceptance and not demands; respect and never condemnation. For those reasons he got you to listen, intently.
"Well Joe," I said, "Where do we go from here?"
"I don't want to walk away, not now," he said, tapping the table as he spoke. "I want something from this. Not just for me but for all of us. A man lies dead in that chamber, and we don't know why. Was he trying to steal the treasure? We will never know. And that is what worries me. But it excites me too."
"Why does it excite you?" asked Grace. "You will have Linda and Emily with you, and their wellbeing is YOUR priority. So don't try and become a hero, Joe."
Grace shook her head in a look of dismay, because she was fearful for us. She didn't say those words. In fact she didn't say anything at all for the rest of that night, but a look can tell you more than a newspaper.

Joe had been planning the trip for days. Despite what I feared, it was not a "grab your coats and away we go" sort of manoeuvre. He was meticulous in his planning.
Emily was subdued. The reality was starting to hit home, and it smacked her hard. Joe's words of warning were necessary, but they added more stress to an already tense atmosphere. The girl was traumatised enough.
"This isn't Hogwarts," he said, in a week effort to add a bit of humour. "And you are not Hermione Granger."
"Stop being patronising, Joe" I said, stopping his antics. "For God's sake, you're not talking to a child!"
I think I took myself by surprise with that little outburst. It displayed an intensity that I normally save for traffic wardens and tax officials, but that one I gave for free.
Emily didn't want to be drawn into a pending argument and switched her attention to the changing scenery. All around us the fields flew by. The tyres made their monotonous thump-thump-thump over the rain-washed motorway and the windscreen wipers battled with them to keep the same beat.
I couldn't stay focused. I closed my eyes, letting my mind fill with music from the radio. That was a help.
We got to Holy Island at 10.37. I remember because it flashed up in red on the dashboard clock. Then Emily drove to the gate by the castle and we unloaded a couple of boxes, placed them on the trolley, and away we went, leaving Emily to park further up the road then follow us to the cliff head. Immediately Joe spotted the old rope ladder, folded exactly where it had been left.
"Someone has been down there," said Joe, sparking fear into us all. "They've brought the ladder back."

I wasn't convinced: "Perhaps it was there all along, and Emily couldn't find it."
Emily wasn't sure. Joe decided to use the new ladder, just in case the original had been tampered with. Unlikely, but possible. He drove the pins into the soft soil and then he clambered down to the rock in double-quick time, followed remarkably quickly by little Emily. She made me look pedestrian; pathetic even. And I was supposedly teaching her the ropes. No pun intended.

I upped my game myself, and dropped in on them in speedy time, leaving my 'girl in distress' temperament up on the cliff. It's amazing what can be achieved with a bit of competition. Thankfully, Joe didn't mock me, probably because he knew I was 'on the edge' after my ridiculous outburst earlier.

Walking inside the cave was foreign soil to Emily, and I kept an eye on her constantly. But she seemed to resent it, as though I was baby-sitting her. There was I accusing Joe of being patronising, when I was no better.

We walked towards the wall and colours merged from daylight into charcoal. On the earlier trip, we decided that we would never shine a torch in the cave because it could attract attention from fishing boats. We all had torches but we saved them for inside the main chamber. Joe feared climbing up and peeping into the cavern, then finding the place had been robbed. Now the boulders had been removed there was easy access inside, and there was nothing to stop anyone taking whatever they wanted. He found his footing and scaled the stones, just as he had done days previous, occasionally glancing in my direction. He didn't say anything but I knew what he was thinking. Had we given opportunists the window to make their fortune?

Meanwhile, Emily clutched her flash-light like a kid with a rag doll. Holding it close to her chest, mouthing words of reassurance. All I could smell was rancid seaweed on damp rocks, and the stench reminded me of when I was trapped underwater when Joe pulled me clear. I had a ridiculous urge to want to wipe those rocks clean just to get rid of that odour.

Joe got to the entrance and poked in his torch, scanning the inside with the utmost attention.

"What do you see?" I asked.

He lost his footing and stumbled back, grabbing hold of a protruding rock to save his fall. Not only did it add to the tension but it frightened the life out of Joe, as he clung on before finding balance once again.

"Yep, it's all still there. I'm coming back down for the bags."

We scampered up and threw the fold up travel bags inside the cavern, before climbing through ourselves. Earlier in the day I would have expected Emily to roll her eyes and say "Nope. No way!" But she was performing beyond our wildest expectations. She didn't say much, just went with the flow, until we clambered through that hole.

If subtitles were required on this fictitious film we were making, they would read in big bold letters: "And then there was darkness!"

Total darkness that robs you of your best sense and replaces it with a paralysing fear. Although the three torches worked perfectly well in the car on the way up (and we did check them) they decided to let us down when we needed them most. Joe's flash-light flickered and twinkled in an unorthodox manner, but it gave us something. Meanwhile, mine was as dead as the proverbial Dodo. I think Emily was so scared out of her wits I don't think she had the

strength to press the button on hers! She stopped in her tracks, faster than a bullet into lead.
"Oh my God!" she cried, and I hurried to comfort her.
"It's OK Emily, nothing is going to hurt you," I said, cuddling her shaking body.
Strange though it may appear, her nervousness was keeping me composed.
Joe was still fighting with his extra large flash-light, trying to get full beam but not quite achieving it. The power was erratic, which infuriated him.
"What the hell is causing this? There are new batteries in all the torches!" he shouted out, shaking his in frustration.
The light would suddenly sag before booting up again. But as I said earlier, at least it gave us something.
"Hurry!" said Joe, "Let's do this and get out!"
I grabbed a bag and dropped in gold rings and trinkets by the score, but Joe insisted, "DON'T take anything that is religious!"
That made a lot of sense.
There were exquisite golden statuettes of the Egyptian bull god Apis, the goddess Isis, a gold Sphinx, but Joe repeated his words, "I insist girls, nothing religious, just take ornaments and jewellery only."
I tipped in bracelets, goblets and coins. Then onto the next bag, and then the next.
Then Emily screamed at the top of her voice and it suffocated my whole body like a musty, thick blanket, clinging to every inch of my skin. A figure appeared from nowhere, quite possibly through the cliff wall, dressed in a monk's habit. Possibly the same creature as before, but it was difficult to tell. He wore a brown tunic, tied around the waist with a leather belt. The garment consisting of a long piece of woollen cloth worn over the shoulders. A hood hid

his face entirely, as though he had no face at all, and around his neck a silver cross flickered as it occasionally caught the glare from Joe's torch.

I was in no position to tell Emily to shut up, I was virtually paralysed from the neck down. But Joe eased her worries and calmed her, shielding her from our visitor. Then, just like before, more monks appeared. Four in total, each shrouded and clandestine as the next. No features or characteristics on display, but they seemed real to the touch. They moved like before, levitating an inch off the ground, buoyant but each in control of their own motion. I cannot explain how it was done, just as I cannot explain what the hell they were. They weren't human, but that's talking in the present tense. Maybe they had been ... at one time.

I knew it right from the start of this messed up drama that we would never win. I predicted it only the evening before. The only reason to venture into that cavern was to join the game - the game where everyone loses - and the only prize is knowing you fought.

As the four monks from the nether world stood before us, Joe tried to usher Emily up onto the stepping stone and over the wall, but the leader of the monastic brethren roared out a question: "What do you fear?"

It still didn't stop Joe, and he launched Emily through the exit hole like a torpedo with very little compassion as to how she landed on the other side. I only hoped she hadn't broken any bones or knocked herself out, but at least she was out of this mess. I thought about going in the same direction but I wasn't going to leave Joe.

Joe turned towards the monks and replied: "I don't fear you."

"Hide your light!" boomed a voice that reverberated in echoes around the cave.

"Know your fear and you can unlock your own cage and step right out," said one of the ghostly figures, pointing a finger in Joe's direction.

Joe didn't answer, he was ushering me towards the exit and either didn't think the question worthy of a reply or he was too occupied. I shook my head and indicated I wasn't going without him.

"Go Linda, get out," he whispered. But I stood still.

"They want us out," I said, always keeping my eyes on the figures across the cave, "and there is nothing stopping us, as long as we leave without the gold."

"I'm taking it," he said, and he really was determined to upset our hosts and go into battle.

"You don't know what you are fighting, Joe. They are not vampires, you can't show a cross or hand them garlic. They are not going to go anywhere."

He bent down and tried to picked up two of the bags but buckled under the weight. One of the monks became agitated and advanced forward, moving within ten feet of Joe. Now we could see his grotesque, withered features, looking like a 2,000 year old Egyptian mummy.

Something touched the side of my cheek and spoke into my ear, whispering words I couldn't understand. I presume it was in Latin. I was transfixed and I felt slightly lightheaded, as though my energy was being sapped away.

Joe must have seen me tottering and stumbling and he moved forward to grab me. It was then that the white translucent figure suddenly emerged by my side and, with the force of a dozen horses, sent Joe crashing against the sandstone wall.

Just for a fleeting moment, I thought I could hear my name being called. It was a deep, absorbing voice, echoing softly, and I could feel my tension evaporating away. The shimmered, hazy, bright blue glow was breathtaking. His form, once again, became a man dressed in a white robe with hands crossed.

CHAPTER TWENTY FIVE

Joe stepped forward to try and touch the white figure. But, just like before, he was catapulted across the floor with ferocious force and he bounced off one of the walls, splitting his head. He took a heavy fall and settled on the sandy ground with blood seemingly coming from his left ear. But he was built of strong stuff and shook it off as though he wanted to return for more punishment. He slowly came forward, risking the wrath of the mighty overlord. For some strange reason my torch burst into life and it disturbed the monks as they all backed away, but the white figure remained ... unmoved. Joe stood face to face with him, dare I say ... looking every inch a comic book hero. If there was fear in his body, it didn't show.
"Are you Cuthbert?" he asked.
No response.
"Are you the mighty Saint Cuthbert? Monk and bishop of Melrose and Lindisfarne."
Still no response.
"Talk to me!" Joe demanded. "Are you defending your treasure?"
The figure raised his head, and for the first time opened his eyes. He didn't look at Joe, he tilted his head back and looked up towards the roof. Slowly opening his mouth but producing no sound. Time moved so slowly with each

movement of his face prolonged, drawn out in a lingering action. Joe looked at me, as if he was short of ideas and needed some advice, but I was rooted to the spot, watching and praying there was going to be a favourable outcome.

"You saw a vision," continued Joe. "A vision of Saint Aidan."

That seemed to bring a reaction as the figure finally looked Joe in the eyes.

"Can you talk?" Joe asked, putting his hands together in prayer. "Shall we pray?"

The figure closed his eyes once more then bowed his head, then in the fullness of time he spoke words.

Words in prayer: "Sanctus Christus Salvator lautem quod Iudaeorum. Sit nobis tandem."

We gave him his moment of grace, staying silent throughout his prayer that I couldn't understand a word of. Then there was a moment of wonderment that defied explanation. Peace and tranquility like nothing else I have ever experienced. I was never religious, but there are times in life when you get inspiration from people that transform your future. I felt a compulsion to close my eyes, my eyelids felt so heavy, and I drifted into a strange semi-sleep that took my mind out of my body. I thought I was in a monastery, kneeling in front of some kind of demi-God. He touched my head. My whole body began to cleanse itself of all repugnant toxins. I felt invigorated. Dare I even say it ... I felt blessed.

The next thing I can remember is Joe holding me in his arms. All the spirits had disappeared and we were alone. I cannot remember clambering through the exit hole, and I cannot even remember walking back into the light. But the next thing I recall was feeling a hug from Emily and rain running down my face, and I felt radiant and cleansed. No pain nor discomfort.

"Where's Joe," I asked.

"He's putting the bags by the dinghy," said Emily in a somber, slightly shaky voice.

"So he got out, then?"

"Yeah," she said, "he got out. I don't know what happened in there but I don't know if it was good or bad. I don't want to take the gold, Linda. I don't want any of it."

"I don't either," I said, hugging her tighter than I can ever remember.

The new plan, devised on the spot, was for Joe to row Emily and me a few hundred yards to the coast towards the Castle. Emily would return to the carpark, and drive down to the spot to meet me. Meanwhile, Joe would ferry the treasure to us by means of his dinghy. It seemed a cracking plan – in theory. And fair play to him, although it had us out in the open and exposed to every 'man and his dog', there weren't that many people about. Thank the Lord for torrential rain.

We didn't want to return to the cavern to go through this again so it was now or never. We had eight large bags that weighed a ton each, so for safety and the threat of the possibility of overturning the dinghy and losing the lot, Joe would ferry them to us two at a time.

But after two runs I felt we were over-stretching our luck. Two men came over and asked what we were doing.

"What's the gentleman in the dinghy doing?" asked a guy with an Australian accent, as his friend took a couple of photos on his phone.

That was disturbing, and I could either reply by telling him to mind his own business or feed him a crock of shit. But first I told Emily to phone Joe and warn him.

My crock of shit: "I'm not supposed to tell you this, but there has been a terror alert in the village. The guy in the dinghy is an S.A.S. officer and there are troops on the other side of that cove. That's all I can say."

"A terror alert?" he asked in shock. "On THIS island?"

"That's all I can say, sir, and I'd appreciate it if your friend deleted those photos. I would hate to think he got his head blown off just for taking photos of an S.A.S. officer at work."

He responded very quickly, "Jamie, delete those photos! Oh my God, are we safe here?"

"I'd appreciate it if you left the island, sir," I replied. "The village is about to become a 'no-go' area. It's for your own safety. Leave and please don't say a word to anyone. We don't want to create a panic."

It worked. You couldn't see their backsides for dust.

Joe paddled on, bringing in all eight bags. We struggled with the last bag together, the heaviest of them all, then deflated his trusty dinghy and put it in the trailer we had attached to the car.

Joe wanted the cavern leaving "squeaky clean". No tools, no evidence, no hint that anything had been taken from the cask.

I had walked along the cliff top and unhooked the rope ladder and dumped both of them into the sea.

Then there was only one thought on my mind, and that was getting the hell off that island.

Emily drove us down the motorway smarting over the fact she had a black eye and a body full of bruises. Joe was sympathetic to a degree, but remained convinced he did the right thing launching the poor girl skyward.

"It had to be done, girl," said Joe, trying his hardest to massage her ego, but no matter how much reflexology he gave her, the tears weren't far away.

"I have never been that frightened in my life!" she said … and I believed her. But we asked her to help us, and without her backup, we would never have got off that island, never mind get away with the stash we managed. That girl is a diamond, and always will be in my eyes.

Talking about the frightening Monks, Joe asked Emily, "You won't have seen a monster before?"

"I've never been afraid of 'monsters' per-sey," said Emily most profoundly. "But I know they exist. I knew a monster once. In fact, I loved him. My monster only scared me when he came home."

I knew who she meant. Her ex-husband had a way with subtlety. One time she told me she couldn't recall how long the beating had gone on for, only the final kick and the sound of her own face hitting the floor. That's what can happen when a dumb-ass jerk mixes jealousy with ten pints of beer.

That journey home, I had the strangest, most intense feeling, from the tip of my head to my damp and grubby toes. Guilt made me feel greedy and dirty. I am not a bad person, but that saga turned me into one, or at least it made me feel that way. And that is tragic on so many levels.

On the other hand, Joe was ecstatic. Never have I seen him so happy.

"Billy Bones called himself 'The Captain' in Treasure Island," I said to Joe. "You deserved a name too. What shall we call you?"

"I don't need a name, babe. Just plain old 'Magnificent Joe the Dinghy Skipper' will do for me."
That had Emily in tears ... of laughter.
Joe had us up there with the all-time greats in piracy: "I've researched treasure maps these last few days and do you know the only pirate known to have actually buried treasure was Captain Kidd? But they never found it. Probably because they didn't have the lovely Emily giving them guidance."
We arrived at Joe's house and the three of us carried everything, lock-stock-and-barrel, up to his bedroom. We sat and toyed with artefacts that were probably produced around the time of Christ, from far away places, taken from people of enormous wealth. A hair-slide of the purist gold that could only have come from a mighty dynasty. An Egyptian queen perhaps; a wife of a Roman Emperor? Cleopatra? Give over ... that was too much to ask.
"What happens to it now?" asked Emily.
"It goes in a safe until I move it on," said Joe. "The wall has been breached so whoever goes into that cove is going to find the rest of the gold. But, is that a bad thing? Nobody knows what was in that wooden box. There was no itemised list. As far as The College, or anyone else is concerned, that could be the treasure in its entirety. And we didn't take anything religious, so our consciences should be clear. There are another two treasure chests stuck up that shaft, just waiting to be found. That should keep The College happy for a few centuries."

I returned home that evening and lay on my bed, holding the only piece I took with me from the chest.
"Don't take anything religious" said Joe. But I broke his rule. I didn't say a word to Joe or Emily, but hidden in one

of the gold boxes I found the cross of Saint Cuthbert. I was holding one of the most celebrated and admired artefacts in European history. That was the actual item that was replaced by a fake during the Reformation when Henry VIII's commissioners travelled to Durham to smash open Cuthbert's tomb and strip the church of its treasure. I was holding the original in my hand.

I switched on the computer. I wanted to look at the photos of the 'copy' that they held in Durham Cathedral. Was it identical? Then it dawned on me that I was the first person in almost five hundred years to compare the two. What I held in my fingers had never ever been photographed.

It's history appeared on the screen: "The Pectoral Cross was removed from the coffin of St Cuthbert on the last occasion that it was opened on Thursday 17th May 1827. Made of gold, the stones are garnets. The cross was discovered deeply buried amongst the robes on the breast. A portion of the silk cord, twisted with gold, by which it had been suspended, was found upon the breast. A tradition, however, says the bones were not St Cuthbert's, these having been removed to safety in another part of the cathedral some time between 1542 and 1558. But the cross may well still have been his, placed with another body as a 'ruse'."

But I had the proof that a copy was made and placed on the corpse.

Despite being buried underground in a damp cave for hundreds of years, and that does not include the 500 years it spent previously in Cuthbert's tomb, 'my' cross was in far better condition than the fake. Both are gold with red rubies up all of the four equal-length arms, finished off with a large ruby in the centre. But, the original has 12 ruby inlays up each of the four arms, while the copy has four missing on the arm facing south. That showed the cast of the fake wasn't particularly good, which gave even more reason to suggest it was never the original. Gold does not rot with time, there simply wasn't enough molten gold to fill the cast. Would such a misshapen item be given to a Saint? I had no intention of keeping the cross. The only reason I took it was because I could not abide the thought of it ending up in the hands of a collector. Its home was rightfully Lindisfarne, but surely not buried underground where no-one could see it.

There was some heavy duty guilt going on in my head and that's something I needed to put right.

I was not a religious person before recent events, but now I wanted God to wipe the slate clean. I wanted to be returned to Cuthbert's Priory.

I was in a bit of a pickle. Having in my possession, arguably, the most precious relic produced in the north-east of England since the Lindisfarne Gospels, I couldn't just place it in the hands of the Royal Mail and post it. Or could I? Would it get to: Lindisfarne Priory, Holy Island TD15 2RX?

In defence of our postal system, I'm sure it would, but imagine the face on the cashier when she got a reply when she asked: "And how much is the item in the box was worth?"

"Oh about fifty million pounds, give or take a penny or two."

Alternatively, I couldn't just walk into the Priory and hand over the Pectoral Cross as though I had found it lying on the beach, saying, "Look what I've found."

Anyway, I didn't want the notoriety or the acclaim, thank you very much. That would have provided them with more questions than answers. I had to keep my distance.
But it was delivered (with a very precise and bona fide letter of authenticity) by a very good friend of mine. What did they make of it? He didn't stay around to find out. But, for the life of me, I didn't expect the outcome.
I had opened a can of worms.

CHAPTER TWENTY SIX

In life, there are no chapters. Unless you are famous, infamous or just plain fortunate, there is no book about your life story. If someone wants to know about it, they should stick by your side and ride the journey.
In Joe's case his journey hadn't ended. Far from it. But this time he wanted to do it alone. We were now on different roads, finding our own individual paths to heaven, and his was the short cut.
I remember seeing the frightening monks for the first time, and Joe and I left the cave together, both on different wavelengths. I was so happy to be alive, but Joe said to me:
"Who said defeating evil wasn't going to be fun?"
He rode the rollercoaster and - come ups or downs - he was always the thrill-seeking barking-mad wacko. We weren't defeating evil. Those creatures, whatever they were, didn't want to harm us. We were EVIL for trying to steal what they had! We were the robbers doing the plundering and the pillaging. How dare we judge them when all we were doing was ripping them off? There was no 'good' side to anything we did.
Emily was now on antidepressants; Grace was at peace with herself now that she had no involvement in our hair-

brained scheme; and me ... well I had returned a piece of jewellery to its rightful owners and I was feeling rather proud of myself. I wanted to call it the last act of the Three Musketeers.
But, because of my actions, Emily and Joe were about to have one last dance with wolves.

I met Joe the following Saturday in Newcastle for lunch down the Quayside. We met at the Pitcher & Piano, the elegant iconic wine bar that sits on the bank of the Tyne, with stunning views of The Sage music venue and the Tyne bridge.
My Musketeer mate was bright and cheerful, as always, but there was a twist to our rendezvous. He was planning to move abroad, which was not unusual because he had spent half his working life on foreign soil, but he went to the bizarre length of leaving everything to me in his Will.
"It's all done and dusted," he told me, laying down the law on what I would officially own.
"The Will is in the hands of my solicitor. You get the lot."
Then he handed me a copy.
"What's brought this on?" I asked, "Where are you going?"
"Somewhere sunny," he said, with the briefest reply that told me nothing.
"Where's that then? Whitley Bay?"
He laughed, but still didn't tell me.
"I get your house? What the hell is this all about? Why me?"
"I had a visitor a couple of days ago," he said, sipping his lager while looking up river and staring at the Tyne bridge. He then switched the conversation in a second: "Do you know that 75 people fell off that bridge when it was being constructed?"

"I'm not bothered about the bloody bridge," I snapped, "who visited you?"

"75 men fell, but only one lost his life, isn't that incredible?" he said, continuing to look away from me.

I didn't react to his facts and figures. I didn't react to anything, I just sat and thought for a few seconds. Were The Invisibles starting to show themselves?

He turned to me and his lips formed a beam of sunshine. We sometimes talk in smiles. We are experts at extracting the most we can from a look, grin or a laugh. He is my Mona Lisa. The eyes give it away.

He finally got back to his story: "The security cameras picked them up. Two men checking out the property, front and back."

"And that is why you are giving me your house! Because you fear burglars?"

"You know what I mean, Linda, it's not burglars. They weren't wearing balaclavas and they weren't trying to hide. They want me to KNOW they are there."

"Why you?" I said, trying to put the pieces together and come up with something constructive.

"They got to Emily, so they must know about me," Joe replied. "That was why Steve wanted to take the phones off the pair of you. Someone was listening in. I don't think they know we took the treasure but they must have known we were planning something."

I wasn't convinced they got much from the calls: "We were very careful what was said in texts and calls, Steve always stipulated that. And we followed it to the letter. They are capable of having CCTV anywhere and everywhere but nothing overlooks the spot where we climbed down. That is one part of the island that is out of view from any landmark. Let's not forget, they don't know where the

treasure is ... or we wouldn't be having this conversation. They would have taken it themselves."
Then I realized by easing my conscience and returning the cross to the Priory I had virtually rubber stamped the fact that the treasure had been found!
I had blown open the whole plan!
"Joe, when you said 'don't take anything religious from the chest'?"
"Yeah," he replied, giving me a curious look.
"Why did you say that?"
He leant forward and held my hand before saying, "What was taken is on my conscience, because you and Emily didn't want any of the profit. The College don't know jack-shit about what we did. It's the end!"
"Where is the gold now, Joe?"
"I don't want you to know," which was probably what I wanted to hear.
"You're never gonna shift it now, Joe. Nobody will touch that with a barge pole. Look what happened to Craig and his mate."
"Selling it isn't the problem," he said. "I know the market, I have a contact in Egypt who will take the lot. It will be OK, I will be fine. There is still a 'plus' side to this, you watch."
"Oh Joe, why did you take it? Why?" I pleaded, but there was little point in adding to his agony. He knew he was up to his knees in trouble when he had to work so hard to justify he wasn't.
"Give it back Joe, I will go back with you. We can take it together. We can tell them where the rest of the treasure is. That must make it right."
Joe wasn't so sure: "Yeah, Steve tried that, didn't he? He returned the Gospel. That didn't stop them. He even told you, 'They don't forgive or forget'"

I looked down at the pieces of paper Joe had given me and flicked through the items betrothed to me. He really was serious about this.
I sat and shook my head and asked him: "Why me? Why is everything left to me?"
He laughed out loud before giving me the most beautiful look: "Because I love you."
"You what?" I replied. "Yeah, but ..."
I didn't know what to say, or think, or do. He held my hand and said: "Whatever happens next, we have to be brave."
And I replied: "We have to be brave alright. More than you can ever imagine. The College know we have the treasure. I sent the **Pectoral Cross back to the Priory**."
Then I explained that I had inadvertently opened the gates to Hell!
Being brave means being afraid, or at least it does to me. The two go hand in hand. First is the fear, then the determination not to be ruled by it. I could do that? Of course I could do that.
Then my phone rang. It was Grace about to break my heart.
"Brace yourself Linda, be strong ... I'm so sorry to tell you this ... but Emily died in a car crash this morning!"

We all know the conversation after death ... about taking people who were far too young, far too good. I didn't pretend to care, I didn't pretend to distinguish. All I knew was that my friend had been taken and it was a catastrophe! All her life all she wanted was a happy ending.It was never going to be 'happy' for those left behind, but for her part she left the biggest and most beautiful footprint I can ever remember.

It was always "poor" Emily, as though life owed her more than she was given. But she was an inspiration because she had it all ... she just didn't realize it.
The results of the inquest were announced long after the funeral, but she was pronounced dead at the scene of the accident and the cause was never truly made known. The brakes on the car were "defective" and investigation showed she made no attempt to slow down when she hit the wall. That put the emphasis on Emily rather than giving a cause for faulty brakes. Why were they faulty? Had someone tampered with them? If the bloody brakes didn't work how could she possibly slow down? The inquiry also played on the fact she was on medication for depression, and that gave off too many wrong messages. What they pieced together was only half an inquest, and that disturbed me more than anything.
The funeral was tough. One hundred and thirty people turned up but we hardly recognized any of them. They were old work mates and a lot of family and friends from London. But her ex-husband was there, and I had mixed emotions about that. He showed respect, and I appreciate he made the effort when he could have stayed away. But I knew the torment he had put Emily through. His flowers were ... how can I put it ... 'spectacular'. They came in a massive box with pretty ribbons and an even prettier price-tag. The higher the price you pay, the more the love, right? But, once again there was I being judgmental. My biggest failing by far, amongst a whole catalogue of shortcomings. I am a self-righteous bitch, make no mistake. And a funeral is not the place to play God and evaluate right from wrong. **Grace made a little speech that tore at the heart strings. Her eulogy:**

"Dear friends and family gathered here today. This day today is a hard one for us all. It is so much easier to mourn in silence, it takes away the worry of not being able to get your words out, or even just simply picking the right words to say. But we are all here together, sharing each other's moments of thought for such a wonderful person, who we all loved, as a friend, a loved one, a sister, a daughter ... our Emily."We will all have our own personal and special memories that she left in our hearts, in our lives and it is very hard for me today to be up here, hearing my own thoughts out loud, trying my best to focus on the happiest times she brought us, rather than the fact that she is no longer here with us. am certain of two things though. She would have been so proud to see you all here today, all of us expressing our happiest thoughts of our times spent together. Secondly ... none of us would have managed to get a word in!"Emily was such a strong character, personality and talker, that we are here today because someway, somehow, she touched us all with her heart ... the heart of an angel. or me, she will always be with me. What I will remember is the most beautiful smile I have ever witnessed. That girl could make all my troubles disappear with the twinkle in her eye and the smile that shone like a rainbow.

"You will all have your very own, special and private moments that you will cherish and keep close to your hearts. My memory is when we called ourselves, 'The Three Musketeers and Joe'. She wanted adventure; she wanted excitement with the enthusiasm of an eight year-old; and she wanted to meet Jesus. We laughed at the time, but she really meant it.

"She took care of her mother when Mary was ebbing away. And I'm sure they are together now in a lovely place. If she

gets to meet Jesus, I'm sure he will be spellbound by the girl we all love and miss.
"I love you Emily – in the past, present and future.Rest in peace my darling."

As I wrote earlier: "Everything that makes you hurt should be disposable. A form of mental dislocation, which would be a blessing for those that could do it. Because some folks just aren't built to withstand such a loss."
A grave had been dug close to a beautiful cherry blossom tree, and I held a bunch of pink roses in my gloved hand, before throwing them onto the coffin. My last respects before we were separated by six feet of earth.

CHAPTER TWENTY SEVEN

I always believed that if there was a nuclear war, two things would survive - cockroaches and Joe. He was indestructible. But for the first time since University I feared for him, and I feared for myself.
We were convinced the brakes on Emily's car had been tampered with, and even the investigation declared there was that possibility.
Death is inevitable. Of course it is. The master up above will turn a blind eye to right and wrong; to man, woman, or child; to good or bad. He does not discriminate. And we had no direct line to our maker. But I sensed something was brewing. I could taste it. I could smell it.
I actually think Joe grieved more over Emily's death than when his own father died. I saw a side of him I'd never seen before. Remind me - what are those five states of the mind after a loss?
Denial; Anger; Bargaining; Depression; Acceptance.

Joe started with 'anger' and that was as far as he was prepared to go.

I never found out what happened to the gold Joe took. He never mentioned it and I didn't pry. The loss of a treasured friend changed the man ... and not for the good. The realisation that WE may have caused Emily's death altered his life for the worse.

I wrote earlier that Joe had never shown fear in all the years I had known him, as though he was immune to it. But friendship, of all things, proved to be his Achilles heel. He still showed no fear, but he should have learnt about the process by which it is expressed. Don't be so arrogant as to think you can control fear. You need to know thy enemy. Know its name. The enemy is 'complacency'. It's when you are on top ... and you believe it ... that your world can fall beneath you.

It pays to weigh up the pros and cons. I can think of many instances where the brave choice was to walk away. When a situation is intractable, when every move is a bad move, it can take courage to take yourself out of the equation.

To Joe 'an ounce of action is worth a ton of theory'. He went into battle with The College and perhaps an ounce of theory would have been more beneficial than a ton of anything else.

Those who don't learn from history are doomed to repeat it. But Joe knew his history. He had to keep his eyes on the horizon and his mind on the fight.

Two weeks after the funeral we went back to Newcastle, to the same wine bar, and talked about what lay ahead for the both of us. Joe was even more down than I had imagined, and he spoke of Emily with a heavy heart. He said he was suffering nightmares periodically, weird dreams of walking

corpses and battles with ghostly monsters, and he worried me. That was what he had become - lovable on the outside; malevolent on the inside. And I struggled with that.
"I know who did this," he said, pointing his fork at me in an irritated fashion. That was another mannerism I picked up on. How he nervously couldn't keep his hands still. He occupied himself by playing with his food, and toyed with anything that happened to be on the table at the time.
"You don't really know, Joe. You think you know."
He placed black and white photos on the table of the guys who had tried to get into his house. He was right when he said they acted as though they wanted to be recognised. As if they were posing for the CCTV cameras. Two white males, in their 30's, wearing dark army trench coats. A sudden flash from the past.
"Are those coats issued as regimental uniform, or can they be picked up in any charity shop?" I remarked sarcastically.
"Have you seen them before?" asked Joe.
"Yes, the two guys Steve 'confronted' in Chester-le-Street and the Danish gentlemen we met in Edinburgh. They were all wearing them. It's like a little secret army of Mafia members."
I knew I had put thoughts into Joe's mind. I only confirmed what he wanted to know. He was on a mission, and neither Hell nor high water was going to stop him.

I hadn't heard from Joe for a couple of days and he wasn't answering my texts. Nothing unusual in that if he was busy with work or in a location with a poor phone signal, and his own house wasn't particularly good for phone reception. However, when he wasn't answering his land-line I suspected something was amiss. I decided it wouldn't harm to pop in and see him.

There was nothing unusual about the house as I approached it, but his car was not in the drive. Then, as I hovered at the threshold, I noticed the door already ajar. I made an obsolete knock, but I knew no-one would come, so I walked into the hallway.

There were shoes lying on the floor in a haphazard fashion, when normally they were stacked in boxes by the door. That could have been nothing and I didn't think much about it, but within seconds of opening the living room door, the story was laid bare.

The stench of dried blood filled the air. I spied a mobile phone on the floor with spatters of blood around it, then I viewed the horror of it all. Blood was smeared on the walls and on the floor, and I saw a body as I looked behind the door. He had a battered face with open eyes staring into space. He lay sprawled on his back, and despite his face taking a beating, there was an entry wound at his temple. A gun shot must have finished him off after a bitter struggle. The blood on the walls was smeared by hand, as I could clearly make out the hand prints.

I made my way to the stairs and there were traces of blood on every step of the carpet, as though someone had been dragged up to the bathroom, losing a lot of blood. I dreaded opening that door, and in hindsight I wished I hadn't. I could hear a dripping sound, as though someone had left a tap running. And after a few seconds of debating "shall I?" I pushed open the door to be met with a horrific sight. The victim was hung on the wall like Christ crucified on the cross. His facial features were totally obscured by dried blood, and his throat was cut. I was terrorized to the pit of my stomach when I saw six inch nails had been hammered through his wrists. This wasn't just revenge, this was morally disgusting.

"Joe," I screamed, "what the hell have you done?"
I guessed they were the men in Joe's photographs, even though their faces were almost unrecognisable, because I recognized their army coats. I couldn't imagine what was in store for Joe, but I had to stay focused, go downstairs and phone the police. I closed my eyes, trying to get rid of the sight of the crucifixion, and I cried my heart out. I was still sobbing when I phoned 999.
The police arrived within five minutes and the social gathering commenced. Every imaginable service turned up. Guys with specialized equipment and white germ-free overalls; finger-print experts; photographers; doctors; and ambulance technicians with body bags.

I was taken to the police station to answer questions, but I only responded to the questions they asked. I gave nothing else away. I was terrified for myself and for Joe because I knew too damn much. I felt it was my right to be dumb, freezing out the facts ... but I told the truth when asked. The officer removed his hat and started his investigation politely and calmly. In that moment he tried his hardest to be human but all I saw was the dark blue uniform and the shiny shoes. I sensed I was acting too defensively for my own good. Maybe he had me pegged from the start, and that worried me immensely, but he didn't show it. It didn't put him off his stride, and probably just made things more interesting for him. He kept looking me up and down, which I thought was most inappropriate, but I couldn't object.
I was taken to a counsellor for therapy and, despite their kind words, I felt so vulnerable and very scared.

I searched and searched, but Joe disappeared off the face of the Earth. His phone was disconnected, most probably destroyed, and his car was never recovered. After Emily died, Joe confided in me he was intrigued by the idea of how to commit the perfect murder, even drawing up a long list of ideas. It was progress in motion. He didn't reveal his exact plans to me, but I knew he had a strategy. A 'masterplan' he called it, and I knew it was going to happen, I was just so sad he shared it with me. He expected 'Mohammed to go to the mountain,' and judging by what I'd seen on his CCTV, it was going to happen.
For a few weeks, he kept the scheme inside his head until the moment that 'they' went calling. The act; the escape; and the cover up was all prepared, just waiting for the foxes to break into the hen house.
Another body was found in Washington (about 200 yards from Joe's house) dressed in the customary army trench coat. The police report claimed: "The man's blonde hair was stained and discoloured when he was found dumped inside the sewer. His lungs were choked with filthy water because he was still alive when the killer had thrown his body down the manhole. He had breathed in sewage with his last gasping breaths. His face was bruised and battered, and three of his ribs had been broken, struck by an extremely heavy object."
Two days later there were more carcasses to bury, although it was more akin to 'disposal'. Their souls had moved on but they were found in shallow graves in woodland next to the Holy Trinity Church close to Joe's house. Their throats cut, each holding a silver cross of the First Satanic Church in their right hand. According to police reports it was "murder with religious links" suggesting the murderer was a Satanist. The two who died in Joe's house also had silver

crosses placed on their bodies. The man by the door had one on a chain around his neck, while the crucified guy had one pushed in his mouth. Personally, I think they were chasing the wrong thread. The murderer wasn't Satanic, he just wanted to send them all to Hell.

Joe's house became a big problem. His family wanted the building for themselves, and although I had the Will, it obviously wouldn't become active until his death. He was a 'missing person' rather than a 'suspect', and who was to say he hadn't suffered a similar fate as the victims? The house was now a place I was petrified of, but I wanted to see out Joe's wishes. What I did with it was irrelevant, although putting it on the market was favourable. No way was I going to live there. Legally his family were his next-of-kin and, unless I could prove otherwise, they were entitled to everything. However, although they didn't want me to own the house, they were happy for me to do the day-to-day maintenance because I lived at close quarters and they all lived in foreign countries.

My legal advisors told me it takes seven years for a missing person to be declared legally dead, and I started to count down the weeks and months because I feared I wouldn't see him again.

Time passed and the loneliness ate me up.

In the eyes of the law, Joe was 'wanted for questioning' but there was no concrete evidence he was involved in any killing.

CHAPTER TWENTY EIGHT

Today the air is sweet, the weather is fine. I switch off the radio and get out of the car and I watch the young children

playing on the beach with their buckets and spades. I check the time. But what does it matter – like any other day – I can do whatever I want - whenever I want.
There's something about the sea that mellows me to the point of evaporation. I lay my towel on the sand and the smell takes me back to my childhood.
I close my eyes and draw in a lung full of sea air. The sound of parakeets flying overhead fill my ears instead of the drone of traffic, and I realize at last that I have found happiness. In this quiet contemplation, I can banish those demons and think about love, the people I cherish and what is right with my life. My only thought of religion is the feeling that God is whispering nice things through the swish of the palm trees. Here the minutes can be split into seconds or the day can be stretched out like a small eternity … it just doesn't matter. I adore this lifestyle. My only worry is "Do I have enough sun lotion on my back?"
The waves roll in white tipped, spreading themselves like fine lace over the beach making a cooling white noise type of splash. Percussive in their regularity.
I open my eyes when I hear my friend approaching with a cold bottle of water. He jokingly drops it onto my lap, making me shiver, then places his towel next to mine. With every step the sand shifts, before he finally settles down to relax.
"Have you brought your bucket and spade?" I ask.
"Nope. Buckets and spades are for tourists," he laughs.
"Are we not tourists? We live here but we can still be tourists. I like being a tourist."
"Linda," he said, shuffling towards me to put lotion on my arms, "you can be whatever you want to be, girl."
As you will have gathered, Joe and I are back together. Living in some place with a 'funny name.' It took an

immense amount of time in the making, and precision planning, but our minds were made up and the job is now done. I won't say there is no going back, because I go back to England on a regular basis. I sold my house, my business is thriving back in Durham, and I live off my own money. No hand outs from anyone.

I suffered immensely during that Holy Island period, losing Craig and Emily, and being taken down the garden path with Steve, when all I wanted was a happy life. I didn't hurt anyone intentionally because I would never do that. I made sure Corrie got the finances to pull her life together, and I paid her from my own money.

Joe has changed. The "happy guy" persona is returning but he has major issues. He runs down every blind alley when strangers ask about his past. The every day things like: where he grew up, what his parents are like, his early schooling ... he fabricates the lot. After six months of living here I have learnt never to join his conversations with tourists, because he changes his stories so often. He doesn't have an accent so he could be from anywhere, and usually he is from anywhere, never tying himself to a specific location.

I reached out with my open heart to find out what happened in his home that particular evening. I saw the consequences, which still haunt me to this very day. Joe insists he wasn't inside the property that night and he can prove it. He insists he saw Steve on three occasions, the final time when Joe ran from the house after finding the dead bodies.

Joe explained: "A guy approached me in a supermarket in Newcastle two days before the murders, saying he would 'sort out the mess' and I shouldn't worry. I didn't know who the hell he was, or what he was talking about. But I saw him again standing in the car park as I went for my car, watching me with a glare in his eyes that I will never forget. When I saw the bodies in my house, I ran because I was scared! The police will have CCTV coverage showing me returning home AFTER the killings. I had every intention of killing whoever broke into my house, because they were out to kill me. But eliminating them would have been seen as murder, not self-defence, because I planned it. It was premeditated. But, hand-on-heart, I didn't kill anyone! As I left my home, I saw the guy standing by a silver Merc a street away, with that same intense glare that could strip paint. It was Steve Campbell. The description of the face, the hair, the ruby ring … it was him!"

As for the other murders, Joe is convinced Steve orchestrated the whole lot of them to protect us both. Satanic charms were left (or tied) to each body, so whoever committed one murder committed the lot.

Joe has a theory: "Steve wanted to send them to Hell, just as The College had done to the people they strung up with rope. I don't believe Steve acted alone. He wasn't the 'Lone Ranger' we thought he was. It took a lot of people to cover up his fake death. That was not something you could do without help. He has some power behind him, and there is no doubt in my mind what he is capable of. He is not taking on The College single handed, he has support from someone. But I see a role-reversal. If The College want to hunt him down to the ends of this Earth, they have a death-wish, because that guy means business."

We made Steve out to be the bad guy, but what he did for us probably saved our lives. Sadly, Emily slipped through the net.

I try not to turn back the pages of that summer and dwell on the finer details. Yes I wished I had never made that trip to

Holy Island and never met Steve. Life then was pulling me forward. One hand was moving into the future; the other was erasing my past. Or that was my plan. But I didn't erase anything, I just uncovered a lot of agony and torment. Joe and I have built a new life for ourselves and we can dream we will be happy.

£1,600,000 appeared on my bank statement one day, from a foreign account bearing Craig's name. That was something else Steve predicted. Despite doubting his every word, he wasn't the liar I thought he was.

I still look over my shoulder occasionally when I walk down the street, and I've noticed Joe does the same. It happened just the other day. For a fleeting moment I thought I could hear my name being called and I could feel the composure that I have built up over the past few months evaporate. That's how we are these days.

I don't know how long we can live in Paradise, or how long the dream with last. But if they track us down and they do their worst, I'm sure there will be very little of us left to bury.

People say that the pain of death diminishes with time, and things always get better because you learn to forget. I don't believe that. I no longer see Craig's face in strangers, and the things Emily and I once shared no longer bring tears to my eyes. But I will NEVER forget them. That is not the way forward. I talk about the pair of them often, but in a happy way, and I feel blessed to have known them. That is the moving-on process in a nutshell. If getting past the pain means forgetting them, well, I'd rather choose to suffer in agony my entire life.

Printed in Great Britain
by Amazon